Infinite Risk

Infinite Security
Book 2

Denise DeMarco

Dedication for Infinite Risk

For Diane and Lenore – Your enthusiasm, support, and friendship mean more to me than you'll ever know. And thank you both for always being there to help me through my plotting dilemmas and writing mania!

Chapter 1

Liam

If the guys found out how he spent a rare summer day off, he'd never live it down.

Doing these things online was more convenient, but sometimes Liam wanted to see with his own eyes what he was going to purchase, not have it filtered through a camera lens. In this case, handling matters 'in-person' was unavoidable.

Head down, sunglasses still on, Liam strode under the royal blue awnings with their crisp white lettering and into the building. In addition to the lights strategically positioned everywhere inside, sunlight streamed through the huge plate glass windows that spanned the whole first floor. Although they looked like regular windows, he knew they were crafted with a protective layer to eliminate harmful rays that might damage any of the valuable antiquities inside. As best he could tell without getting close to them in a way that would arouse suspicion, the windows were impact resistant as well.

The well-dressed man who greeted him was attired to meet expectations for the ritzy Park Avenue address in Midtown Manhattan. Liam had been here many times and was familiar with the layout already, but a certain level of procedural decorum was expected in these places. Hands loosely linked in front of him, the auction house representative still managed to grip a small tablet device. In-house communications, perhaps? The man's posture managed to be both relaxed and attentive, and he was friendly in a practiced, professional way.

"Good morning, sir, and welcome. How can we help you today?"

"Good morning," Liam said. "I'm here for the rare book auction."

"Excellent. There's quite a lot of excitement for that auction today. I'm Brett. I'd be glad to be of assistance."

Liam smiled politely, knowing full well that the same exact sentences were said to everybody who was there for an auction. Nothing here was personal, and he wasn't going to let the obsequious behavior distract him from his goal.

"Do you wish to review anything about auction procedures?" Brett asked.

"No. I'm good." Liam had already had enough of the niceties. "Lower level?"

Brett checked his tablet. "The Cascadian Salon." Then he added what was obviously a customary line. "Have a winning day."

"Thanks."

On the first floor was the boutique, where a wide array of luxury goods and collectibles were available for immediate purchase. Liam had bought more than one gift for his grandmother over the years from among the frequently rotating merchandise. On some of the upper floors were the auction house personnel necessary to run this location.

In the back of the building and in the rear of the lower level were the auction rooms. They ranged from very large to extremely small, depending upon the type of items being auctioned and the size of the group of attendees invited or expected. Liam knew from experience that today's auction was likely to be small.

After being advised of the room number he needed, Liam made his way to the elevator tucked discreetly in the southwest corner. He could deal with tiny places again, but he still preferred not to. He hadn't suffered the type of torturous PTSD that plagued so many other veterans, but memories of being trapped on that last mission still reared up when he least expected them. No point inviting them if he could avoid it.

Liam pushed through the door beyond the elevator and moved quietly down the steps. The staircase ended two flights down and he emerged into a tastefully appointed hallway. Elegant directional plaques affixed to the wall indicated the path to the room he sought.

He tucked his sunglasses in his pocket. The only noise in the hall was the quiet hum of the central air conditioning, so the loud metal squeal of the door hinges was startling when he pulled it open. Liam stepped through, letting the door close behind him with a dull thump.

A woman softly snickered. "No one can sneak in here; that's for sure."

He looked in her direction, and it required effort to hide his reaction. Women who looked like her never showed up at events like this – at least none he'd ever attended. If they did, he'd always attend in-person when he could, even if he had no interest in what was being auctioned.

Not that he was looking for a woman. Or a relationship. What he'd gone through after Kelsey had taught him that romance hurt like hell. It was unnecessary pain, something better experienced through words in a book rather than in person.

He wasn't going to risk going through *that* again.

That didn't mean he didn't still appreciate beautiful women.

And this woman had plenty of reasons to be appreciated.

At first she seemed to be about 5' 7", but then he realized her shoes were making up nearly four inches of that height. A snug, knee-length, gunpowder-grey skirt appreciated her curves in a way only well-tailored fabric could. Her hair was a glossy dark brown, and he noticed glimmers of auburn within it. The abundance of her tresses were gathered up at the back of her head in a way that was ordered enough to be professional but relaxed enough to be casually sexy. If only she'd worn glasses, she'd have fulfilled a naughty librarian fantasy he hadn't even known he had until that moment.

"You'd think they could invest a few dollars on lubricant." As he said the words, he realized how they might sound to her, and quickly clarified, "WD-40. For the hinges."

Liam didn't know who was more surprised at his slightly awkward comment, him or her. A stodgy, high-end auction wasn't the place for innuendo, accidental or otherwise.

He held her honey-eyed stare, wondering if she'd reply to his words with outrage, offense, or if she would be obtuse about the double meaning in his words. She didn't miss a beat,

"Maybe I should do a good deed and loan them some. I usually have a tube in my purse," she said. Her lips quirked upward on one side, like she was resisting a laugh. "Lubricant, not WD-40."

Well, that was unexpected.

"Generous of you," he said at last.

"I try." She gestured with her chin in the direction over his shoulder. "You'd better check in, even if you're only here to watch."

The words were said with a slight but mischievous smile on plush lips that were tinted a rich red color. It reminded him of the wine his buddy liked to drink. Next time, instead of teasing Mason about his choice, he'd be thinking about her lips.

She turned around and walked away. Rounded hips shifted hypnotically as she moved. When she'd been facing him, he'd struggled to keep his eyes respectfully above the generous curves that strained the buttons of her white blouse. During their all too brief encounter, Liam had noted manicured fingernails kept slightly long. The color matched her lips. There were no rings on her hands, which made him give a mental fist pump. They were soft-looking hands with long, slender fingers that would feel amazing wrapped around his --

"Sir, you have to register even if you're just observing." The comment was addressed to him, and the auction house representative sounded irritated. "We start shortly. You must register or leave."

"Got it," Liam said, pulling his gaze away from the beautiful stranger.

The older man shrugged and looked at her too. "I understand. I wasn't always this age."

"Never too old to appreciate beautiful women, huh?"

"Exactly. Just too old to appreciate them the same way I used to," the older man added.

Because Liam was pre-registered, it only took a few minutes to get his paperwork and bidding paddle in hand.

"I'm Tom, and I'll be here for the duration of the auction." The other man told Liam. "Any problems or questions, you can come see me or talk to another representative in the salon itself."

"Thanks, Tom." Liam leaned in a bit closer. "I have a permit to carry concealed, and I am. What's the current procedure here?"

"Speak to security at the metal detector and show them your paperwork."

Tom indicated a doorway across the room and a metal detector there, flanked by two security guards. It was a smooth process to get through security after Liam gave them his identification and quietly alerted them about his weapon. He was ushered smoothly around the detector and into the larger room on the other side.

Liam had missed the auction item viewing opportunity that had been made available to bidders, but he'd looked over what was in preview online and read the comparative reports. The way modern auction houses simultaneously coordinated live streaming bids, regular online bids, and in-person bids was always impressive.

He already knew the item he wanted to win. It was a beautifully bound edition of poetry written by Percy Bysshe Shelly and published not long after the poet's death in 1822. There was a chance the final price would end up outside his budget, but there was an equal chance he'd walk away with the book as his own.

The room was small compared to most venues for these things, but still large enough for at least four dozen chairs neatly set in rows. Each chair was a few feet from the one next to it, the placement clearly trying to make bidders feel they had a bit of privacy. Along one wall were auction house representatives standing with their clipboards and communication devices, ready to place bids by proxy for customers who couldn't be there in person.

The air was efficiently kept cool, providing a respite from the sweltering world outside the doors, and optimal conditions for the items up for bid. Each item would be brought out when it was officially presented and put up for auction. The atmosphere in the room buzzed with the excitement of the thrill of the hunt, money and stress, all tastefully subdued.

Liam was focused on acquiring a single, specific item. Nothing else.

Now, as he enjoyed the sight of the alluring woman again, he realized he suddenly had two interests today. Liam headed to the vacant chair closest to her. Her attention was now focused on the auction catalog, and it didn't escape his notice that she now wore eyeglasses with black frames.

Hello, naughty librarian.

Chapter 2

Sarah

The skin on the back of Sarah's exposed neck tingled, and it wasn't from the air conditioner circulation system. He was watching her. She could feel it.

Men who looked like him never showed up at events like this. Sure, sometimes there were handsome men at auctions. This man, though, was unexpected. He reminded her of a not too clean-shaven Chris Hemsworth. Hair with shades of blonde and dark red scattered through it, grey-blue eyes, and a face that was all sharp angles and surprisingly symmetrical bone structure. A long-healed scar marred the skin just under his left cheekbone, but far from being repugnant, it somehow added to his appeal and kept him from being too handsome.

Sarah was accustomed to getting hit on. After her curves bloomed as a teen, she quickly learned how to handle male attention. She received a lot of attention, but most guys didn't get hers in return. It wasn't that she had some crazy high standards or expected them to meet unreasonable expectations of her own. She simply never felt much of an urge to reciprocate. Looking at this guy, though, was certainly making her feel something.

Black jeans and round-toed black boots made him look even taller than he was. The blue shirt that showed beneath his open leather jacket complemented his eyes. It was a hot day for a leather jacket, even a thin one, but he looked at ease in it.

Did his wife or girlfriend buy him that shirt?

Sarah told herself to knock it off. Hot Auction Man and his relationships or lack thereof were none of her business. Looking for available men was not her purpose today or any day. She needed to win the auction for lot L615217. That was it. Maybe Lot 615223.

Why hadn't Collins' last set of pre-auction instructions come through yet?

Sarah checked her business phone again, adjusting it on her lap with her small iPad. No notifications. After indecisively gnawing her bottom lip for a second, she quickly texted her client, "Have you decided regarding Lot 615223? Auction starting soon. Will move quickly."

She stared at the screen, tapping her thumbnail against it. Still no new messages.

"We're neighbors today," Hot Auction Man said as he claimed the chair to her left.

Sarah tried but couldn't stop the laugh that escaped her when she looked at him.

"That doesn't look like a comfortable neighborhood for you," she said.

It really didn't. His big body made the small chair look even smaller. It was a fancy folding chair designed to have an elegant appearance, not to be comfortable.

"You'd think they'd want people at an auction to be comfortable," Sarah continued.

Shifting slightly in the chair to face her more directly and, he said, "It makes cruel sense when you think about it. If you're uncomfortable you think less about your bid and place it faster because you want to get up and get feeling back in your legs."

"Interesting theory."

The downturn

"It's more than that because I have proof of it." He shrugged. "At least about other times when being extremely uncomfortable made me think less and move faster so I could try to win the day and be done with it."

Before Sarah had time to think about what seemed to be some subtle innuendo, he extended a hand to her. "Liam."

She shifted her belongings and shook his hand, "Sarah."

At the clasp of their hands, a jolt of awareness sparked through her. Her stomach swooped like she was on the freefall portion of the high roller coaster. She wondered if he felt it too, or if men were immune to that sort of thing.

A loud voice over a microphone startled Sarah, and she dropped his hand, suddenly realizing she still clasped it.

"Ladies and gentlemen, we have a bit of a technical issue."

The gray-haired man speaking into the podium microphone adjusted the lapel of his pinstriped suit. The younger man to his right clutched a black clipboard and pile of paperwork and looked nervously around the room. The first man continued,

"The technical problem is something that must be handled before we can proceed and it's being taken care of as I speak. We anticipate a delay of approximately 3 to 3 ½ hours total. Once the problem has been fixed, all procedures must be tested several times. I'm sure you can understand that accuracy and reliability are critical."

The grumbling and complaining got louder. The auction house official raised his hands beseechingly, "I have been assured the problem will be resolved as quickly as possible. I understand your frustration but ask for your patience."

"What are we supposed to do for *hours?*" shouted a woman at the back of the room.

The representative replied with forced excitement,

"We have all your mobile phone numbers and will contact you as soon as we have a new start time. Meanwhile," he raised his voice in response to the still increasing level of grumbling, "we have gift cards for each of you to use for a meal or whatever you'd like. We put together a list of nearby restaurants and stores, for those of you not familiar with this part of Manhattan. We've also arranged for two shuttles to drop any of you off at Times Square or 5th Ave if those areas interest you. Trust me, you don't want to drive yourself."

The assistant started handing out the papers he'd been clutching. When Sarah received hers, she saw there was a Visa gift card clipped to a printed list of restaurants and shops, plus an area map. There was still grumbling in the room, but it was quieter now. No matter how much money people might have, everybody liked free money.

"I assure you the technical issue will be resolved as quickly as possible. As stated in the paperwork you've been given, once you are notified that we are ready to proceed, you will need to be back here in 30 minutes for the start of the auction." He clapped his hands together and forced another smile. "Now, for security reasons I must ask that everyone leave this area. If you don't want to leave the building yet, feel free to explore the boutique on the first floor. Thank you for your kind understanding."

Sarah tucked her papers and everything else she was holding into her black Kate Spade tote bag. Liam followed silently as they joined the line of people exiting into the hallway. The tiny elevator held at most three people at a time.

Sarah gestured at the door to the stairs.

"I'm taking the stairs. You're older than me, I believe, but do you think you can handle it?"

She heard what she was saying but couldn't stop herself. It was like her mouth was speaking without her brain's permission.

His eyes narrowed a little. "Just how old do you think I am?"

"Well, I don't think you're 40 or 50 yet." Actually, she'd guess he was somewhere between 30 and 35.

"You don't, huh?" Liam looked at her steadily, arching an eyebrow imperiously in that sexy way that some men could. "Stay right there."

He opened the door to the stairwell and stepped inside it. Less than a minute later Liam opened the door again and indicated that she should join him.

"Were you expecting a problem?" she asked.

"Can't be too careful," he said. He gestured for her to ascend the stairs in front of him. The staircase was wide enough for two people to pass one another or walk side-by-side, so it seemed strange for him to follow behind her.

"Hey, are you checking out my... my...", Sarah's voice trailed off.

"Your ass?" His low laugh was quick, but she felt it resonate within her. "Any heterosexual man would have a tough time not checking it out."

"Really?" The disbelieving question slipped out before she could stop it. She really had to get better control over her own mouth.

"Damn right."

They'd reached the top of the stairwell and paused at the door that led back into the first floor of the auction house. Facing him directly again, Sarah could feel the strangest sensations, like her skin was humming. Or was it the air between them?

"Sarah, if you tell me your ass and everything else about you isn't beautiful, I just might have to spank it until I get you to see reason."

Sarah froze for a moment. Well, that was unexpected. And hot. Her mind raced as he pushed open the stairwell door. Was he into that or was it a joke? Was he flirting? Teasing? Being an ass? She was a modern, confident woman who didn't need validation from a man; she should be offended by his comment. Why wasn't she?

Liam opened the door into the main part of the building and held it while she moved out of the stairwell. He certainly had good manners. Well, if you didn't think it was bad manners to comment on her ass. It took less than a minute of self-reflection for Sarah to decide that she didn't have a problem with it at all.

She walked with him through the array of people quietly talking and perusing the offerings in the boutique area. By silent mutual agreement neither of them stopped to look around at all. Even with tinted glass to mute it, the August sunshine beamed through the plate glass windows.

Liam held open the door to the street, and Sarah slipped past him. She didn't want to shop in random New York City stores for two or three hours. Abruptly, perhaps, she decided she wanted to kiss this man and see if he tasted as delicious as he smelled. But how was she going to make that happen without looking desperate or ridiculous?

She didn't even know if he was married or committed to someone. Another thought grabbed her. From his comment on the stairs, she knew Liam was into women. But what if he wasn't that into her? That would be more than a disappointment today.

"Want to come with me, Sarah?" Liam asked in his smooth baritone. Even in the glare of the sunshine she could see that his gaze was heated and hopeful.

"Sounds much more fun than coming alone," she quipped.

Aliens must have taken control of her body because she never acted this way. Maybe she was ill. That had to be it; she was developing a fever. It was the only explanation.

Maybe he'd like to play doctor?

Chapter 3

Liam

Sarah's comment caught him off guard, but he'd received the not subtle message she was sending. With women, he was never at a loss for words, so it was a disconcerting experience. Liam knew he was generally regarded as a quiet guy. It wasn't a label that bothered him. People who knew him well realized that he wasn't shy. He just didn't believe in speaking simply to hear his own voice. Sometimes he had something to say but then chose not to because it wasn't necessary. Right now, he didn't speak because he was startled.

The woman was feeling him out without feeling him up. He'd been right about the 'naughty' part of naughty librarian.

"Sarah."

"Liam?"

She met his gaze directly, tilting her chin up so she could look into his eyes. He liked that.

"Come with me. I know where we can eat. Talk. Explore this." He gestured back and forth through the air between them.

The heat in her eyes was banked by uncertainty. "I don't know you. Not at all."

"You know my name," he pointed out. "You know the auction house vetted me."

"I know your *first* name, and I'm not interested in your financials."

"Liam Connolly."

Sarah tilted her head, "So, Liam Connolly, what's the 'this' you want to explore?"

"I think you know exactly what 'this' is. *This* is why your face is flushed and your nipples are hard." He heard her sharp inhalation. "It's why the pulse in your neck is pounding, and your pupils are dilated."

He moved a little closer to her. Sounds from the street and sidewalk in front of the building were those of a typical Manhattan day. The vehicular traffic was loud, and the foot traffic jostled them on both sides as people rushed about their business.

Liam was sure he wasn't reading the situation wrong, but if she didn't want to explore the obvious attraction between them, he wasn't going to try and force it or pressure her. He could try and fan the flames, though.

"I made the suggestion, Sarah. You make the decision."

"I'm not sure what I'm deciding about." She licked her bottom lip.

Liam bent closer, not aggressively but with determination, casting a shadow over her beautiful face. "Let's start by considering this."

He grasped her left hand and gently but firmly pulled her aside, so they were standing against the building. Out of the flow of pedestrians, Liam cupped her jaw with his hand, his eyes intensely focused on hers. He swept his thumb over her cheekbone. Beyond the heat of the air surrounding them, he could feel the distinct heat of her gentle breath, her respirations increasing as the energy flowing between them also increased.

"I want to kiss you now, Sarah. If you don't want that, I need you to tell me."

Even in her 4-inch heels, there was another 4-inch difference between their heights. Sarah pressed up on her toes and slid her free hand up to his shoulder. He hadn't taken off the light jacket he'd worn inside the auction house, but through it and his shirt he could feel her gripping the rounded muscles capping his shoulder. Liam realized she was probably sure she was making her assent clear, but he said,

"I need the words, Sarah."

"Yes. Yes, please."

His lips brushed hers, once, twice. Then again more firmly, his tongue now licking at her bottom lip where hers had a moment ago. His hand still cupped her jaw, angling her head the way he wanted it, deepening the kiss while he pressed his thigh between her legs with a rocking, lifting motion that made her clutch his biceps. Liam didn't know if she was simply enjoying the way he felt under her hands, or if she was steadying herself because the rising passion between them was making her feel unsteady.

He imagined her sweet little clit was throbbing the way his thickening cock was, behind the cruel zipper keeping them apart. She was making needy little sounds in her throat that he could feel, and that made his pulse pound. Her right hand slid up further and then around the back of his neck. Liam held her closer, kissed her harder.

The day was hot, the kiss even hotter, and her hesitance vanished like the occasional breeze.

Holding her tightly still, Liam ended the kiss and drew back enough to speak softly by her ear. "I've got a hotel room a couple blocks away."

He exhaled gently by her neck, nuzzling the soft skin there, "There's a restaurant in the hotel." Liam used his other hand to slowly caress her side, running his fingers close to her breast but not quite touching. "Or there's room service."

"Room service?" she echoed, shivering in response to his touch despite the heat.

"Options, Sarah." He lifted his head so he could look in her eyes. "We can just have lunch. Talk –."

She interrupted him quickly, "Options sound good."

Chapter 4

Sarah

Liam was staying at an elegant hotel close to the auction house. The Barrington Arms was well known, even to people like herself who could never afford to stay there. When he told her where they were headed, she'd been able to picture it immediately from photos she'd seen, and from walking past it a couple of times when she was in New York City.

Liam Connolly was an interesting guy. Military bearing, motorcycle clothes, unexpected taste in reading material, and evidently a healthy bank account – although that last part she could have guessed by him being at the rare book auction. And she was going to have lunch and probably something more with him. At the Barrington Arms.

Liam put his hand at the small of her back to guide her across the street at the crosswalk. The high temperature today was supposed to be 88 degrees, but at barely 10:00 AM it was already at least that if not more. Where his hand was touching her felt hotter still.

Manhattan was loud, as it always seemed to be during the daytime. On the far side of the crosswalk a vendor sold fresh fruit and stood just a few feet from a vendor selling donuts, muffins, and some kind of breakfast wraps.

It was often said that in New York City people rushed around and ignored each other. Sometimes that was true, but Sarah had often noticed that even though they were rushing, pedestrians sometimes acknowledged each other with nods of the head and occasional muttered words. When there were so many people around, you just couldn't take time to chat with even the people who looked approachable. The people, the traffic, the food, the trash – it all combined to make the city smell like, well, the city. Unfortunately, August was probably the worst time of year because of both the smell and people's impatience with everything and one another.

The very last thing she ever expected today was to be where she was, right now, with this man. Was she really thinking about getting intimate with this man whom she just met this morning? Sarah wasn't a prude, but she also wasn't a wild party girl.

Do not hyperventilate. You can do this. Guys have casual sex all the time.

As they approached the front door to the stately hotel with its French art deco-inspired facade, Sarah shoved her hand into the bottom of her purse, searching frantically for a breath mint. Where were those things? Not that it mattered. They'd kissed already. If you could call it kissing. It was more like devouring. She'd been basically humping his leg. Her panties were damp just from those kisses.

She could have spent this unanticipated break working on her iPad or making phone calls to clients. She could have reviewed her notes about the auction today, done some research about upcoming auctions. All smart choices. She was a smart woman; she knew that. Sarah was still questioning that self-assessment right now. She was excited and felt empowered somehow, but she wasn't sure that the decision to come here was a smart one.

Just because she met this man at a book auction in a prestigious auction house didn't mean he wasn't a serial killer. Or a first-time killer, looking for a victim. Or a sex trafficker, trolling for women in unusual places.

Another stray thought hit her. *Are my legs stubbly? What about my 'you know what'?* She rolled her eyes at herself. *You're thinking about fucking this man and you can't think the word pussy? Get a grip, Sarah.*

She mentally answered herself. *I'd like to get a grip on him. On what just a few minutes ago she'd been practically climbing on the city sidewalk, right outside the auction house. Classy.*

The uniformed doorman touched his cap and greeted them politely. Sarah wondered for a second how the man was tolerating this beastly weather in a full uniform, hat and all. At least the man was wearing what appeared to be a summer-weight uniform with short sleeves. He pulled open the heavy-looking door with its huge brass handle and the air conditioning from the hotel swept over her like a cool river.

Liam gestured with his open hand. "After you, Sarah."

"Thank you." she smiled but shifted awkwardly, not sure what to say or do.

He eased the moment by taking her hand and leading her farther into the hotel. It was a beautiful place, decorated in a modernized take on an old-world style with furnishings that were dark and stately but upholstered in light, lush fabrics. The lighting was just enough to be welcoming, and light fixtures that were created in a modern inter-pretation of Victorian style.

"As far as I'm concerned, they can take as long as possible to fix their technical issues," Liam said.

"I'll take that as a compliment, I think," she said.

"It is."

He escorted her across the lobby. There were at least a dozen people scattered around the space, some alone and others in small groupings. A stylish middle-aged woman softly played a baby grand piano on one side of the expansive space. In a far corner an archway led into a restaurant decorated in shades of cream and hunter green.

It was all a world far removed from the sweltering city on the other side of the heavy brass doors. Even the air was lightly scented – eau de Jasmine and money. None of it was heavy-handed, though, or made her feel like she didn't belong.

Liam nodded towards the restaurant. "If you changed your mind or you're having second thoughts about going upstairs now, tell me. We can just have lunch and talk down here."

"No!" Sarah cringed because she sounded louder than she intended in the quiet lobby.

Sarah lowered her voice while they waited for the elevator. "I want to. I've just never done this before so I'm not exactly sure what to do."

"You've never done this as in you've never had – "

"Sex? No, no, no, Of course, I've had sex. Plenty of it. That's not what I mean, either –." Sarah brought her hands to her face in embarrassment and smacked herself in the chest with the bag she'd forgotten she was holding.

The elevator arrived, giving her a moment to regroup as the passengers stepped off. Again, Liam graciously gestured for her to go into the elevator before him and kept his hand on the open door protectively until she was inside the compartment.

He continued, "So I guess that going to a hotel room with a guy you've just met is not something you're used to doing." This time he couldn't stop his smile. "By the way, as happy as I am to hear that you've had plenty of sex, I was referring to brunch in Manhattan."

The first part of his statement was so accurate that Sarah had to laugh, and the second part made her cringe in embarrassment again.

"I meant what I said, Sarah. If you'd rather eat at the lobby restaurant, we can absolutely do that."

"I'm not nervous about being here with you. Like you said, I know you're registered with the auction house, and they do background checks." Her eyes were fixed on the intricate brass details on the elevator panel. "I trust my instincts, and I feel comfortable with you."

A muted chime sounded, and the elevator doors swooshed open. This time, instead of indicating that she should exit before him, Liam indicated she should wait. He stepped out of the elevator himself, and she watched him quickly look both ways while he held an arm out, blocking her from exiting.

Was he looking for danger, or for witnesses?

"Is there something wrong?"

"No, and I didn't mean to alarm you or anything like that. I'm just safety conscious."

"Smart." Liam reached out to her, "Let's get to that room service menu and order fuel for the auction."

When she took his hand, Sarah felt the same little jolt she'd experienced when they shook hands at the auction house. Never in her life had she experienced anything quite like it before. It was as exhilarating as it was alarming.

Still holding her hand, Liam led the way down the hall and stopped in front of door number 1411. After he withdrew his key card from his pocket, Liam paused,

"Sure you're okay eating up here?"

"I'm sure."

It was immediately apparent that the hotel room was really a hotel suite. The small entryway in which she stood opened up into a room set up like the living room in a lavish home. There wasn't a bed in sight, so clearly one of the doors or archways in the room led to a bedroom area. To her left, wide windows looked down onto Broadway, and a door handle clued her into the fact that one window was really a glass door that opened onto a balcony outside the room. Everything was decorated in shades of cream, burgundy, and gold. It was both understated and opulent.

Liam had moved over to the round table positioned near one of the large windows. He picked up a portfolio-type folder off the table.

"We should order. No telling how quickly the auction house will call us back." "Good idea." Sarah shrugged her tote bag off her shoulder and hung it on the back of the chair nearest to her.

"Ladies first." He handed her the thickly padded menu.

The hotel offered brunch every day, according to the menu, which was very appealing. Sarah requested the quiche Lorraine with a side of fruit and wheat toast, then passed the menu back to him. He dropped it on the table without opening it and picked up the phone to place their order. It amused her that they'd each chosen stereotypical items – the quiche and fruit for her, steak and eggs for him. He added a couple of additional side dishes and carafes of coffee and orange juice after checking to see if she had any other preference.

Liam hung up and moved to a 4-foot long freestanding bar positioned near the wall.

"Glass of wine or something else? Or is it too early for alcohol?"

"I have to pass on the wine; technically, I'm still working. But I think a mimosa would be okay, if it's mostly orange juice."

As she walked closer, Liam crouched down and she realized there was a small refrigerator behind the bar. She couldn't see what he was doing but she heard the seal on the refrigerator releasing when he opened it, followed by the gentle clinking of bottles being rearranged as he looked for what he needed. He stood up with a split of champagne in one hand and orange juice in the other. Liam put both on the bar in front of him and reached for a couple of champagne flutes from the decorative display rack on the wall behind the bar.

"Not my usual choice, but a good option for this time of day," he commented.

"You look comfortable playing bartender," Sarah said, watching him fill about 1/3 of each flute with the orange juice and then open the small bottle of champagne. She didn't recognize the name on the label, but she didn't know much about good champagne. Her ex-fiancé had bought a bottle of Dom Perignon to make a toast when he proposed, and when she was in college she and her friends sometimes bought cheap champagne.

"A good skill for a gentleman to have, I think, so thanks," Liam said, pouring champagne to fill a little more of the flutes. The continually brightening sunlight refracted off the crystal and glittered almost hypnotically.

He handed one to her, then came out from behind the bar.

"I'd like to make a toast." He raised his glass slightly, the crystal looking even more delicate in his large hand.

"Please do," she said, pleasantly surprised.

"To an unexpected find at the best auction I've ever attended."

"The auction didn't even really begin yet," Sarah said, laughing.

Liam laughed as well. It was a sound that she felt like a blush beneath her skin.

"Well technically it did. It's just on pause."

"Can't argue with that, I guess." She raised her glass. "Cheers."

Sarah sipped and wandered back over to the wide windows. Typical Manhattan traffic clogged the street below, although no sound filtered up into the room. Iconic yellow cabs jockeyed for position, moving bumper-to-bumper with the other vehicles. On both sides of the street messenger and delivery bikes zipped by, and foot traffic was plentiful. Men in traditional suits walked briskly past people wearing clothes more appropriate for the sweltering weather.

"On days like this, I really appreciate air conditioning," she told him, turning around to face him again.

"Can't argue with that."

"I wonder what other people are doing to fill the unexpected break."

"Some of them are probably still yelling," he said.

"People can be ridiculous. So much technology involved, things happen."

Liam opened his mouth to reply and a brisk knock on the door interrupted. He put his champagne flute down on the little table next to the door and looked through the peephole and confirmed for her, "It's room service."

"That was incredibly fast!" Sarah said.

He pulled the door open and spoke quietly to the person on the other side. When Liam stepped back, he gestured for the attendant to enter. The young man who walked in pushing the room service trolley was smiling and nodding.

"Brunch for two, sir. Where can I bring this for you? This room, balcony, bedroom?"

Gesturing at the table by the window, Liam indicated his preference.

"May I set up for you?" the young man asked politely.

"Do your thing. Thanks," Liam said.

Sarah watched as the uniformed waiter acknowledged her with a friendly smile, then quickly set up place settings, glasses of water, the beverage carafes, and multiple covered dishes. As a final touch, he produced from the bottom shelf of the cart a small white vase with several flowers in shades of lavender and blue.

Liam pressed a tip into the young man's white-gloved hand. Sarah had no idea what he gave the guy, but the "Thanks so much, sir!" was given with enthusiasm, and followed up with an awkward little half-bow along with one more sincere comment.

"We want every guest to leave The Barrington Arms feeling satisfied."

Chapter 5

Liam

The food was excellent, as expected. One of the reasons Liam stayed at this hotel when he was overnight in the city was that the food alone was worth the cost. At least to him, it was. Years of eating military food and fast food, field rations and frozen meals, all made him appreciate a great meal when he had a chance to enjoy one.

"Are you an auction regular?" Liam asked as they each enjoyed a cup of coffee and lingered at the table. He made a mental note that she liked it light and sweet.

"Somewhat. It's part of how I earn my living," Sarah said. "What about you?"

"Just a bit of a hobby," he admitted.

"You collect rare books?" she asked with what seemed to be genuine interest.

"Not collect so much as pick one up here and there." Liam was intentionally somewhat vague. He got teased so much by the guys about this that he wasn't sure he wanted to share with a beautiful woman.

"By a particular author or something?" Sarah asked.

He cleared his throat, hesitated, then told her, "Poetry. Mostly 19th-century."

Sarah didn't seem to try to hide her surprise, or then, her pleasure. Her smile was bright and genuine. "Not what I was expecting, but better."

"What were you expecting?"

Now *she* looked embarrassed. "I'm not sure really. Maybe military history type stuff, old engineering texts, architecture, things like that."

"Manly kinds of stuff, huh?" Liam couldn't resist teasing her. The soft blush that appeared on her lovely face was his reward.

Sarah quickly responded, "No. Well, maybe, but not in a bad way."

"What about you? At the auction it seemed like you were trying to get in touch with someone. Business, or personal?" If she was involved with someone, this was definitely going to be a platonic meal. Just because *he* didn't want to be in a relationship didn't mean he'd be involved in messing up someone else's.

"Business." Her answer came without hesitation. "I'm something of an expert on certain types of rare books, and occasionally act as a buying agent."

"Meaning you place bids for somebody else."

"Yes. Not my favorite thing to do, but the pay can be good." She frowned. "Some clients are more difficult than others, though."

"Don't take this the wrong way, but you seemed very stressed waiting for the auction to begin. Maybe more than the usual stress level people have from waiting for proceedings to get started." He didn't want to overstep, but Sarah had been more nervous than he'd expect a professional to be. "I don't know your usual pre-auction demeanor, of course, but it makes me wonder if today's client fall into the category of *more difficult?*"

By that he meant *asshole,* but he didn't want to say that to her.

"I don't think it breaches any type of confidentiality so, I can tell you, yes, he definitely does." Sarah's frustration was clear. "Actually … Excuse me a second while I check messages again?"

Liam watched silently while she turned over her phone that was resting face down on the tabletop. After looking at it, she murmured an apology and got up from their brunch table. Sarah picked up her tote bag and pulled her iPad from its depths. Her unhappy expression was the same when she checked both devices.

"Bad news?" he asked, pushing back from the small table.

"More like no news." Sarah responded, shaking her head. "I haven't heard from him since yesterday."

"Not typical, I guess?" Liam closed the small space between them, standing close enough to enjoy the subtle fragrance she wore.

Sarah looked up into his eyes, her honey-brown ones bright and clear. "Definitely not. This client is usually very clear about what he wants in terms of bidding. Sometimes he's so determined to win that he has me jump in the sequence of bids to make sure he gets the win. He overpays as a result."

"Do you work with this guy a lot?" Liam asked.

"I don't know if I'd call it a lot, but probably a half-dozen times."

"I know it's none of my business, Sarah, but do you think he intentionally overpays?"

Although it wasn't an area of specific expertise for him, he recognized that it sounded shady. Even the wealthiest people didn't intentionally overpay for things again and again.

People looking to launder money would do that, though.

"It really *isn't* your business." Sarah's posture had stiffened, and he knew he'd pressed too much.

Liam wanted to shake himself and find his usual common sense. This was supposed to be a meal with a beautiful woman who shared mutual interests with him. Maybe even a quick hook-up, if it worked out that way. Sarah was not a damsel in distress. But still…

"I have a rare day off today," he told her. "My usual work has nothing to do with books or auctions or anything like that, but if you need help.…"

Sarah was standing completely still now, phone still clutched in her hand. "Okay?"

"I work in security," Liam said.

Now she looked confused. "Like store security?"

"No. Bodyguard work, protection details, and all kinds of things having to do with legal and illegal undertakings. It's why I truly understand confidentiality and discretion."

"So you're like James Bond or Jason Bourne with rare books in your hands?" He liked that she could tease him even when she was clearly under a lot of stress.

"I guess that's one way to look at it. Another way is that if there's something hinky with your client, I can help."

"No offense, Liam, but you could be some basement gamer with an active set of delusions."

He pulled his mobile phone from his pocket and dialed it, on speakerphone. Liam stayed focused on Sarah's eyes as he dialed.

"Infinite. May I help you?" Jillian answered.

"Things busy today?"

"*Liam?* Why are you calling the main line? Aren't you still on vacation?"

"I am." Jillian was going to wonder what was going on, but he'd deal with that later. "I'm here with someone, Jillian. Can you do me a favor and explain what it is we do at Infinite?"

When Jillian answered, her confusion was evident. "This is one weird phone call, even for you."

"Jillian."

"Okay, okay. Mystery person, whoever you are, Infinite Security handles all types and levels of security issues, domestic and international. Our teams of skilled operators are the best in their respective fields, and are supported by the latest in available technology and resources. Do you need a consultation, mystery person?"

Sarah was still staring at him, now wide-eyed. He held the phone out toward her, offering it to her.

"I guess I just have one question right now," she said to Jillian. "Is Liam Connolly one of your... operators?"

Jillian hesitated. "We don't usually discuss names over the phone, but since he made the call, I suppose I can tell you that yes, Liam is one of ours. And he's one of the best there is at what he does."

Liam asked Sarah quietly, "Is there anything else you want to ask right now?"

Instead of answering him directly, Sarah said, "Thank you for your help, Jillian. I think I'm good for now."

Liam said, "Thanks, Jillian."

The woman at headquarters started to ask him something else, but he moved his thumb and disconnected the call. He knew without a doubt that Jillian would tell Dax about the call, and there'd be a whole bunch of questions about it later.

"I know that doesn't tell you a lot," Liam said, trying to decipher what Sarah was thinking.

He took it as a good sign that Sarah hadn't fled the suite, retreated across the room, or done anything else to close herself off.

"It's a lot to process, Liam, but yes, that helped. I doubt you have a professional- sounding receptionist at your beck and call to support delusional claims about being some kind of superhero."

"I'm definitely *not* a superhero. Not by any stretch of the imagination. And if you meet Jillian, you'll find out she's way more than a receptionist and most definitely isn't at my beck and call."

"If I take your word that you are what you say you are, why do you want to help me?" Sarah shook her head as she spoke. "What's in it for you?"

Liam shrugged slightly. He didn't want to be cavalier about it, but he didn't want to belabor the point either. "I want to help you because I believe I can. What's in it for me is the satisfaction of doing the right thing."

He let the ensuing silence sit between them while she thought it over.

Sarah took a deep breath and let it out slowly. "You asked about whether today's client intentionally overpays for auction items?"

"Yes."

"I have thought that a few times, which doesn't reflect well on me because a good buyer's agent helps you not overspend." Sarah shook her head slowly, thinking while she spoke, "Most of the time there was at least one opposing bidder driving the price up."

Liam had to put it out there, "Any chance he wants to pay too much or more than he has to?"

"Money laundering?" She correctly named what he was referencing. "I've wondered, but there's nothing concrete to indicate that. If there was, I wouldn't ever work with him again."

"But the possibility worries you," he said.

"Of course it does! My reputation is a big part of what I have to offer." There was no mistaking the tension in her body language or her words. "I don't have any *reason* to think he's doing something illegal, just an uncomfortable feeling."

"If you find that you do need help, you can reach out to me," he offered.

He wasn't going to be able to solve her problems right now, even if she wanted his help. It didn't make sense to add to her stress level before they had to go back to the auction. It was time better spent in other ways.

"Sarah..." Liam slid one arm around her waist, slowly but with deliberation. "Instead of spending the rest of however much time we have right now, focusing on stressful things, I'd rather focus on you. What do you say?"

She sighed into him. "Yes, please."

He brought his other hand up to the right side of her face, gently cradling her cheek in his palm. Liam brushed it back and forth across her cheekbone. Her eyes fluttered closed, and he heard the hitch in her breath.

"Let's focus on something else for a while then..."

Chapter 6

Sarah

Liam's hands were big and warm, confident but gentle. She never could have anticipated something like this happening today, but she had no complaints. She was single and unattached, enjoying the undivided, very much welcomed attention of the sexiest guy she'd ever met.

Liam pulled her closer, his arm now a snug band around her waist. The hand on her face gently tilted her head and then he was exploring her mouth with his own. He tasted faintly of the cinnamon that had dusted their coffee, and a practical part of her brain silently gave thanks that she hadn't had anything with garlic or onion in it for brunch. He gently nipped her bottom lip and ran his tongue across the seam of her mouth. When she opened to him, the growl that rumbled from deep in his chest was something she felt right down to her core.

Liam explored her mouth with his while his right hand caressed her back, then her hip, then her lower back and to the curves below. His left hand slid from her face to the side of her neck, where his thumb continued its hypnotic stroking.

"Do you taste this good all over, sweet Sarah?" he asked when the need for breath separated their mouths.

"Is that some of your own poetry?" she asked, her voice soft as she tried to catch her breath.

"My poetry is awful. If you want a poem, the most classic of all time suits you." And then this tall, strong man with his unusual gray eyes looked into hers, "Shall I compare thee to a summer's day? Thou art more lovely and more temperate: Rough winds do shake the darling buds of May, And summer's lease hath all too short a date."

Sarah felt again like a naïve teenage girl charmed by a sweet-talking man. But at 28 years old she was certainly not a naïve teenage girl, and he definitely didn't seem like the type of man to be a sweet talker. Although he also didn't seem like a man who'd enjoy 19th century poetry, so what did she know?

"Sounds like you don't just read poetry, you know it." she said.

"I know what I like." He moved in closer again, nibbling at the sensitive skin by her ear. "Me, too." She slid her arms up around his neck.

The next kiss they shared was even more powerful than the first, and Sarah willingly moved with him to the sofa. She was kind of surprised he hadn't instead headed for the adjacent bedroom.

Proud of her own temerity, Sarah plucked open the top buttons on his shirt, revealing more of the broad expanse of his chest.

Liam tugged her shirt from her waistband.

"I'd love to take your hair down, but I don't want to wreck you for when we have to go back."

"It's okay," she reassured him. "I can fix it fast."

As she was finishing her sentence, he was already plucking out the tiny hair combs and pins that kept the heavy mass in place. The auburn highlighted dark waves tumbled down around her shoulders. Liam gently pushed her now opened blouse off those shoulders and she helped it slide down her arms. Sarah watched as Liam's eyes took in the white lace that cupped her.

"I know white is boring, but –."

"Stop. Nothing about you is boring, including every lovely thing you have on your luscious body." He stroked the upper curves of her breasts with two fingers.

The very slight roughness of his hands made her shiver. His lips took possession of her mouth again in a kiss that was anything but gentle or sweet. Liam feasted on her mouth, and she met him in her own hungry quest. Sarah couldn't stop the embarrassingly loud moan that escaped from the passionate place inside he'd awakened.

Sarah's heart was hammering. She could feel that her generous breasts were swollen even more with her arousal, the lace edges of her bra cups digging into her flesh with a pinch of pain that somehow heightened the pleasure. She couldn't remember ever feeling so incredibly turned on and was desperate for more of this man who'd come into her life today.

Anxious to get his shirt off, Sarah fumbled with the remaining buttons. Liam's hand came up to cover her own and he helped her quickly slip them free. She slipped it off his shoulders and he pulled his arms free. Skin tanned a golden brown made a rich backdrop for the couple of tattoos she could see. There was a military insignia on his left bicep and another type of official looking crest on the right. She thought she'd seen it before but couldn't quite think of where. His nipples were perfectly placed copper discs, accented by just a perfect amount of dark blonde chest hair. His abs flowed smoothly with every small movement he made. The man looked great in clothing, but he was beyond her imaginings without it. And this was just with no shirt – what would it be like if he ditched the pants as well?

She caressed his arms with both hands, lightly tracing the outline of the strength beneath. Again, he kissed her, this time the exchange involving tongues and touches, exploration and adoration with mouths and hands fanning the flames. His scent, their combined scent of wild arousal was intoxicating.

Sarah heard an unmistakable groan of male hunger in her ear and then he slid his hands beneath her, "In my lap, honey."

As her thighs split around his, he helped hike up the snug black pencil skirt that had evidently kept drawing his eyes to her behind. But now he was tonguing her right nipple through the white lace of her bra, seeming to be equally enjoying those curves too. Her blood ran hot and heavy through her veins, and she could feel the wide ridge of him pressing against her swollen lips where they were nestled behind black lace panties.

Liam moved his mouth to her other needy nipple and gave it the attention it wanted, groaning around her, "White bra and black panties, saint and sinner."

He tugged the bra cups down with his teeth and hissed when her dusky pink nipples were completely revealed. "That's how the world sees you, isn't it, honey?"

He sucked on one and lightly pinched the other, switching sides between his words. "Such a proper appearance for the world to see and such a dirty girl underneath."

She could barely catch her breath, his words as hot as his actions.

Liam caressed her through the black lace, "Soaking wet. I know you're delicious, aren't you?"

He was everywhere at once, or so it seemed. One hand stroked her hip and her ass, the other teased her through the growing wet spot on her panties, his fingers devoting increased attention to applying more pressure along her slick slit.

She was rocking against him, her clit rubbing against his fingers, her achingly empty core pressing against his hardness, a length she now desperately wanted to possess.

Sarah felt the pressure building, her mind focused on nothing but the pleasure Liam was giving her. She gripped his arms more tightly, trying to hold on to something stable in a world that was spinning crazily on its axis.

"Feels good, honey, feels so good doesn't it?" He was scattering kisses on her neck, working his way back up to her mouth, "Come for me, Sarah, I want to feel your honey soak my pants."

His wicked words, the feel of his hard chest against her soft one, his scent surrounding her, his heat filling her even though he himself wasn't yet ... It all combined to send her shuddering into a climax that stole her breath.

She collapsed against him, gasping for breath, trying to figure out how this had happened, how this man she barely knew had wrecked her so completely. Liam kept rubbing her back in soothing circles holding her close to him, letting her gently come down from her peak.

Two different phones ringing almost simultaneously shattered the silence.

Chapter 7

Liam

Damn. Couldn't the auction house IT people have been a little less efficient? Maybe two or three hours less effective? He wasn't ready to relinquish Sarah back to the world outside the hotel suite. Not only was she bright and beautiful, it sounded like she also had a potentially serious problem on her hands with the buyer she'd been talking about today. Liam's sense for danger and his inherent need to be a protector were colliding too loudly to be ignored.

Sweet Sarah looked flustered and embarrassed, which didn't surprise him that much. She didn't strike him the type of woman who took her clothes off so quickly with a man she barely knew. In fact, he'd been surprised she'd even agreed to go up to his room with him.

Guys in his profession tended to have reputations for treating women like nameless, faceless objects. Liam had never behaved like that, and he never would. He had to guess that his decent manners and respect for her as a woman had come through during their time together, along with the physical chemistry that sizzled between them.

"Wait here. I'll grab the phones," he said as he gently moved her off his lap and onto the couch. Still shirtless, he walked across the large room to grab his phone from the bar top and hers from the small table with the flowers.

He glanced at his own and saw it was as he expected; a message from the auction house requesting they return promptly.

Damn.In the 90 seconds that had taken, Sarah had already put on and buttoned up her blouse, hiding away her sexy bra and the bounty within.

Deciding not to comment, Liam handed her phone to her. "Problems are fixed so we have to be there in 30 minutes."

She darted a glance below his belt, blushing furiously, "Our problems aren't fixed yet. I can take care of that for you…"

He took her hands and tugged her up to stand. "That is not a problem. It's just a reaction to how incredibly beautiful and sexy you are."

She buried her face in his bare chest. Her words were muffled but clear, "It's not fair to leave you like that."

Liam ran his fingers through her hair, still amazed at its silky softness. "I'm a grown man, honey, and I've known for 20 years that an unanswered hard-on isn't fatal. Your concern is as sweet as you are." He kissed her forehead and hugged her before releasing her and stepping back.

"Why don't you use this bathroom to get yourself together and I'll go inside to the other and do the same."

She finally looked at him and nodded. They went their separate ways, and when Liam returned to the main living area, Sarah was ready to go. Nothing about her immediately indicated that she'd just come apart in his arms, but he could see it in her softened, more relaxed expression.

When they left the room, this time he had his arm around her waist and kept her tight to his side. He wanted to make sure she didn't feel like anything they'd done had somehow been wrong or tawdry.

When they left the hotel lobby it was immediately obvious the temperature and humidity had already risen dramatically. It was like standing next to a blast furnace, though it wasn't anywhere near as bad as the Middle East had been in his military days. And you might get the occasional crazy scene into Manhattan, but there were no snipers or IED's waiting for you. He could've sworn he felt a twinge in his left ankle at the memory, but he quickly shook it off, knowing it was just his mind messing with him.

It felt right walking with Sarah by his side. Different somehow.

As they walked, Sarah was texting and emailing her client, and then leaving the man a voice message. She had to speak loudly over the sounds of traffic, and Liam picked up that the client's name was Edward.

By the time they reached the auction house, Sarah was even more frustrated than she'd been before. It occurred to him that he needed to get her naked in his bed, so he could spend a couple of hours putting her in that relaxed and satisfied zone again.

And again.

Everyone was a little on edge going through entry procedures again, people's days having been put out of order and off schedule because of the delay. There was still an air of excitement, as always, but it was tempered by impatience.

Liam and Sarah were among the first people back, probably because his hotel was so close to the auction house. Tom was once again at the check-in table inside the auction room doors. The older man looked from Sarah to Liam and back again. When he gave Liam a signal to continue on, Liam was sure the-oh-so-serious worker had winked at him.

They sat next to one another in the small sea of white chairs. Sarah continued to monitor her iPad and phone. He understood her nervousness and agitation, given the ongoing silence from her buyer. The cynical part of his mind insisted on pointing out that he was going on instinct with her – and now and then even *his* instincts could be wrong. His ankle twinge as if in agreement with that reminder.

Maybe the client was running a racket, and she was complicit?

Just because Sarah kissed like Aphrodite didn't mean she was a goddess of truth.

He leaned close to her, keeping his voice as low as possible. "Sarah, if you don't hear from him and can't do the transaction, is it that big a financial hit for you? You weren't guaranteed a commission anyway if you didn't win the auction for him. Right?"

Liam tried to get a better understanding of her situation, without being aggressive about it. They barely knew one another, and he had to be mindful of that. He'd gotten over the first hurdle toward getting her to trust him, but he knew she wasn't all the way there yet. How could she be?

She looked at him with those beautiful eyes under delicate brows that were pulled together, forming a slight crease on her forehead, and he could see how troubled she was. Sarah spoke as quietly as possible, "No, I'm not guaranteed commission if I don't win the specific lots. But he authorized me to spend a lot of money and I have a duty to do my best to win for him." Sarah leaned towards him a little more. "The instructions are unusual, so I really wanted to ask a couple more questions."

"Are your instincts generally good?" he asked.

"Yes," she said.

"What are those instincts telling you?"

"Nothing good," she said. "Nothing safe."

As the last word left her mouth, her phone buzzed. Sarah scanned the message and her lips tightened. It didn't take Special Ops body language training to recognize that whatever she'd read wasn't good.

"Tell me," Liam said.

"Confidentiality requirements preclude me –."

"Sarah," he interrupted her. "I'm getting the feeling this is more serious than confidentiality requirements. If your health and well-being is at risk, is that really what you signed up for with this person?"

The buzz surrounding them in the room continue to grow as more people took their seats. Sarah's face was expressive, and he could see her thinking everything through. Trying to make the right decision.

"He just doubled the money I am authorized to bid, tripled my pay rate when I succeed, and made it very clear that I am expected to succeed." Her anxiety was clear to see. "The initial amount authorized was already way over the expected gavel price."

His mind processed that quickly. If the buyer already gave her authorization to bid well above the amount at which the gavel was expected to fall at the conclusion of bidding, why would he double it? Liam wasn't a professional at this the way Sarah was, but even he realized that was suspicious behavior.

It didn't matter that he'd just met Sarah today. Liam felt mission-level focus click into place like a tangible thing. He was going to help her and make sure she wasn't in any kind of danger from whoever had hired her.

"What's his last name and anything else you can tell me quickly?"

"Liam, you know I shouldn't even be discussing this with you." Sarah shifted in her chair. He didn't know if she was physically or ethically uncomfortable.

"Sarah, you know something's not right here." He leaned his head into hers as he spoke, keeping his voice barely audible. "Let me help you figure this out before you get caught up in whatever he's using you to do."

The hum of voices and other sounds in the room was growing as more people took their places to wait for the cause auction to resume. Well, since the proceedings hadn't even started earlier, he supposed they all were really waiting for the auction to begin.

Sarah's eyes moved as she looked around, but it was clear to him that her real focus was on her own thoughts. She grabbed her phone so tightly that her knuckles were pinched white from the strain.

"Why would you help me?" she whispered.

It was a reasonable question. He'd addressed it with her at the hotel, but he understood it hadn't been enough. They'd known each other less than a day.

Why do I want to help her?

It only took Liam and a moment to realize that the answer was obvious. He couldn't *not* help her. He liked her, he was intrigued by the situation, and most of all, he wanted to spend more time with her and get to know her better. Much better.

Not for a relationship, though. He was done with those.

Sarah was a risk because he truly didn't know her. But she was a risk he was willing to take. He could help her without them having a romantic relationship.

Instead of going into all that, Liam simply said, "I have the ability and resources to help you. Let me do it."

A couple of people in the row in front of them were discussing too loudly what they did during the unexpected break. It was irritating, but at least those closest to them weren't interested in his conversation with Sarah.

Sarah shifted again in her seat. He knew she was still debating with herself. Her next comment surprised him.

"I suspect you're here to bid on one of the books he wants." Her tone was rueful. "If you try to do something now you might miss your chance. That wouldn't be fair."

"You're more important than a book, Sarah," he said. "In fact, don't worry about me at all. I need you to do whatever it is you would normally do. Give it your best effort to win for this guy. It'll help us figure things out."

She made a sound that was really a disbelieving snort, not at all in keeping with her professional appearance and demeanor. Sarah put her hand out towards him anyway, "Give me your phone, I'll write out the basics quickly."

After opening a Notes screen for her, Liam gave her the phone. He watched closely as she typed out several lines of information.

When Sarah gave it back, he glanced at what she'd written.

"I'll be right back. For now, if the items come up, follow your client's instructions." He could tell the fine line stood, needing to find a quieter corner. "Just do your thing the way you normally would."

Liam didn't know if she'd listen to his advice, or if what he said was anything different from what she would've done anyway. Sarah could simply be placating him, and he'd understand it if she was.

There were a number of alcoves built into the far wall, and one of them was fortunately unoccupied. It wasn't the best place from which to view the auction proceedings and items closely, but it was perfect for conferencing with someone, having a quick private conversation, or making a call when you didn't want to leave the room because of the auction.

Liam added some basic information to the note Sarah had written. He provided her name, their location and purpose, and a couple of observations he'd made about her and the situation.

Not having enough time for full security protocols, Liam dialed Dax directly. If the Founder and Director of Infinite Security didn't answer, he'd try Mason, their second-in-command. And if necessary, Rick, their lead tech expert.

Liam was running possibilities through his head when Dax picked up.

"Calling me on your day off? I thought you'd be at the beach, scoping out bikinis," Dax said. It sounded like he was in an unusually lighthearted mood. "But I was expecting your call after what Jillian told me."

Liam fleetingly wondered how quickly Jillian had reported that phone call to Dax, but it didn't really matter and he didn't have time to dwell on it.

"I need you guys to check someone out. Sending you the info now." Liam dropped the Note into a condemned special agency encryption on his phone and then used a VPN piggybacked on the auction house Wi-Fi.

He hesitated, then sent an additional request for them to find out what they could about Sarah, as well. He thought she was being truthful with him, but he needed to be sure. Definitely a situation of "trust but verify."

A few seconds later Dax confirmed, "Both sets of info received. On it. Let me know what else you need."

"That'll depend on what you come back with."

There was silence on the line, and Liam could sense that Dax wanted to say something but wasn't doing it. It wasn't like the other man to hesitate speaking his mind.

"What?" Liam prompted. He wanted to get back to Sarah's side.

"How does this situation involve you?" Dax asked. "Do you know this woman well?"

"No. That's why I sent her info to run, too." Liam answered truthfully but didn't volunteer details. He would tell Dax what he had to share, and he wouldn't lie, but he wasn't going to volunteer too much information, especially not information about Sarah.

After another beat of silence, Dax said, "So again, how does this involve you?"

"She needs help."

"She asked you for help?"

"No. That's why I sent *her* info to run, too."

Liam ran a hand through his hair, trying to keep his gaze on the back of Sarah's head as best he could from behind rows of mostly occupied chairs. His eyes scanned the room for a minute, looking for anyone who seemed out of place or inordinately interested in Sarah.

"Liam."

The sound of his name pulled Liam's attention back to the phone conversation. He understood his friend's confusion. None of them went around involving themselves in other people's business. Operatives at Infinite Security didn't announce their identities. They stayed in the shadows unless the case required otherwise.

Dax wouldn't let it go.

"You still haven't told me how you got involved in this."

"I can't turn my back on this situation. That's the best I can explain it."

Liam himself couldn't figure out why he was so determined to help Sarah, so how was he going to explain it to Dax? Dax knew him well enough to know that Liam wasn't interested in having a relationship with anyone. He knew about Kelsey.

Maybe for that very reason, Dax apparently decided to stop pushing for an explanation.

"Roger," the other man said then hung up.

Liam ended the call on his side and shoved the phone in the front pocket of his current pair of trousers. He'd been unable to wear the trousers he'd worn this morning. Those, Sarah had blessed during their interlude back at the hotel. There was no way he'd be able to stay focused with the scent of her passion on him. He could maintain focus for hours in uncomfortable positions and dangerous situations but wearing the other pants right now would've been too much of a challenge even for him.

Despite all his training and experience, he was still just a man.

Chapter 8

Sarah

Sarah struggled to stay focused on the bidding. Normally she was unshakable in the hunt for the prize she was chasing – on what needed to be done to acquire the items wanted by her clients. Today, though, her mind wouldn't settle down. Something was going on with her client, Edward Collins, and instinct told her it wasn't good. Nobody was ever ready and willing to pay too much for an item unless there was sentimentality attached. More than that, he wanted her to bid outrageously high. Auctions just were not done that way.

Maybe she could see the big picture more clearly if her mind wasn't buzzing from her time at the hotel with Liam. The curved scar on his left cheek was the only thing that kept him from being *too* handsome. Sarah wondered where he'd gotten it. Then she wondered if he had any others elsewhere on his body. Would she ever get a chance to find out?

Sarah shifted in her seat. Adjusted her grip on her phone and checked again for messages, even though she couldn't have missed one. *But can you ever be completely sure?* Maybe the reception wasn't good in here? Even as she had that thought, she swatted it away.

Auction houses consistently maintained top-tier connections and checked them constantly. If it wasn't for that, maybe they wouldn't have even been a delay earlier.

She wanted to look around and see where Liam had gone, but she couldn't take her focus off the auctioneer. The man spoke quickly, not as loudly as if it was a livestock or outdoor auction, but if she didn't pay attention she could lose the flow.

"Ladies and gentlemen, lot number L76342 in your catalog." The auctioneer droned on about title, publishing date, and all the other details before opening the bidding. Sarah's eyes drifted to her phone and iPad again. No new communication.

She knew Liam was behind her before he slipped back into his chair. It was like her body was attuned to his already. Sarah knew he was looking at her but the first lot Collins wanted should be up next if the catalog order was still being followed. She glanced at him to acknowledge him and tilted her chin to the front of the room, trying to indicate that she had to keep her focus on the action.

Liam said, "Got it. Just follow the instructions he gave you."

There were polite murmurs and a scattering of applause when the gavel clapped down to close the lot.

Sarah turned slightly toward Liam and said, "But what if, you know..."

She didn't want to say it out loud, but hoped he might understand her expression. If Collins was doing something illegal and she participated in it, wouldn't that make her some kind of accessory to his client? The worry was overwhelming.

Without the additional funds Sarah needed for her father every month, her dad wouldn't be able to get by. Even worse, if she got in trouble with the law, it would wreck them both.

"I've got your back, Sarah." Liam sounded so confident. "Do your best to win with whatever he authorized you to use, and however the client instructed you to do it."

Her stomach was in knots. She wasn't used to letting someone else make her decisions. Right now, both Collins and Liam were giving her instructions – although Liam was telling her to do as Collins said, so it was more an echo of the client's directions than a different set.

She was confident in her knowledge and skills. That also meant she was always willing to listen to advice, do research, take things seriously, and get the facts as best she could. As part of her process, Sarah had extensively studied the auction catalog as soon as it became available. She also learned as much as possible about the two books her client wanted from this auction.

The auctioneer dropped his gavel to get everyone's attention and announced the start of the proceedings. Sarah watched the nervous-looking auction assistant from early in the morning bring out the next tray with a book upon it.

"Ladies and gentlemen, may I present to you lot number L753 – A09, an excellent example of carefully preserved American heritage in the form of a book of poetry by Henry Wadsworth Longfellow. As you can see, we are starting off this auction with this highly antici-pated volume of Longfellow's work, published in 1880."

It was a lovely book, but not what her client was seeking. As the auctioneer droned on and the bidders bandied about their offers, Sarah kept trying to figure out why on earth Collins was anxious to spend so much more than he might need to. It made no sense.

When money matters didn't make sense, there had to be a reason. Sure, sometimes the reason could be an eccentric bidder with deep pockets, or a sentimental desire for a particular book. Sarah really didn't think that either was the case with Edward Collins.

The first book Collins wanted came up on the screen that showed next to the auction. She clicked over to her notes on that item. At its introduction, Sarah made the opening bid. In quick succession, three other bids were placed. She raised her indicator again, and was recog-nized by the auctioneer. The three other interested parties placed additional bids, and then a bid was presented by an auction house rep manning a telephone.

Sarah bid again, followed by two of the other original three parties, and then the unseen person on the telephone. Again, Sarah raised her bidding paddle. One of the original three opposing bidders dropped out that time, and the auction house facilitator placed another bid for the party on the phone. When Sarah bid again, both of her remaining opponents bowed out, leaving her the winner.

She maintained her calm, professional demeanor, but inside she was pumping her fist in the air and jumping out of her chair. Every time she won an auction for a client, the triumphant feeling was fantastic.

As the next several books came and went on the auction platform, she darted a couple of glances at Liam. He looked so relaxed. When he caught her eye, he winked.

It was so unexpected that she did a double-take as if trying to confirm what she'd just seen. Liam was so serious that he'd gotten others involved, but he still managed to distract her.

"Ladies and gentlemen, may I present to you lot number R-317279 a beautifully bound 1823 edition of selected works by Percy Bysshe Shelley, the first one published after his death. Your catalog contains a detailed description and listing of the specific works within." He indicated the large screen behind him and several of the same positioned around the room. "If you look to the displays, you can get a very clear view of the original silk presentation cover that came with this volume of poetry. As you can see, the condition is pristine."

Sarah's eyes flickered to the board where a close-up view of the book was displayed along with the lot number. She squared her shoulders and took a steadying breath, then waited for the right moment to enter the fray. She expected it to be more challenging than the last lot had been.

She needed to secure the books Collins wanted, because she had big bills to pay, and the cost of nonpayment would be much too difficult to bear. And not just for herself.

Chapter 9

Liam

Sarah had won both books her client was seeking. When the gavel dropped on the second one, the Shelley volume, there were still two items remaining in the auction catalog. Those had closed quickly. He'd only been interested in the Shelley volume but didn't bother bidding on it; he couldn't compete with the obvious wealth of Sarah's buyer, and he didn't want to give her any more stress. When she looked at him in confusion during the bidding on that item, he simply smiled and shrugged.

While Sarah concluded her business on one side of the auction room, Liam stood in the back of the auction gallery, in the same rear alcove as before. Most attendees were already gone from the room. Several people, like Sarah, were still filling out paperwork with auction clerks. They were kept widely separated to maintain privacy and an air of discretion.

Even though the alcoves offered some privacy, Liam consciously kept his voice low so no one would overhear his telephone conversation.

"What do you mean he doesn't exist?" Liam kept his eyes on Sarah while he repeated what Dax had just told him.

"I mean exactly what I said. They can't find an Edward Collins involved in book collecting, or anything similar."

"It doesn't make sense. I even saw one of the messages she received from the guy," Liam said. "They've done business before. He has transferred money to pay for his transactions, and a portion of her commissions."

Sarah had explained to him that the remainder would be paid to her upon delivery of the books to her client. It made sense to him.

"The name could be an alias," Dax pointed out, then hesitated. "You don't know this woman well at all. You don't know what her game is."

"I think she's being honest. I feel it." Liam pinched the bridge of his nose. "What would be her endgame in lying about this?"

"I don't know, man. Did you mention you are bidding on the same thing as her or something like that? Was she trying to reduce the competition?" Dax theorized.

"I don't see how. She'd already told me some of this before we may have mentioned book preferences." Liam thought about it for another few seconds. "I don't even think we ever mentioned titles specifically."

With his eyes still on Sarah, Liam tried to replay their conversations in his mind with as much detail as possible. No, she hadn't been lying to him. He knew how to spot the clues and cues people gave when they were lying. She didn't show any of them.

Dax interrupted his thoughts again. "You said she won both auctions. That means it doesn't really matter now, does it?"

Phone in one hand, Liam shoved the other in his front trouser pocket. "I'm telling you, Dax, something's not right with this. And I don't mean Sarah's behavior." He watched her shuffling through the small stack of paperwork she'd been given by the auction house representative. "When she got the last messages from this Collins guy, she was distressed. Genuinely upset." Liam recalled how her face had paled and the speed of her breathing had visibly increased. "She said she thinks he's up to something. She's worried."

"Liam. It's not your responsibility." Dax was very matter-of-fact. "She can alert the auction house if she thinks something is off about it."

"And make herself the target of some guy who could be a criminal?" Liam shook his head even though Dax couldn't see him. "That doesn't work for me."

"You feel protective of this woman so quickly?" Dax said. It was a question but spoken as a statement.

Liam tried to decide what to say in answer. He went with the simple truth, which wasn't that simple after all. "Yeah. Can't explain it, but I do."

Silence bounced loudly between them.

Finally, Dax said, "We'll keep digging. Let me know if you get any other information from her." Dax fell silent again, but it was the type of loaded silence that Liam knew portended something more to come. He didn't have to wait long. "Liam, you know we have to investigate her, as well."

"I know." He *did* know. He didn't like it, but he understood that it was necessary. Infinite never took on a client without a background check and some level of investigation to make sure (as much as possible) that the person was being honest with them.

"Okay," Dax said.

"Looks like she's done with the forms she was signing. I'll update you when I can." He pressed the red dot to end the call and slipped the phone back in his pocket.

Sarah shook hands with the auction house representative and turned in Liam's direction. For someone who had triumphed in bidding wars for two lots at the auction, she looked decidedly unhappy. He took a step or two towards her but waited for her to come to the quieter area where he stood.

"Everything okay?" Liam could see on her face that it wasn't but didn't think telling her so was the right approach.

"Not really," Sarah shook her head slightly. "Would you come with me? I have to go upstairs to the main level and then take another elevator to the business offices so I can accept the lots and complete the money transfers."

"Of course."

Liam walked with her back to the entrance to the salon, then accompanied her in the etched bronze- looking doors to the elevator. She pressed the "up" button so they could head upstairs to the main level. He couldn't help but notice that she looked even more upset than she had moments earlier.

"Sarah. What's going on?"

She hesitated for several seconds, staring at the arrival indicator plaque above the elevator. He knew she'd heard him, so he remained quiet.

At last, she looked his way and replied. "Collins texted me three times while I was doing all the paperwork with the guy from the auction house. He wants me to call a number he gave me for details, but he wants me to deliver the books to him in some Chicago suburb." Her eyes were locked onto his. "I've worked with him a few times before on smaller deals. He never did that."

The chime of the elevator announced its arrival on the first floor. With barely a sound, the shiny doors parted, revealing the carpeted interior. He put his arm against where one of the doors had retracted to make sure it didn't close too quickly. He let her step off first.

"What did you do those times to deliver the books?"

Sarah walked past him and down the hall to another elevator. The transaction offices were on an upper level. "I had the auction house ship them to whatever address he specified."

They stepped into the second elevator when it arrived. She pressed the number for the floor they needed. Sarah clutched her belongings to her chest in a protective stance.

"This time, though, he wants me to bring the books to him personally. In a Chicago suburb," she said. "He didn't even give an explanation, just told me to come to Naperville, Illinois and call him from there."

"Why doesn't he just let you have the auction house ship them, like you said he usually does?" Such a drastic, sudden change in procedures was a bright red flag.

"I don't know," Sarah said. "I told him I couldn't talk now, and that I was concluding the transaction."

A gentle chiming sound announced their floor. When the doors splid apart, they revealed two men in suits waiting their turn to board. Liam stayed close to her side as they exited the elevator and kept himself between her and the men. He glanced over his shoulder to make sure they both got on the elevator. Then he followed Sarah's lead; clearly, she knew her destination.

He kept his voice as quiet as possible, "How did you leave off with Collins?"

"That I'll call as soon as possible. Within a couple of hours." Sarah stopped outside the third door on the right and double-checked a blue form in her hand. "This is where I need to complete the transactions. You don't have to wait for me. From this point, it's usually fairly quick, but you never know." She shrugged. "It varies."

From his own experiences, he understood.

Liam nodded. "Not a problem. If anyone insists I can't wait here, and I can't convince them otherwise, then I'll be in the shopping area of the front of the first floor."

There is no way I'm leaving this floor he thought, but he didn't tell her that because he didn't want to give her something else to worry about.

"Thanks, Liam."

Sarah knocked lightly on the door, then opened it slowly. Liam could hear the muffled tone of the woman's voice greeting her. Sarah looked back at him with what looked to be a forced smile. The stress showed clearly in her stiff posture and in the way her normally full lips were pressed so tightly together in a grim line and in her stiff posture.

Instead of standing directly outside the door like a bodyguard or creeper, Liam continued four doors down to the end of the hall. Two wingback chairs that looked like they came from a royal palace stood in the corners at the end of the hall. They were flanked by a pair of matching mahogany side tables with intricately carved legs. He leaned against the wall between the stately chairs, relaxed but on alert, and called the office.

Dax answered on the first ring.

Liam asked, "Anything?"

This time, Dax was completely serious, with none of the teasing from earlier. "Edward Collins is not an uncommon name. Rick finally came up with one guy in particular who is involved in auctions, particularly book auctions." He paused. "We've been doing a deep dive on him. Some of his associates are bad characters, Liam."

Liam had straightened his posture as he listened. "Bad, how?"

"Forgery. Counterfeiting. Money-laundering," Dax said.

Liam shared with Dax the new information about delivery. "In multiple prior transactions, Collins instructed Sarah to have the auction houses ship the books she acquired on his behalf directly to him." Liam ran a hand through his hair, tugging at the ends. "This time he wants her to hand-deliver the items to him in a Chicago suburb."

"Did he tell her why?"

"We didn't get to talk about it in detail yet," Liam said. "She's finishing up here."

"What do you want to do?"

It was a fair question. Liam wasn't sure what to do right now. There were too many unknown variables for him to decide the best way to proceed. He leaned his head back against the wall, then quickly straightened up to continue monitoring the hallway and the door through which Sarah had gone.

The outline of a loose plan started to take shape.

"I want to bring her to headquarters. Get more Intel. Figure out how to keep her safe." Liam paused. "I'm not leaving her alone to deal with this. From what I do know already, there are multiple red flags."

He waited to see if Dax would object. If he would point out that

Sarah wasn't a paying client of Infinite. That they hadn't fully investigated her story yet. Liam was prepared to hold his ground; Sarah needed help and he was going to make sure she got it.

"Roger that," Dax said. "We'll keep digging. Let me know when you're en route."

"Will do."

Liam disconnected the call, surprisingly relieved that Dax had agreed so readily. He glanced at his watch, surprise at how much time had passed. When he'd won books in the past, this part of the process had gone quickly. He wondered if it had something to do with the price of the auction lots.

* * *

More than twenty-five minutes after his call with Dax concluded, Sarah finally emerged from the office where she'd been handling final details for Collins. In addition to her tablet, she carried a bag from the gift shop on the first floor.

Liam moved to her side. "All done?"

She nodded, lifting the bag slightly. "Yes. Both lots are under all this tissue paper, disguised as gift shop merchandise paper."

"Clever."

Though he hadn't known Sarah long, her ongoing tension was readily apparent to him. Liam realized that not only did he want to help her, but he *needed* to help her.

He spoke quietly, but he didn't try to hide the intensity of his statement. "Sarah, let me help you deal with this guy."

She started walking in the direction of the elevator. "My problems aren't your problems," she said. "You hardly know me."

She sounded like Dax. Liam knew she was right. He also knew it didn't matter.

Liam kept pace with her and banished her protest as easily as he did the one Dax made. He'd spent his whole adult life taking care of other people's problems. No reason to stop now.

He stood next to her in front of the closed elevator doors and nudged her with his shoulder. "Our impromptu breakfast at my hotel got us knowing one another quickly."

Sarah laughed. She couldn't stop the blush that colored her face, even if she might've wanted to. "I can't argue with that, can I? But – "

The now familiar melodious chime announced the arrival of the elevator. Liam was glad there were no other passengers. Still, he spoke quietly. "Would you come back to my hotel with me to discuss the situation? I spoke to my team leader, got more info about your client." He turned toward her more completely. "We can help you."

"Like I said, though, it's not your problem. I'm not trying to be ungrateful, but I still can't understand why you want to help me."

He gently caressed her cheek before dropping his hand back to his side. "I can't *not* want to help you. I don't think I can explain it better than that."

Chapter 10

Sarah

Why did Collins want her to hand-deliver the books this time? And since when was he in Illinois? He'd never had her ship to him there. She knew he traveled extensively, but she definitely remembered him mentioning that he was out of the country this week. Of course, it wasn't any of her business. Not really.

Except when it impacted her directly, like now.

Liam walked closely by her side, holding the bag from the auction house in the hand closest to her and away from the street. He walked more quickly than he had earlier, and she kept pace with his more purposeful stride as best she could in her high heels. He spoke to her so quietly she struggled to hear him over the sounds of the city traffic.

"We're going to stop just a few minutes for me to grab my things from the hotel. We can talk more on the way to my headquarters." He squeezed her fingers. "I'll figure this out with you so you can get the packages to your client safely and be done with it."

Sarah wished she felt as confident as he sounded. They reached the hotel even more quickly than they had that morning – or maybe it just seemed that way. This time, she couldn't take a few moments to look around and appreciate the beautiful, albeit imposing space. Her mind was racing, and she appreciated the way Liam's grasp was helping to keep her grounded.

She stood just inside the entrance to the hotel suite, holding tight to her personal belongings. Sarah gently tugged the bag from the auction house away from him.

"Do you have a car in the city somewhere?" he asked.

"No. I used public transit."

"Okay, that makes it easier." Liam held her gaze steadily. "My company's headquarters are out on Long Island. You know I was vetted by the auction house, and everything we talked about before. Are you comfortable coming with me so we can help you?"

Before she could reply, he frowned. "I guess Collins was also vetted by the auction house, so maybe that doesn't carry much weight with you."

"I'm not comfortable with anything having to do with auctions or Collins right now," she said. "But I have to admit that I do trust you." She blew a heavy breath out through pursed lips. Even though it was embarrassing, she said, "Obviously, I trusted you this morning, or else I wouldn't have been intimate with you. Why stop now?"

His facial expression shifted from concerned to relieved to pleased.

"I won't let you down on this either," he assured her.

Sarah's eyes fluttered closed as he leaned closer to seal the promise with the gentlest of kisses. When he pulled back, she leaned forward and rested her forehead on his chest. She was an expert on old and rare books, *not* potentially shady dealings by a potentially criminal client. Much as she wanted to be independent and handle everything herself, there was no denying the fact that she'd benefit from help.

When she straightened again, she told him, "Thank you."

Liam turned in a circle, and it seemed that he was looking for something. He took a few steps over to the table next to the couch in the sitting area where she'd gotten so comfortable with him that morning. He grabbed something off the table, and she realized it was the remote control when he pointed at the flatscreen television set mounted on the wall. He turned it on and clicked through several screens. She watched him utilize the quick check-out feature on the hotel channel. Liam dropped the remote and the room key cards on the table at which they'd sat for breakfast that morning. It wasn't even really nighttime yet, but it had already been a long day.

"I'm checked out," Liam said. "I only need a couple of minutes to pack my stuff."

"Of course."

He headed for the doorway into the bedroom, leaving it open. She hadn't gotten a chance to see it that morning, and she was curious, so she followed him.

Sarah stood in the doorway to the bedroom with its burgundy and cream decor. She watched him pack his clothes into a large duffel bag he pulled from the closet. She studiously avoided giving the bed more than a passing glance.

"You put everything in the drawers." She couldn't stop from sharing the observation. "Have you been in the city a while?"

"Just a couple of nights."

Something else popped into her head and she had to ask. "Are you on vacation or something? Were you supposed to be here longer, and I screwed it up for you?"

He responded immediately as he tossed the last of his clothes into the bag. "No. And it wouldn't matter anyway. Nothing is more important to me right now than getting this resolved for you."

Before she could even form a reply to that incredible statement, Liam moved into the bathroom to get his toiletries, she allowed herself to look at the king-sized bed that dominated the room. If they hadn't been interrupted this morning, would they have ended up right there?

She knew the answer even as she posed the question to herself. Based on what had passed between them in the outer room, they would have not only ended up in the bed, but they would've also practically set it on fire with the heat that burned between them.

"I've been thinking about us in the bed, too." Liam stood in the doorway to the bathroom, toiletry travel case in hand. Watching her.

Was there any point denying the truth? He wasn't embarrassed by his thoughts, so why should she be?

"Great minds think alike, and all that?" Sarah said lightly.

"Absolutely." Liam dropped the toiletry case in his open bag. He stepped closer to her, reached out and pulled her tightly against him. "We'll get there. And when we do, it'll be phenomenal."

Her hands came up automatically, one to his waist, the other to his shoulder. Liam was warm and strong and felt so good under her hands. "Confident about your abilities, aren't you?" she teased.

He lifted a hand to her face, traced her cheekbone with his thumb, something she'd noticed he liked to do. "I am, but I'm more confident in the power of whatever this is between us."

When his mouth descended upon hers, she met him more than halfway, and the kiss that followed left no doubt about the truth in his words.

Chapter 11

Liam

Depending upon the day of the week, time of day, route selected, weather, roadwork, season, and other random variables, the drive between Manhattan and Infinite headquarters on Long Island could take anywhere from thirty-five minutes to a couple of hours. Today, the GPS was predicting an hour and twenty-four minutes.

It was a good chance for him and Sarah to get to know one another better. He'd already learned more about her because it hadn't escaped his notice that her hand was in her bag, likely clutching her phone in case he did anything she didn't expect, and she needed to call for help. Sarah had entered the address of their destination from the GPS into the maps program on her iPad, a smart way to keep track of where they were at any given time. She'd know right away if he deviated from the expected path.

Liam kept his mouth shut about those indicators that she wasn't completely sure he could be trusted. He knew it wasn't personal; she was trying to straddle the line between accepting help, and being suspicious of that help, in the form of *him*. It was good fortune that he happened to be at the book auction today, but that coincidence could also potentially look suspicious.

He couldn't quite believe it himself.

"Would you like to listen to the radio, or listen to me talk about myself and Infinite Security?" He glanced in her direction. "Me talking won't be as entertaining, but it might help you relax a little bit."

"Are you trying to warn me that you'll be so boring it'll relax me? Because I doubt that's true." Sarah spoke lightly, but he could hear the underlying tension.

In his peripheral vision he could see she was maintaining her careful positioning, one hand in the bag and the other on the iPad.

"I should probably start with some more about me, then." Liam clicked on the turn signal and changed lanes to get out from behind a car driving too far under the speed limit. "I finished high school at seventeen and joined the Navy a year later. Served a total of about twelve years, ten of those as a SEAL."

He certainly didn't need to give her details about the ambush that led to the injuries that resulted in his honorable discharge before his second contract had finished up, or about those injuries.

Liam continued, "Within six months after I left the military, I was contacted by Dax, a guy I served with for a few years, and recruited to join a security agency he'd helped establish."

Again, he was leaving out some information, like how Kelsey had died because he was so wrapped up in feeling sorry for himself. Sarah didn't need those details, either.

Sarah asked, "I think I'm not supposed to ask about what SEALS do, right?"

"It's not that you can't ask, so much as it is that I can't answer anything but the broadest questions."

"From what I've heard and read about over the years, it's an extremely dangerous career," Sarah said.

"Can be." The ache in his leg, the scar on his face, and the variety of healed wounds and other service-related injuries that littered his skin gave silent testimony to that.

"But you joined a security company that, as you told me before, handles a big variety of cases. Including dangerous ones, right?"

"Yeah."

Sarah was silent for so long he wondered if she was ending the conversation. Then she asked, "Did you miss having a dangerous job?"

Now she thinks you're an adrenaline junkie.

Liam tried to answer carefully, with honesty, and a conscious effort to not put her off.

"I'm someone who likes to fix things. To make things right. That's always been the way I am, and it was one of the main reasons I joined up. Having the opportunity to still make a difference, now in the private sector, is important to me."

Traffic was moving at a crawl again, and he took the opportunity to look over at Sarah for more than a couple of seconds. She'd taken off her sunglasses, and the natural light coming in through the windows accentuated the brighter tones in her caramel-colored eyes.

"I think I understand better now," she said.

Liam returned his attention to the road. "Understand what?"

"Why you're willing to help me."

"Good."

"Liam, this may be a waste of time," Sarah said. "I really can't afford to pay for professional people to investigate Edward Collins. Or to escort me to Illinois."

"Infinite routinely does a certain amount of *pro bono* work. When I spoke to Dax from the auction house, he already agreed that this would qualify."

Sarah made a sound that could best be described as a decidedly unladylike snort. "What, the nerdy book lady discount?"

He had to laugh. "Between you and me, I'd prefer to call it the naughty librarian discount."

"You did *not* just say that!" she exclaimed, reaching as if to shove his arm but then stopping herself. No doubt she realized that pushing the driver of the vehicle while in traffic on an expressway wasn't a great idea. It helped that she didn't know that he'd had to fight off armed bad guys while driving. Or while the bad guy was driving.

Liam hastily dispelled any thought she might've had that he'd shared their intimate moments with Dax or anyone else. "Sarah, seriously though, I didn't and wouldn't ever share what went on between us with anyone else. Our personal business is just that. Ours."

Finally at the Glen Cove exit, he flipped on his turn signal. When they exited the expressway, the heavy traffic immediately started steadily dwindling down. Proceeding north on Glen Cove Road, he guided the SUV through the increasingly scenic shopping area. The road finally narrowed, until it ended at a T-shaped intersection. He turned right and started the last leg of their drive to Infinite headquarters.

Although the estate had a front entrance, he used the small access road on the east side, which brought them to the rear of the renovated carriage house. There were multiple cars parked on the gravel apron behind it, but Liam used an opener tucked into his visor to release the garage door. Two of the spots inside were empty. He pulled into the one on the far end and closed the door behind them. Once it was secured, he released the vehicle locks.

Sarah had closed the cover on her iPad and was already taking off her seatbelt. Her other hand was still in her bag. Even though she looked more relaxed than she had an hour ago, Liam knew she had to be wary.

"I asked Jillian, who you spoke to earlier, and Callie, another one of my colleagues, to meet us here. I didn't want you to feel overwhelmed and outnumbered by just the male members of my team," Liam said.

As if on cue, an access door toward the front of the modified garage opened and two women came through it. Jillian was tall and willowy, with tanned skin and glossy, shoulder-length dark hair. In contrast, Callie was several inches shorter, with pale blonde hair pulled up into a high ponytail and fair skin.

Sarah smiled at Liam. "I appreciate that. Very much."

Glad that his idea had helped the situation, even if it was only a little bit, he swung open his door. "Let me get your door for you."

He walked around the front of his SUV while she checked herself in the visor mirror. She didn't have to look; he could have told her that despite the stress of the day, she looked impeccable. A little tired, perhaps, but gorgeous.

Sarah slipped her iPad and mobile phone into the tote bag and pushed the whole thing up to the crook of her elbow. Liam wanted to take her hand while she stepped down, but he forced himself to let her do it on her own and not invade her personal space.

Before Liam could make the introductions, the women introduced themselves to one another. The immediate niceties concluded, Jillian beckoned toward the inside door. "Why don't we get you inside? I have a couple of simple forms I need you to fill out and sign, and we can grab you a cup of tea or coffee or whatever. Liam, Dax and a couple of the guys are in conference room B. I'll bring Sarah down when she's ready."

"That okay with you?" he asked Sarah. "I can go with you."

"No, it's okay." Sarah looked calm and at ease. He wished he was sure if it was the truth, or if it was a professional mask she knew how to wear. *She's an adult*, he reminded himself. *If she needs you, she'll say so.*

Chapter 12

Liam

Not even an hour later, Liam held Sarah's hand in his own and rested both on his right thigh. The meeting was small, just them with Dax, Mason, Rick, and Callie. He could see that Sarah was stressed, but she was holding it together.

"Have you worked with Collins before?" Dax asked.

"Yes," Sarah said. "A few times over the past year or so."

Dax leaned back in his chair. "Since you worked for Collins before, you must not have been uncomfortable with the experience or you wouldn't be working for him again, correct?"

Sarah shifted slightly in her own seat. "Clients aren't friends. I don't work with someone based on if I like them or don't. They have to be able to communicate with me what it is that requires my knowledge and skills. They must be able to pay for lots they win, plus the fees, and my commission."

Liam resisted the urge to take over the conversation, although it was a struggle. He wanted to help Sarah, not add to her distress. It was important that the team ask necessary questions, but he could at least make sure she knew he was there with her. For her.

"And with Collins those things worked out okay in the past?" Dax confirmed.

"Yes," Sarah said. "But this time has been different."

"How?" Dax asked the logical follow-up question.

"Collins was very specific about what he wanted me to acquire at the auction, but he wasn't merely hopeful that I would be successful for him. He was ... *insistent*. Auctions don't work that way. Not really. You just never know who the other bidders are going to be in person, on the telephone, and online."

"Walk us through your client process." Dax asked.

Sarah's eyes went to Liam, who nodded at her in silent encouragement.

She took a moment to gather her thoughts, then started with some basics.

"Sometimes a client has a particular auction lot or multiple lots in mind. Other times they have me be on the lookout for them among upcoming auctions." She didn't know how familiar the other men were with auction lingo and procedures, so she kept it simple. "In both cases, we talk about the item, and then we iron out specifics about what they are willing to pay."

Across the table, Mason nodded in acknowledgment of her statement. He asked, "Are you in touch with clients during the actual process?"

Dax added, "Walk us through the auction."

Again, Sarah seemed to consider her thoughts before she replied.

"If I'm not constantly in touch with the client during the live auction process, then we are usually at least reachable by phone and by text. I work from written instructions setting the parameters. Mostly things like how high the client is willing to go in pursuit of winning the auction lot." Sarah paused again, then continued, "An auction lot can be a single item or can include really any number of things to be bid on together."

Liam appreciated the seriousness with which she was handling the discussion. Truth be told, it bordered on being more of a polite interrogation than a discussion. He didn't like it, but he understood the need for it.

"Collins wanted more than one auction lot today?" Mason asked, clearly looking to verify what Liam had already told the team while Sarah had been busy with Jillian.

"Yes," she confirmed, and then elaborated, "A volume of poetry by Percy Bysshe Shelley and a collection of poetry by lesser-known 19th-century authors."

Mason followed up with another question. "What was different in dealing with Collins for the transactions today?"

"He let me know how determined he was to win the two particular items he wanted. Determined enough that he ordered me to make very high bids right after the opening of bidding for each."

"You mean instead of bidding in sequence?" Dax asked the question while he kept making notes on a yellow legal pad. He underlined something he'd written. From his vantage point on the other side of the table, Liam couldn't see what it was.

"Yes," Sarah nodded.. "And the initial bids he told me to place were above what the items were expected to go for. He is experienced enough to know that isn't how it's done."

When she stopped speaking, Liam squeezed her hand under the table in what he hoped she understood to be a gesture of support.

He added onto her last comment, "Expectations aren't always met at auctions. Lots can go for a lot more or a lot less than what was expected, or not even be sold at all."

Dax tapped his fingertips on the table. "Sarah, you didn't think that simply meant Collins really wanted to win?"

"I don't." Sarah answered immediately. "If he just wanted to win, why not let the auction process play out and authorize me to go to his maximum bid? That's what would make sense." She was emphatic. "It doesn't make sense to increase the bid amounts so aggressively."

"Give me your opinion," Dax said. "Why would he do it that way?"

Liam was certain Dax was of the same opinion he was. Money-laundering, or that combined with some other purpose. But he wanted to hear Sarah share her own thoughts.

She let go Liam's hand and put both of hers on the table, clasped in front of her. "I can't help but think he wanted to open the bidding high because he had some other motive."

Dax' gaze flickered to Liam, then focused again on Sarah. "What kind of motives do you think he could have?"

"I've been thinking about that all day." Sarah spoke slowly and thoughtfully, as Liam had already realized was often her way. He reminded himself that she wasn't accustomed to dealing with criminals and conmen the way he and his team were. She continued, "Some kind of money laundering, maybe? Especially if he knows the sellers."

Liam hadn't thought of that. He asked another question of his own. "Do you think Collins knew the sellers? They were different sellers for the two lots, right?"

Sarah half-turned toward him when she answered. "Supposedly. But real identities can be hidden, can't they?"

She was more aware of criminals and conmen than he'd thought.

Rick spoke up from his seat at the far end of the table. His ever-present laptop computer was open in front of him. "Were the auction lots worth hundreds of thousands of dollars?"

"No, nowhere near that much," Sarah said. "Not in my opinion."

"Why don't you show them the items you acquired for Collins today?" Liam phrased his words as a suggestion, but they were clearly an instruction.

"Sure."

Sarah picked up the bag from the gift shop from where she'd placed it on the floor by her feet. She set it on the table in front of her. Next, she dug a small bottle of hand cleaner/disinfectant out of her purse. She quickly rubbed it between her hands and gestured to the other occupants of the room. "If anyone else wants to examine the books, I'd ask that you use this first.

Sarah withdrew the books from the bag and unwrapped them both.

"No gloves?" Mason asked

"No." Sarah smiled at the other man, and Liam was surprised at how much he didn't like that.

Sarah took a moment to explain what many people outside those who dealt with old books didn't know.

"Most people who deal with old and rare books don't wear gloves, because it affects how safely and securely they can be gripped. More damage is caused by dropping things and accidentally tearing them than by simply handling them with clean hands."

Gingerly, she held one of the books out to them for their perusal. "Percy Bysshe Shelley died in 1822, at the age of 29. He drowned when his boat capsized in a sudden storm off the coast of Italy. When it happened, he was already a renowned poet. His widow, Mary Wollstonecraft Shelley, was the author of *Frankenstein*."

Sarah held the book up higher and turned it slowly. "You can see this book has a removable cover, something of a precursor to the modern book jacket. It's basically a silk gift wrap and was secured with a wax seal." Slowly, she traced two fingers along the side of the volume. "Would've been published in 1830, by which time it was very chic to give a book as a gift."

Sarah turned the book around to show them the back, holding it away from her body and turning first to her left and then to her right so everyone in the room had a clearer view.

"You can see that the seal was broken, no doubt by the original recipient. So, since then, the silk ribbon holds it all together."

Sarah took a couple of minutes to walk around the room with the book in each hand so she could show everyone an even better view of them, then she returned to her seat. Carefully, Sarah wrapped them up again.

"Having the original silk cover on the Shelley book makes it even more valuable because so few of the covers have survived."

"Sarah, explain about the change in delivery plans," Liam said.

She gently laid the books on the table next to the bag from the auction house. "When I worked with him before, Mr. Collins let the auction house ship to him. Today, though, he told me I have to bring him the lots. Out of state."

"Where?" Dax asked.

Gracefully, Sarah sat down in her chair. Outwardly she looked calm, but Liam heard the note of nervousness in her voice when she spoke. "Naperville. In Illinois."

Liam gently laid his hand over one of hers where it rested in her lap.

Dax's frown mirrored Liam's own. "And he didn't discuss that with you ahead of time?"

"No." Sarah shook her head. "I wouldn't have agreed to that." She paused. "Or, at the very least, I would've demanded a higher commission rate or some additional compensation." Her eyes shifted to the table top. "I have arrangements to make. It's very difficult for me to just up and leave."

"How are you supposed to pay for the travel?" Liam's own anger at her client's behavior surprised him.

He wasn't a relationship guy. Not after the pain of losing Kelsey. But he could be there for Sarah now, and until this Collins business was done.

"He said to get my ticket, and he'll reimburse me," Sarah said.

"Not cool to spring it on you like that," Callie said. "Rude."

Mason remained focused on the bigger picture. "If it's not money laundering, what else could this be about?"

"I wish I knew."

As interested as Liam knew she was in the conversation, it was obvious to him that Sarah was fighting the need to yawn. She'd mentioned earlier that she had been awake for 18 hours or more and had barely slept the night before. That, combined with the tension she had to be feeling was clearly making her terribly tired.

"When does he want you in Illinois?" Dax asked.

"Two days, tops."

"There are too many red flags here," Liam said. "Something's not right."

"I don't like it." She was stressed and tired. Worried.

Liam watched her press her lips together and fight to smother another yawn. At least the third since this meeting had begun.

He knew he wasn't going to let her deal with this strange situation on her own, but they couldn't solve everything immediately. They didn't have all the answers. Not yet, at least.

However, there was *something* he could fix right now. "Sarah, we're going to look for more information, try to come up with some ideas that might help. That's what we do." He squeezed her hand where he still held it under the table, then gently rubbed his thumb over her knuckles. "There are a few guest rooms here. Why don't you try to rest a little bit? Give yourself a break."

Liam could see the indecision in her expression. She was probably torn between her mind wanting to stay in the conference room, and her body needing to rest.

He could already read her well enough to see when she'd made a decision.

Sarah lowered her eyes and when she spoke, her voice was suddenly very quiet. "I think that's a good idea."

Chapter 13

Sarah

Sarah kicked off her shoes and opened a few of the dresser drawers. As she'd been told, there was an assortment of clothing in them, each piece in several sizes. It only took a minute to choose sleep pants and a loose T-shirt that she should be able to sleep in comfortably. The room had an *en suite* bathroom nicely stocked with travel size toiletries, individually packaged toothbrushes, and other various items, including feminine care products and condoms. The latter was a surprise and made her think of Liam.

She wondered for a moment if he'd show up at her door tonight, even though he'd said good night to her when she walked off with Callie. Sarah banished the thought.

Sarah stripped off her clothes, folded everything neatly, and stacked them on the side of the dresser. After she finished washing away the long day, she dropped the used towels into the hamper under the sink. It seemed presumptuous to put her clothes in there, so she didn't.

She'd hoped the warm water would relax her, but when she stretched out on the bed the tension running through her was no better than it had been before.

Sarah looked around the room more thoroughly than she had before. It wasn't lavish by any means, but it was nicely appointed, kind of like a moderately- priced hotel room. It certainly was nothing like the fancy hotel suite Liam had rented in Manhattan. This room was decorated in shades of tan and cream, with accents of blue; overall, it had a corporate sort of vibe.

Never in her life had she envisioned the existence of a real company like Infinite Security. Sure, there were things like it in movies and some fiction books, but not in actual reality. Since arriving, though, she'd met five or six rugged and handsome men who looked like they were action figures come to life, and two beautiful women who were also sharp and obviously well-respected by their male colleagues. Sarah had glimpsed other people here and there, each of them totally fitting with the general vibe of the place.

She'd seen multiple military and government commendations framed and displayed on some of the walls. Sarah hadn't asked to examine them for authentication purposes, but to her trained eye they look like the real deal – or at least, top-notch forgeries.

This place engendered confidence.

The queen-sized bed was surprisingly comfortable. Sarah twisted just enough to plump up the pillow under her head. She was looking forward to sleeping.

Instead, Sarah stared at the off-white ceiling for a while. She hadn't turned on the light fixture in the middle of the ceiling, instead opting for one of the lamps on the two nightstands that bracketed the bed. She closed her eyes. Opened them again. Turned onto her right side, then tried the left. After a few more minutes passed, Sarah sat up again and wiggled herself backward until she was leaning against the headboard.

Even as tired as Sarah was, her body wasn't ready to fall asleep yet.

When Liam had noticed her fighting a yawn for what he said was the third time, he'd suggested she rest a while in a guest room that would be hers for the night. At the time, part of her had wanted to deny, but she couldn't deny how weary she was, or how grateful she was for the offer.

Now, though, she couldn't rest. Her mind was twisting.

Sarah swung her legs over the side of the bed and scrunched her toes into the soft carpeting. After eyeing the giant chocolate chip cookie she'd brought with her to the room, she picked it up off the nightstand.

She wasn't much of a gym person and could never appreciate the "joy" of jogging. It was obvious to anyone with eyes that the people who worked at Infinite Security didn't share her feelings about exercise. They all appeared to be extraordinarily fit.

Stationary cycling, some basic yoga, and somewhat balanced food choices were the best she could do to stay in shape. Sarah took a bite of the sweet treat. Maybe most of the people who were employed here didn't indulge very much, but they certainly had good cookies on offer in the break room.

Everyone she'd encountered at Infinite headquarters was polite and professional, but could they really help her? Did she really *need* help?

Maybe Collins was just another eccentric client. She'd certainly had a few of those over the last couple of years.

Even as she tried to convince herself of that, Sarah knew it wasn't reality.

What was Collins up to?

Sarah took another bite of her cookie and followed it with a sip of water.

What am I going to do?

Abandoning the rest of her cookie on the small table, Sarah lay down again. She folded her arms around a pillow and clutched it to her middle.

She slept fitfully for a few hours, then woke again. After more tossing and turning, sleep claimed her for several more hours. When she woke again, the unfamiliar surroundings confused her for a moment before all the details of the last day dropped into place in a rush. The worries were no less overwhelming than the night before.

All the uncertainties battled for top billing.

The concern that won was her decision that unless Liam and the Infinite Security people came up with some definitive reason she couldn't go out of state to meet with Collins, she was going to have to do it, despite how much she didn't want to. The world of rare books and book auctions was too small to risk her burgeoning reputation.

She needed her commissions. Her dad's care was incredibly expensive, and she was barely keeping up with the necessary payments on what insurance wouldn't cover. If she had to go to Naperville, then so be it.

Her dad wouldn't even be aware that she wasn't near enough to visit. It'd been more than three years since the accident, and his condition still hadn't improved at all.

The doctors all said that traumatic brain injuries were unpredictable at best. The road to recovery could be slow and erratic. It could also lead nowhere. Recently, there'd been a little bit of improvement in his grip strength and cognitive function. But in the grand scheme of things, was the cognition level of a six year old child really all that much better than that of a four year old? The man she visited as often as possible wasn't her father in any way she could recognize; except, of course, for his basic physical appearance.

Overthinking wasn't going to accomplish anything. Sarah reached for her handbag where she'd dropped it on the nightstand. She unzipped the top and dug around in the center compartment, searching for her cell phone. 6:22 a.m.

"Highland Hills, how can I direct your call?" The receptionist for the nursing home and rehab center was cheerful as always.

There were four primary receptionists who rotated shifts behind the desk in the mail lobby. By now, Sarah knew them all as well as one could know someone in this kind of situation. It was formal, but somehow intimate, too.

At each level of interaction with staff at Highland, the structured intimacy grew more comfortable and therefore also more uncomfortable. Part of their professionalism was in trying to make the terrible situations surrounding the residents easier, which therefore involved helping family members feel more relaxed. The lines blurred strangely at times, because no matter how anyone dressed up the situation, it still sucked.

"This is Sarah Prescott," Sarah replied. "Unit three, please."

"How are you, Sarah? This is Casey." The receptionist lowered her voice. "I saw your father with a nursing assistant last evening. They were on their way to sit outside. He looked good! At least, to me he did."

"That's great to hear," Sarah said. "Do you remember which assistant?"

"Joanna." Casey raised her voice again. "I'll put you right through."

Before Sarah could thank her, the line at the desk on the unit was ringing in her ear. Mornings were especially hectic on all the units and she wouldn't normally call at this time, but she didn't know where this day would lead. She just had to know how he was doing. On the fifth or sixth ring, someone picked up.

"Unit three, Jamie speaking. Can I help you?"

Sarah didn't know if Jamie was a nursing assistant, an aide, a supervisor, a nurse, or an administrator. She could also be a physical or occupational therapist who happened to be standing there, or a volunteer helping out by picking up the phone. Not that it really mattered at the moment.

"This is Sarah Prescott. I'm calling about my father, George Prescott. Room 310. I'm sorry to call at such a busy time of day, but is there someone who can give me an update"

"Sure. Let me get you the CNA assigned to him this shift." The other woman spoke quickly and then was gone.

Sarah put her cell phone on speaker mode. It could take a minute for the Certified Nursing Assistant to pick up the phone, or it could take a half-hour, or anything in between. At first it'd been frustrating when she'd call and have to wait what felt like forever. Then her regular visits quickly taught her that the environment on the floor at Highland was controlled chaos. Witnessing it gave her a whole new level of patience and understanding.

Shifting on the bed to get more comfortable, Sarah also tried to ease the tension in her neck and shoulders. The first care facility she'd gotten her father into had been a rude wake-up call and a lesson about how badly those places could be run. Overcrowded, too many patients and not enough staff, staff members who really didn't give a damn, cheap supplies, unsanitary conditions, inattention... it hadn't taken long for Sarah to decide to find something else. Something better.

Her mother died of an aneurysm when Sarah was just three years old. Sarah had a couple of pictures of the woman, but no real memories. Lucky for Sarah, her loving father had provided her with the best education possible, from kindergarten through to her graduate degree. Tutors, extracurricular activities, vacations, he'd done anything he *could* do to make her life better. Easier.

There was no way she would ever even consider not doing the same for him.

"Ms. Prescott?"

Sarah immediately recognized the lilting Haitian accent of the woman who picked up the phone.

"Yes. Hi, Rose."

"He's having a good morning today," the older woman told her. "Mr. George was outside for a while after dinner yesterday, and he's been telling me about it. He's had breakfast, and is dressed, and now he's resting and watching television before speech therapy at eight."

Sarah's shoulders slumped in relief. It was good he wasn't starting the day already agitated.

"I'm sorry to have called so early, but I may have to go out of town for a few days for work. I wanted to check in first because I probably won't have time to stop there before I leave. I'll be reachable on my cell phone. And I'll visit as soon as I'm back in town."

Sarah could hear more voices in the background as traffic in the hallway at Highland gradually increased. She could picture the tall woman adjusting her eyeglasses and turning toward a wall to focus on their conversation.

"You do what needs doing. Your father is okay." Rose said. "I tell you again, you visit much more than most family members do. You can't live here."

"I know."

It wasn't the first time Rose had said so. Knowing that other people treated their family members poorly only made Sarah feel more badly for patients and residents. It didn't make her feel less guilty about not spending more time with her dad.

Sarah plugged the phone back into the charger and walked over to the *en suite* bathroom. There was no way she was getting any more sleep, so a shower and a change of clothes was in order.

Chapter 14

Liam

Liam paced around the small octagonal table hidden within the larger of the two gazebos in the rear gardens of Infinite headquarters. The removable white latticework on the eastern side of the structure obscured the view of them from the mansion. Today, the panels on the eastern side were off, allowing for a cooling breeze from the Sound to wash over them.

Dax was usually the one who couldn't sit still, but today he observed silently as Liam took the path he himself usually trod. "I thought you'd be glad to know she lives alone, has no husband, no ex-husband, and no boyfriend."

"I already knew that," Liam retorted. "She would've told me if she was with someone." He wanted to say that she wouldn't have found her pleasure on his lap if she was involved with someone, but he wasn't about to reveal anything that had passed between them to this crew. Hell, he wouldn't reveal that to anyone. He'd never disrespect Sarah that way.

"So you found out she's been doing this as long as she said, and that she lives alone." Liam stopped walking and faced Dax directly. "Why do I feel like there's some kind of problem?"

"Not necessarily a problem, but maybe some of the motivation she has to see this through," Dax said.

"Come out with it already." Liam wasn't one for beating around the bush; he much preferred to be direct and honest. At least whenever possible.

Dax gestured to Rick, who took off his glasses and told Liam, "Sarah's father, George Prescott, is in Highland Hills. It's a nursing home and rehabilitation center near Westchester County."

That was something Liam wasn't expecting. "Is he ill?"

"In a matter of speaking." Rick leaned back in his chair. "He was severely injured by a hit-and-run driver several years ago. His case is —"

Liam held up a hand to forestall him. "I don't need to hear anymore unless she shares it with me. I hate that we invaded Sarah's privacy like this."

"I get that," Dax said. "It does explain why she is so determined to make sure her client pays what he owes her. Care at Highfield isn't cheap."

It certainly did give him a window into understanding even more clearly why her career was so important. Why every client, including Collins, mattered so much to her. If she was responsible for paying his medical expenses, it had to be a big monthly expense.

He eyed Rick. "I don't suppose you looked at Mr. Prescott's financials or insurance info?"

The other man smirked at him. "You know me so well." He didn't even have to check his screens or his files. "Medical insurance isn't that great, and what it does cover was maxed out for the year a while ago. He has very little left in savings."

The information confirmed what he'd already surmised about her character. "Sarah is picking up the difference to keep him there." It wasn't a question. He hadn't known her long, but he *knew* her. Knew that Sarah would do what she believed was the right thing to do. Knew that she'd worked tirelessly if it meant she could provide the best possible care for her father.

Knew that he'd probably never be able to convince her to let someone else handle the book delivery.

And he also knew that he was still going to try. He was going to be there for her. He failed Kelsey, but he wasn't going to fail Sarah. It wasn't the same situation, but he'd be damn sure there wasn't the same end result.

Liam leaned against one of the pillars that supported the gazebo structure.

"This guy is insisting Sarah meet him in Naperville, Illinois, to deliver the books. Says he'll give her the address when she gets there, because he's not sure exactly where he'll be." Liam scowled. "Sarah tells me she's dealt with him three times. She said although he had her bid more money than she thought made sense, he didn't do anything like he's been doing this time."

"What's your take on it?" Mason spoke up for the first time. Because he was a mountain of a man, people tended to underestimate how smart and serious he was. Instead, they focused mostly on his size.

"I think she should go back to the auction house and get them to ship to Collins, but she says she can't do that because it's not his instructions. And she doesn't have a definitive address to use."

Liam ran a hand through his hair for what had to be the seventh or eighth time during the conversation. "Plus, she already took posses- sion of the lots. Signed all the closing paperwork. I don't think the auction house will undo that without authorization directly from Collins."

"Can't somebody go to Illinois in her place?" Dax asked.

"I offered when we were on our way here," Liam said. "She insists that under the contract the lots are her responsibility and must be in her control until she hands them over. Or they have to be under the control of a licensed and insured carrier agreed upon by her and the client." He crossed his arms and made eye contact with each of his colleagues "I'm going with her, whether she likes it or not."

"You have a reason to think she won't want that?" Rick asked, eyeing him over the top of his open laptop.

"No, but if she argues, I need you guys to back me up," Liam said.

Dax nodded. "You're right; she shouldn't go alone. Maybe it's legit, but the way this Collins guy is going about it makes the situation strange at best."

Rick posed another question. "Where do you want to fly out of?"

LaGuardia Airport was primarily focused on serving domestic flights, and Kennedy International Airport focused on international flights, as the name indicated. Then there was MacArthur Airport, a much smaller one further out on Long Island. Even though Infinite headquarters itself was on Long Island, the Queens airports were often closer in terms of travel time because of traffic.

Liam thought it through yet again. "I think the least obvious choice would be out of JFK, since it will be a domestic flight out of an international airport. That's the best bet." He looked around the room. "Anyone disagree?"

"Makes sense." Rick was typing again, probably already searching for flights.

Dax had his arms crossed and tapped the fingers of his left hand silently against the top of his other arm. "Are you expecting trouble?"

"Not really," Liam admitted. "But I'm not taking unnecessary chances with her safety."

"When does she need to get there?" Rick interrupted. "Does she have instructions about that? Do you want to go into O'Hare? Or Midway?"

"Yesterday Collins told her two days."

The sudden change in delivery procedures, the tight timeframe, the whole thing had Liam's internal warning systems raising all the alarms. He damn well wasn't going to ignore the noise.

"Any preferred destination airport?" Rick repeated his second question.

"What airport is closest to Naperville?"

"Midway," Mason said.

"How did you know that?" Liam asked. If memory served, Mason was from the DC area, not the Midwest.

Mason didn't answer, just gave him a blank stare. The guy was steadfast and reliable, always dependable no matter the situation, but Mason never shared anything personal about himself. Not that Liam was much better. He'd shared some key things about Kelsey with Dax, though. Maybe Mason also shared personal info about himself with the head of the company.

"Can you find something into Midway?" Liam directed his question at Rick.

"On it," Rick said.

Liam couldn't shake the feeling that making this trip was a mistake. He was going to try again to talk Sarah out of it. There had to be another way to complete the delivery.

* * *

"You don't have to go with me, but I'm going."

"You said yourself he's never done this before," Liam pointed out. "On top of his uncharacteristic bidding instructions, it's a big red flag."

"I also don't need you to treat me like a child," Sarah said. "I'm aware that the situation is odd. Eccentric bidders are not unusual in my field of work. Bottom line is, the contract I signed with Edward Collins did not specify delivery instructions, and that was my mistake."

The expression on her face showed how frustrated she was by that fact. He felt like an ass throwing the next question at her, but he had to do it. "Why did you overlook that?"

"Foolishness. Stupidity." Sarah crossed her arms at her waist. In self-protective, defensive position. "He offered me such a high commission rate but time was of the essence to accept it, or he'd move on to someone else."

Collins had manipulated her. He knew or suspected Sarah couldn't pass up the lure of a big payday and reeled her in.

Liam's intention hadn't been to embarrass or upset her. He needed to understand as much as possible about the situation, and how Sarah had embroiled herself in this mess when she was a woman who had impressed him as being sharp and savvy.

Not only did he have a better understanding now, but it also revealed that Collins must have found out about Sarah's personal situation, the way Infinite had found out. Her client knew she had extraordinary financial obligations pressing down on her. It made sense for a buyer to check into the professional credentials and success record of someone they might hire to represent them during the bidding process. Maybe even pull a consumer credit report to make sure the person wasn't likely to abscond with anything he won. But that required obtaining consent.

"Did you give Collins your Social Security number and permission to run a credit check?" Liam asked.

"No. He never asked for that." Sarah said. "Why?"

"I'm trying to figure out how much Collins knows about you, personally." Liam rested his hands on his hips. "Trying to get in his head."

"I don't much care what's going on in his head. I just need to get him the books and get my money. That means making the delivery myself and not causing problems or giving him an excuse to say I didn't abide by the terms of our contract."

Chapter 15

Sarah

John F. Kennedy International Airport was a massive, sprawling complex. For a few months after high school graduation, she'd worked for an aviation maintenance company located in the cargo area. More recently, she had read an article that out of the more than five thousand public airports in the United States, JFK continually ranked among the five busiest. Arrivals, departures, cargo areas, parking, long-term parking, eight terminals, eight train station stops, and a slew of other things all made up what amounted to a small city unto itself.

At such a busy location, no one was going to be able to find and bother her and Liam, or the expensive items she carried.

And why would anybody want to do that anyway? The books were valuable, but not *that* valuable. No one would be seeking them out. She knew that. But theft was always a worry when valuable books were in her possession. They were her responsibility until she handed them off to a designated party.

The only one outside the auction house (and a few people at Infinite Security) who knew she had the books was Collins, and she was bringing them to him anyway. No one else would even think she had the lots on her. Most buying agents would have shipped them already. Even if someone *did* know she still had possession and wanted to steal the books, they'd have no way to know where she was. They'd never know she was traveling out of state.

She was sure she was perfectly safe.

Liam was handsome, compelling, and protective, but he was also being paranoid. Sarah had to admit to herself that his overprotective concern was flattering, even if it was also unnecessary. It probably went along with the requirements of his job, though, so she could understand it.

She couldn't deny that she was rattled by the order to meet Collins in another state. But not so much that she wouldn't deliver the items and make sure she got paid. Anybody could be eccentric, and in her experience, wealthy people tended to be more eccentric than others. The commission she earned from winning the auction lots Collins wanted would cover several months of care for her father, plus her personal monthly expenses for those months. That made the unexpected request worth the risk.

Sarah could admit the request did seem strange, but that was primarily because it was not preplanned. If he had requested it at the outset, she'd have asked for more money, yes, but she would've done it. Maybe Collins was going to give her a bonus for accommodating him in this? He had to be pleased that she'd achieved his objectives, right?

Feeling quite satisfied with the common sense of her logic, Sarah secured the non acidic paper more snugly around the books she would be transporting to Illinois. They were such wonderful volumes; it was a privilege to even touch them. It irritated her endlessly that some people only valued old or rare books because they were worth money and didn't appreciate the history that went along with them.

How many hands had held these books? Who had read these verses in these exact books to help win someone's heart? Which poems about far-away lands had inspired people to travel, in the days before airplanes, trains, and motor vehicles?

A soft knock at the door interrupted her thoughts. Sarah quickly crossed the room to answer it. Within Infinite Security headquarters she certainly didn't have to worry about who was on the other side of a closed door.

When she opened the door and their eyes met, Liam said, "You didn't ask who was knocking."

He was as handsome as ever, and his smile again made the butterflies riot in her stomach. Being with him made her feel like a young teenager crushing on the senior quarterback. Except Eddie Galway had never noticed her, and Liam not only noticed her – he kissed her and touched her like a dirty dream come true.

"I figured it was you," she said. "But if it wasn't, I know that in this building, I'm safe."

"I can't argue with that." He leaned his left shoulder against the door frame. "Can I come in?"

Sarah stepped back, pulling the door open further, embarrassed that she'd been standing like she was intentionally blocking the entrance. "Of course."

When Liam stepped past her, their bodies brushed against each other. She closed the door. They'd been intimate yesterday morning, but it seemed like a long time ago already. Too long ago.

Yesterday she'd been confident and bold. Today, she felt awkward. Unsure about how to behave with him now. It was like she had gone from being a self-assured, modern woman and regressed to being a shy, insecure teenager.

Fortunately, Liam displayed no hesitation at all. He gently but firmly tugged her into his arms. "How are you doing, beautiful? Talk to me, Sarah."

His nearness, his heat, the scent of his skin, made it hard to catch a full breath.

"Well enough, I guess. The room is great. Everybody's been very nice." She hesitated. She needed to speak her mind so she directly met his gaze. "I don't understand exactly why you all think this could be some kind of dangerous situation, instead of simply an annoying one. His behavior doesn't necessarily mean he's dangerous. He's probably just another quirky client."

"Let's sit down." Holding her hand, Liam led her over to the royal blue two-seater sofa against the wall.

It didn't escape her notice that he hadn't addressed her comments.

"Is there something you haven't told me?" Sarah asked. She hated how nervous she sounded.

Liam sat so that his body was angled toward her, one of her hands still in his. His voice was calm, his eyes steady on hers. "From what the team has discovered so far, Collins is associated with some shady characters."

"Shady?" Sarah repeated. "In what way?"

"He has business and social dealings with people who function on the wrong side of the law," Liam said.

It was obvious to Sarah that Liam was choosing his words carefully, and that made her even more nervous. Was he wary about saying something inaccurate? Or about frightening her?

"You don't need to dance around whatever you're trying to say, Liam."

"Look, Sarah, this may have nothing to do with whatever else Collins is or isn't involved in. But it's also strange that he's demanding you bring the books to him in another state when that wasn't part of the agreement, and you said he's never asked you to do that before." He paused. "And then there's the fact that he instructed you to basically overbid to a degree that raised red flags for you." Liam leaned closer to her. "All those things add up to something suspicious going on with him. You're a smart woman, Sarah. I know you're concerned, and I am, too. So I'm going with you."

"I agree that something isn't right, but it doesn't mean I'm in danger." She shook her head, then tried to make her voice as calm and reasonable as possible. "I saw all kinds of commendations and certificates of appreciation downstairs. Your company handles major issues. This isn't a major issue. It's an issue about an eccentric collector. I don't need a protective detail or a bodyguard, whatever you want to call it."

"Then don't think of me as a bodyguard. I'm just a fellow old and rare book enthusiast who can't resist your charms and wants to spend time with you," Liam said.

Sarah wasn't going to let him charm his way around her valid points. "You *are* a bodyguard, and that's why you want to go with me to Illinois."

In the second before he answered, his facial expression tightened. "Yeah, that's part of it," he admitted. "But another part of it is that I want to spend more time with you." Liam looked awkward and slightly embarrassed as he told her, "I haven't felt this way about anyone in a very long time."

"Me either," Sarah admitted, feeling just as awkward. Then she squared her shoulders.

"So are we going to treat this like a date?" Sarah smiled at him. "A first date doesn't typically involve traveling to a different state by airplane."

"Think of it as me being someone who goes the extra mile. Or the extra 800-miles."

Chapter 16

Liam

Liam had traveled in and out of JFK International more times that he could remember, and some part of the hectic airport was always under construction. This time the backups started on the Belt Parkway as they made the approach to the main entrance of the airport. Even though Liam was in the backseat with Sarah, he could hear Mason grumbling under his breath about the traffic.

"You didn't have to drive us, man," Liam said. "I could've taken my car or called a rideshare or something."

"We do appreciate it, though," Sarah hurried to add. She elbowed Liam none too gently, and he realized she thought he was being rude.

He slid his arm around her shoulder and hugged her, whispering, "It's okay. He enjoys being grumpy."

"I heard that," Mason said, catching Liam's eyes in the rearview mirror. Then the big man said more mildly, "Happy to help *you* out, Sarah." When Liam gave him the one-finger salute, Mason laughed.

The traffic on the approach to the airport was a mass of speeding cars and lane changes that frequently seemed death-defying. The well- marked airport exit was a wide access road with brightly colored signs.

The airport property was highly organized chaos with detailed signage, number keys, and color-coding. All the drivers seem to be exceeding the posted speed limits. Sarah simultaneously braced her right hand on the seat in front of her and tangled the fingers of her left with Liam's. Mason maneuvered the SUV smoothly into the passing lane.

"Delta Airlines," Liam reminded Mason. "Terminal 2."

Mason replied with a sound that was a grunt more than a word.

The vehicle rounded a curve, then another. Then Mason pulled into a turning lane for a parking lot marked for Terminal 2.

When she'd argued with Liam against driving to the airport, Sarah had told him that the last few times she'd used this airport, she'd accessed it via the simple and efficient air train. This time, instead of repeating that, Sarah simply said, "Can't you just drop us off at departures? That way you don't have to park."

Liam shook his head. "We're both going in with you. Mason's not going to Illinois, though, just to the gate."

"It's already overkill for you to go to Naperville with me," Sarah said. "There's no threat or anything against me. No one even knows who I am, or what I'm carrying with me. Even if someone saw books, they wouldn't even realize they are something special." She withdrew her hand from his. "Being accompanied by two big guys makes me stand out more than if I'm just traveling alone, anyway."

"What you you want me to do?" Mason asked, again looking at Liam in the rearview mirror.

Liam thought it through again, quickly. Yes, Sarah was right, there was no overt threat or anything against her. But he just knew something wasn't right with all this. It was that old and unwelcome feeling again; anytime he'd ever ignored it, he'd regretted it. He was not taking a chance like that again, especially not with something involving this woman.

He shook his head and spoke firmly. "We have enough time

before the flight to not take chances. See how close you can find a spot, or if we have to take a shuttle bus."

Sarah sighed, but Mason nodded and stayed in the turn lane.

For all the traffic and chaos of people and luggage moving in all directions, they'd parked and made it into the terminal with surprising speed.

Neither he nor Sarah had any bags to check. It was going to be a short trip and a quick turnaround. Liam adjusted the small duffel bag on his shoulder and his grip on Sarah's tiny carry-on suitcase. She insisted on holding her big handbag, her "personal item", which she had slung across her body in a safety hold.

Mason accompanied them as far as he could without an airline ticket, which was to security. Some airlines offered gate passes, but Delta didn't. At least not yet.

At the security checkpoint, Liam kept a close eye on their belongings and Sarah while going through the body scanning metal detectors. He grabbed their things from the plastic bins. After making sure he had the three correct items, he jammed his feet into his boots while standing; Sarah pressed a hand against the wall to do the same. Looking over the crowd, Liam caught Mason's eye and gave him a chin lift in thanks. The other man reciprocated and vanished into the crowd.

"We have a little time. Do you think we could grab something quick to eat when we get closer to the gate?" Sarah asked. "I know it's a short flight, but..."

"Sure. There won't be meal service, and a little bag of pretzels isn't going to cut it." He shouldered his duffel, with the handle of her suitcase again on that same side and took her hand with the other. "Let's see what looks good."

Chapter 17

Sarah

The main food court was crowded and loud. Sarah would've thought that the vaulted roof would have amplified the sound, but whoever the architect had been designed it so that the acoustics weren't overpowering. Men's, women's, and children's voices rose and fell in waves of sound, multiple languages wrapping around one another in unpredictable harmonies.

The vast space could've easily felt dark and tight, but an array of glittering skylights brought in plenty of natural light. The huge sheets of glass made the crowded space seem much less overcrowded than it might've been otherwise.

Every table Sarah could see was occupied. Although at this point no one was carrying luggage to be checked, there was still plenty of small carry-on suitcases, backpacks, storable duffel bags, shopping bags, and assorted other carry-on items all over the crowded space.

"What would you like? I see a bunch of the standard options. Burgers, Asian, chicken, vegetarian, a sandwich place." Liam observed. "Any of that sound good?"

"A burger and fries, or mixed vegetables and rice. A simple turkey sandwich. I'm good with almost anything, really," Sarah said.

Out of the corner of her eye she spotted a man and woman with a young child in a stroller with a huge gate claim ticket attached to the handle. The woman was gathering their belongings in preparation for getting up from a square table some five feet away from where she and Liam stood.

"I'll see if I can grab this!" she told him, hurrying in the direction of the small family.

Smoothly, Sarah maneuvered over to the now nearly empty table-top. She smiled at the toddler in the stroller. The little girl smiled back and waved her plush unicorn toy excitedly. Sarah addressed the woman who had her hands on the handle of the stroller and was taking the parcel in the basket beneath it.

"Are you finished with the table?" She felt almost silly asking the question, because it was so obvious they were done, but it wouldn't be right to simply assume.

"It's all yours," the other woman said.

The blonde man with her had thrown away the trash and now stacked the family carry-on bags one atop the other. He somehow latched them together and grasped the handle of the top one

Sarah slid onto one of the chairs. "Thanks so much. Safe travels!"

They walked away with their stroller, their little girl who was chattering away, and their happy smiles. Sarah allowed herself a moment to wonder if they were going on a much-anticipated vacation, or to visit family somewhere. Sarah envied their happiness and how carefree they appeared to be – and she hoped it was a reality for them, not just a façade. Appearances could be deceiving; people thought she was happy and content also.

Liam was next to her before the other couple had even vanished from her line of sight. Looking around, he frowned in Sarah's direction. "We should stay together. I'll take the bags, just come to the line with me."

"This is still right in the food court," Sarah said. "You can leave the bags with me and free your hands to carry food."

He put a hand on the back of her chair and leaned over so his face was close to hers. "I can't protect you if I'm not near you."

"Liam, like you agreed before, there's no threat against me or anything like that. Collins is behaving strangely, but he's in Illinois waiting for me. Not here in New York."

Sarah appreciated his concern and diligence, and she knew that he'd already told her he was a protector by nature. But she also knew she was right in what she said – no one knew what she was carrying, and there were no threats against her.

"Liam, either you stay with the packages and the table, and I'll get the food, or the other way around. Or we both get the food, we lose the table, and then we'll have to sit on the floor in a corner to eat. That will make me uncomfortable and unhappy. Or I can sit here, *safely*, and you grab the food. But one way or the other, we're running out of time," Sarah said. She beckoned him closer and said quietly, "There are no threats to me. Please."

Hands on hips, Liam turned in a slow circle, obviously assessing the situation as best he could from their vantage point. Facing her again, he dropped a quick but thorough kiss on her lips. He waited until she was settled in a chair facing in the direction where he was going to be grabbing food for them.

"Stay alert, Sarah. If anything seems wrong or anybody bothers you, yell for me. Get someone's attention. Okay?"

"I will," she assured him.

She watched Liam walk away in the direction of the popular fast food chicken place that was between the hamburger joint and the sandwich place. He was tall, but at a certain point it was still hard to see where he was in the crowd.

Sarah adjusted the long strap of the cross-body bag over her shoulders and tugged both her little suitcase and Liam's small duffel bag even closer to her feet. She'd traveled enough to know that during the boarding process at the gate, airline agents would ask again if the carry-ons had been in their control and possession the whole time.

No way was she going to put herself in a situation where she had to lie; she was a terrible liar.

Her stomach rumbled.

Like she'd promised, instead of allowing anything to distract her, Sarah watched the people within her field of vision as best she could. It was no exaggeration to say that crowds in the area continued to grow, maybe because it was afternoon now. Maybe the delicious aroma of food was pulling more people in. Maybe there were simply more flights at this time of day.

People watching was always entertaining, especially where so many diverse people were gathered. Sarah found herself wondering where particular people were headed. The guy in the three-piece suit on such a hot day, was he off to an important business meeting in a faraway place? The two young women in flip-flops and cut-off shorts, were they traveling to beaches on the other coast or on a Caribbean island? The mother with four small children, was she wrangling them alone or did she have a travel companion currently buying food for them all?

Where is Liam?

Sarah looked at her phone and wished she'd done so when he'd gone to get *their* food. He had to have been gone 15 or 20 minutes by now. The food court area was so crowded, they might end up having to rush after all if they were going to eat and make their flight.

The hair on the back of her neck prickled in a strange way, and she stiffened. Before she could look behind her, a hand clamped down on her shoulder with a punishing grip. Sarah twisted in an attempt to see who was grabbing her so tightly that it hurt.

"Hey!" Sarah exclaimed to the person who wouldn't let her turn all the way. She could see the hand on her shoulder though, and it was definitely that of a man.

"Shut up and smile," the man snapped at her. "Where is it?"

He still wasn't letting her turn enough to get a good look at him; all she could see was that he was burly, with a plain black baseball cap pulled down low, dark jeans and a black windbreaker.

"What are you talking about?" Sarah demanded, angling her head and trying desperately to spot Liam. She fought the urge to get hysterical. This had to be some kind of misunderstanding.

"Keep your voice down," he warned her, then continued, "You know what I'm talking about." The man used his grip on her shoulder to shake her slightly. "Fast, or your boyfriend there is going to get a sharp greeting from my associate."

Her mind seemed to stutter as she tried to decide what to do, then she told him, "I don't understand!"

Was this about the books? *What else could it be?*

"Gimme the fucking package or your boyfriend gets cut. Right there in the food line. Clear enough?" He shook her again, more roughly this time.

This time, Sarah was physically frozen as her mind raced. Shock had her hearing her own heartbeat in her ears. The moments were distorted, as if in slow motion.

The guy grabbed her arm and hauled her out of the chair. He bent and picked up both the duffel and the suitcase and roughly pulled her away from the table. She stumbled after him, trying to keep him from dislocating her arm with his merciless grip.

What are you doing, she silently yelled at herself. *Scream! But what if Liam or someone else gets hurt because I scream?*

Then it was like a switch was flipped on inside Sarah. Suddenly everything was moving in real-time again. The need to act stomped over her internal worries. She heard herself screaming so loud it echoed in her head and in the huge space.

Sarah dug her heels into the tile floor as best she could, trying to slow down and twist away from the furious stranger.

Bystanders were scattering in all directions. Sarah heard people yelling, and several shouts of "Stop!"

The would-be kidnapper veered to the left. She didn't know where he was heading but she wasn't going to stop struggling and make it easier for him to haul her along. Sarah tried to grab onto anything she could, but he didn't let go of her. She almost tripped over the luggage he abandoned. He moved faster and slammed his way through a door at the end of the intersecting corridor.

His grip on her wrist was so tight she could feel the bones rub together under her skin. Sarah stumbled behind her assailant, trying to keep up so she didn't fall but also trying to make him stop. One suitcase escaped his hand and bounced down stairs. The noise echoed like they were in a wide canyon instead of a narrow airport stairwell.

Her attacker yanked her down the first set of stairs and around the turn at the bottom but before he started on the next set of steps, he shoved her against the rough wall, his arm brace on her throat, pinning her in place.

"Where's the fucking package?" He snarled the demand in her face while he scrabbled at the handbag securely draped across her upper body. He couldn't dislodge it, especially as Sarah slapped at him while trying not to increase the pressure against her throat.

"Leave me alone." She tried to yell but couldn't take in enough air to support a lot of sound. "Help! Help!"

"Shut up," he snapped at her, clearly frustrated at his failure to get her bag free. He started pulling her down the next set of steps.

Sarah grabbed at the metal banister with her left hand, trying to slow their descent enough to wrap her arm around it.

Above them, the metal door banged open and brought with it an influx of sound. Multiple voices. Some kind of alarm. Running feet. And above everything, Liam's voice, shouting, "Sarah!"

Her attacker hesitated, apparently torn between abandoning her or still pulling her along. Above them, the door to the stairwell banged again. And then again. More voices echoed in the passageway as additional people arrived in pursuit. The assailant made his decision clear by shoving Sarah to the concrete floor and taking off, jumping down several steps at a time.

Sarah pushed her face up off the ground and struggled to catch her breath. Her heart pounded, accompanied by the sound of her own heavy breathing.

Then Liam was there, crouching next to her.

Her attacker was gone. The sound of running footsteps were fading as he escaped down the stairs.

"I'm TSA Officer Kyle Minton. Are you both okay?" The introduction and question came from someone nearby but positioned several steps above them. "What happened?"

"White male, 5' 10", black windbreaker, jeans, black baseball cap, hightops, running down the stairs," Liam said quickly, and snapped, "Give chase and seal the exits."

Even as Sarah tried to process what had just happened, she noticed how confidently Liam spoke to the officials. He wasn't one of them, but he was obviously used to taking charge of situations.

As he spoke, Sarah shifted up to her knees. With trembling hands she checked that the bag containing the books remained safely strapped around her. That the slight weight of it wasn't some figment of her imagination.

She turned her head and saw two men wearing the royal blue shirts of airport security go racing down the stairs in pursuit of her attacker. The other man in the same uniform, Officer Minton, was on a phone or radio, giving instructions to someone else.

"Did he hurt you?" Liam spoke quietly, calmly, but she could feel the tension radiating off of him.

"I don't think so," she said hoarsely. Her voice was rough from screaming and dry from fear.

"Hold on to me," he told her as he lifted her into his arms and stood.

The comfort of Liam's hold banished Sarah's instinct to make a self-deprecating comment about him not hurting himself by carrying her. She buried her face in his neck, breathing his comforting scent, her right hand holding tightly to the muscles in his shoulder, her left gripping his bicep.

"He said if I didn't cooperate his "associate" would stab you or something while you were in the food line." Sarah tried to push away and get a better look at him, but it was impossible from high up in his arms. "Are you sure you aren't hurt?"

"I'm fine, honey." Liam kissed her forehead. "I have to ask you the same question. Are you sure *you* aren't hurt? You just flinched like you're in pain."

"No. Not really," she said.

There was no need to tell him she was sore in so many places from the guy's rough handling. Sarah lifted her head to look him in the eyes. "He said he wanted "it" and referred to a package. It has to be the books. But how would they know I was here? I don't understand."

"I don't either. Yet." He stared at her, and Sarah could see that he was still assessing her condition. "Do you think you can stand?"

"Yes," she said and nodded.

"Are you all right, Miss?" A woman in an airport security uniform joined the man with whom they'd spoken previously, and both were now standing close to them. Sarah wasn't sure how much she wanted to say in front of them.

The female officer spoke again, "I'm TSA Officer Angela Nichols. Do you need medical attention?" The woman had her radio in hand. "I can have EMS here within a few minutes."

As soon as she finished speaking, the male officer said, "Was anything stolen?" Before Sarah could respond, he also told her, "We have officers in pursuit. I need to take a full report from you, Ms....?"

"Prescott." Sarah filled in the blank for him. "I'm Sarah Prescott." She looked over to the female officer. "I'm shaken up, but that's about it. Thanks for the offer, but I don't need EMS."

All she wanted was to get out of there. Get to where she could think through what had just happened and try to make sense of it. The questions she'd had about Collins' strange behavior had been magnified by what just went on. Was there a connection? Could the attack be truly random? Based on what the attacker had said, the answer was an emphatic "No!".

Even in an airport as huge and metropolitan as JFK International, any crime was taken seriously. Sarah and Liam were escorted to an office in a private, lower level area of the terminal. Their carry-on luggage had been safely retrieved from the food court, untouched. In fact, one of the TSA officers told them that another traveler had stayed with the bags where they'd been abandoned near the stairwell, in an effort to protect their belongings.

Sarah was grateful for the unexpected act of kindness on this hellish day.

Sarah and Liam sat across from Officer Minton with a small silver desk separating him from them. The chairs were also small and silver, and uncomfortable. Or maybe it was her sore body making the seat uncomfortable. Whatever the reason, she felt lousy.

The first few minutes were spent on rudimentary information. Name, address, contact information. A copy of her ID. Employment information. Then came the tougher questions, trying to determine if she could have been a target.

She couldn't verbally discuss it with Liam, but Sarah was certain she didn't want to share her suspicions with these people. It was too complicated. Too speculative.

"I'm an expert on rare books and certain types of antiquities," Sarah explained when Minton asked for details about her career.

"Do you carry valuable items with you?" was his follow-up question. Minton studied her over the frames of his reading glasses.

"No." Sarah kept her answers as short as possible. "Auction houses typically ship the items directly to the recipient."

After another few questions, Liam interrupted. "I already advised your associate that we are not going to be traveling today after all. Sarah needs to rest after the trauma she went through. Are we done here?"

As he asked the last question, he was already standing and reaching out a hand to help Sarah do the same. She put her hand into his, glad to have him taking charge of the situation.

"I suppose we can be." Officer Winton sounded less than enthusiastic about finishing up, but he cooperated anyway. Maybe his issue was more the fact that Liam had ended the interview instead of him doing it.

Sarah settled her cross body bag around her again and picked up her tote. "Thank you so much, officer." She offered the best smile she could manage. "Will you let me know if you catch the man?"

Winton also stood. "Absolutely. Even though he eluded the officers on the scene, we are reviewing camera footage and will continue our efforts to find him."

Sarah doubted that was true. The man hadn't succeeded in stealing anything. He hadn't severely injured her or killed anyone. With such a vast airport property to police, the TSA and Port Authority Police Department, as well as the NYPD in Queens and the rest of New York City had much more pressing matters to focus on than what amounted to a random, unsuccessful mugging attempt.

Chapter 18

Liam

Mason drove more sedately back to Infinite headquarters than he had on the way to the airport. There was no plane to catch now. No point attracting attention or skirting any laws.

Liam had extricated them from airport security, the Port Authority Police Department, and anyone else wanted to talk to them. Fortunately, Sarah had gone along with his lead, equally anxious to be out of there. It's not like the authorities were going to get to the bottom of what was going on. There was no point in trying to explain to them the nuances of Sarah's job, her interactions with Edward Collins, their suspicions, and so forth.

Liam was certain what happened to Sarah wasn't an "ordinary" mugging carried out by ordinary criminals. But he wasn't going to tell law enforcement that and muddy the waters. Port Authority police would look at security cameras and the like. If they found anything of note, he knew they'd be in touch.

He also knew it wasn't likely the authorities would find anything at all.

Liam was acutely aware that he could've lost Sarah today. It didn't matter that they'd known each other for less than a week. She mattered to him. She mattered a lot more than should even be possible.

Sarah shifted in her seat, angling her body a little more forward. "I have to call Mr. Collins and let him know what happened."

"Don't worry about that right now," Liam said.

She was in pain. Collins would have to be dealt with, but that would happen later, after Sarah was checked out medically and he'd had a chance to think this through. Liam was damn sure that Collins knew exactly what was going on, anyway. Still, it wouldn't be wise for Sarah to let her erstwhile buyer know that *she* was aware *he* was up to no good.

"How many times do I have to tell you this?" Sarah snapped. "This is my career at stake here."

"I understand that, Sarah. I do." Liam tried to walk a fine line between sounding empathetic and sounding like he was placating her. "I absolutely respect that. But we need to look at this from every angle we can to figure out how you need to deal with him right now."

Sarah stilled beside him. "Do you think he was behind this? Why would he try to steal his own property?"

"Give us a chance to work through some of the possibilities. That's all I'm asking."

She didn't answer for a full two or three minutes. Then, she conceded, "I can't wait long. But okay." Sarah settled back against the seat and then quickly leaned forward again.

He knew she'd been hurt more than she'd admitted to back at the airport; the back of her shirt was visibly damaged. Liam hadn't called her out on it there because he understood, in the logical part of his brain, that the injury must not be bad enough for her to want to bring it up then and delay their exit.

But she'd been hurt. His dismay about that came through in his voice, and he didn't prevent it from doing that.

"The back of your blouse is torn. Almost shredded in places. I'm going to have Callum examine you when we get back."

"Callum?" she repeated. "Who is he?"

"He's a medic. Knowledgeable and experienced." Liam gripped his own knees, determined to keep his hands to himself.

"I haven't met him," Sarah said.

"You weren't at headquarters very long."

Sarah made an indistinct sound of agreement. She rolled her neck gingerly from side to side. "I could use some aspirin or something."

His eyes snapped in her direction again. "You should've said something at the airport. You could have taken something already."

You should've asked her if she needed something because you knew she was hurt.

"I didn't want to have any reason to stay with those people any longer." Sarah turned her head to gaze out the window at the other vehicles. "They're not going to be able to help us." She paused, then looked at him over her shoulder. "Right?"

Liam wanted to hold her. Comfort her. But he didn't really have the right to do that, did he? Sure, they'd shared some passionate time together. They weren't dating, though. He wasn't anything to her except a guy who happened to be in the right place at the right time to offer assistance amidst a terrible situation that was unfolding around her.

When the words left his mouth, he knew they sounded harsher than he intended. "How the hell did that guy and whoever he's working with know you were at the airport? That you had the books?"

Liam was generally good-natured. It was a quality he tried to maintain despite all the stressful facets of his past and current careers. Being a sniper required a level head and patience. Assessing battle damage and spotting necessary coordinate adjustments for airstrikes necessitated clear thinking. He couldn't let pressure rattle him.

His ability to think clearly had apparently taken off at the airport, even though he and Sarah hadn't.

Liam didn't want to distress Sarah more than she already was, but there had to be something they were missing about the situation. None of it made sense.

"I don't know," she said quietly.

Of course she didn't know. He felt like a piece of trash for even asking the question.

Sarah leaned her head back carefully against the seat and they lapsed into silence. The remainder of the drive passed quickly; the midday traffic was nearly nonexistent. Sarah kept her eyes closed and Liam thought she might be feigning sleep. When her breathing changed, he decided she had truly fallen asleep.

Instead of forcing her to talk, or staring at her like a creeper, Liam continued updating his team in a group text. He also put Callum on alert.

Keeping his voice quiet, Mason finally asked a question. "How sure are you about their motives? That it was about the books?"

"Based on what was said to Sarah, very sure," Liam said.

Mason absently tapped the heel of one hand on the steering wheel. "What did you tell airport security?"

"That it'd been a botched luggage theft."

Mason caught Liam's gaze in the rearview mirror. "You think they bought that?"

Liam shrugged. "Yeah. It clearly wasn't terrorism, and that's their main concern. What I said helped them quickly categorize it as an attempted mugging. With their daily caseload, it made their paperwork easier."

Chapter 19

Liam

Liam paced back and forth in the hallway outside the room Sarah had been assigned at Infinite Security headquarters. He'd been banished while Callum checked her out, medically. Despite the fact that he'd known the other man for years and trusted him implicitly, Liam still didn't like the fact that he, himself, wasn't in there to make sure Sarah was okay. That she was comfortable with Callum.

He forced himself to stop walking. Took up a position on the wall across from her door. Fell into the patterned, regulated breathing he utilized in his role as a sniper. Called upon that feeling of control.

The familiar self-discipline helped, but not enough.

What's taking so long?

Maybe Sarah had a concussion from being thrown to the ground? Or from something that had happened when she was out of his sight? He never should've let her be out of his sight at all. Liam hadn't really thought Sarah was in danger, especially when not around her client, and that was a mistake he'd never make again.

The door to Sarah's room suddenly opened, and Callum was in the doorway.

"Want to join us?" Callum was looking at Liam like he was holding back a smile. What the hell was so funny?

Liam was pushing past him and into the room in a matter of seconds. His eyes landed on Sarah, who was sitting on the edge of the bed, facing the doorway. Immediately, he noticed the gold-toned hair clip that held back a swath of hair from her right temple, revealing a small bandage. Instead of the rest of her hair being pinned up, it flowed loosely around her shoulders and down her back; he couldn't see it all from his position, but he knew how beautiful it was.

She'd changed her clothes. The pale blue blouse Sarah wore caressed her curves and complemented her coloring. It looked as soft as he knew her skin to be. Sarah's tailored black pants were professional. The high heels he was accustomed to seeing her wear were absent, replaced by flat black shoes.

Sarah's beauty overwhelmed him enough that it had taken him a moment to truly notice the bruise that had darkened around her right wrist, and the bandage that peeked out the right side of her collar.

"Hi," Sarah said quietly.

"Hi." He didn't like how pale she was. "How do you feel?" Liam said it to Sarah, but looked at Callum, who stood nearby with that annoying expression still on his face.

In the blink of an eye, that hint of amusement vanished, and Callum said, "Sarah says she feels fine, but I'd venture to say she's in some pain."

Liam's gaze had returned already to Sarah. She was avoiding his eyes now, apparently finding the photo of the gardens to be completely captivating.

Callum continued, "Since Sarah already gave me permission to share information with you, I can tell you that she has a variety of cuts, scrapes, and bruises, the worst of which are on her back. She described to me what happened, and what I'm seeing is certainly consistent with what she went through."

Sarah finally returned her eyes to Liam. She spoke firmly. "It's not that bad."

Liam crossed his arms over his chest and schooled himself not to say anything in response. He wasn't going to argue with her, but he suspected she'd say it wasn't bad, no matter what she was feeling.

Callum continued, "I disinfected everything, applied antibacterial ointment, and nonadherent bandages. The cut at her hairline was deep but not long, and I don't think it needs stitches. It's closed with a butterfly bandage. Once it has started to heal, there is another ointment she can use on it to help prevent scarring."

"I'm sure it'll be fine." Sarah seemed unconcerned about the possibility of a scar.

"Precautions? Limitations? Instructions?" Liam snapped out his questions for Callum one after the other, and never took his eyes off Sarah.

"Antibiotic cream for a week. Limitations as needed because of soreness and to not tear open small scabs. Instructions are to keep watch for any signs of infection, some increased rest to let her body recover from the experience, change bandages daily or more as needed. "

"Why would more be needed?" Sarah asked. She studiously avoided looking at Liam.

"If they get wet, or dirty, or loosen up too much, have any blood that seeps through –."

Liam interrupted him. "Why would blood come through if the injuries aren't bad?"

"I don't expect that to happen," Callum said. "But a lot of movement, reinjury, or worsening can potentially cause that. I need to cover all possibilities, Liam."

Liam grumbled, but he didn't say anything discernible and Collin finished his instructions to Sarah.

"Don't hesitate to take acetaminophen as needed, up to every four hours. I don't think you need anything stronger than over-the-counter meds. If you think you need anything else, let me know. Okay?"

"Yes." Sarah bestowed a soft smile upon Callum. It was so warm and friendly that it made Liam hot under the collar. "Thanks so much for taking care of me today."

Liam reached out and clapped a hand too hard on his friend's shoulder. "Yeah, thanks a lot. I've got her from here."

Liam pulled Callum around and steered him toward the door. "I think Mason was looking for you." It was a complete lie, but who cared?

Callum's medical bag was on the small table to the right of the door. Liam grabbed it and shoved it at his friend's chest. "Here you go. Thanks again."

Callum was laughing as Liam practically pushed him through the doorway. He closed the door firmly and flipped the lock. When he turned around, he saw that Sarah had moved to the tufted couch that was positioned against the wall closer to the attached bathroom.

Liam slowly crossed the room and sat down on the couch next to her, close enough to Sarah that he could indulge in her perfume. The soft floral scent had an undercurrent of something almost spicy, and it suited her perfectly. He wanted to hold her again but reminded himself that they weren't dating.

Not for the first time he thought about how they'd known each other for two days. It could be measured in hours. It didn't *feel* that way, though. Yes, they'd messed around in his hotel room, but that was all. He didn't have the right to haul Sarah into his lap – no matter how badly he wanted to do just that.

"We'll figure this out," Liam tried to reassure her. He wanted to get rid of the worried expression on the beautiful face of his "naughty librarian."

"I know," Sarah said. She gave him a small smile and he had the sense she was trying to reassure *him*. "I've been trying to figure out how they found me." She turned towards him more. "How small can tracking devices be?"

He immediately understood what she was getting at. It was a

thought he'd had and discarded as impossible. "You think someone concealed a tracking device in those books?"

"I think if it was tiny enough and light enough, it might be possible. I've never known anybody to do that, but that doesn't mean nobody would."

"Let's say somebody did do exactly that, in a way that got by the auction house officials," Liam said. "To what purpose?"

"I have no idea." Sarah admitted. She adjusted her eyeglasses on the bridge of her nose. "I've been trying to figure out how somebody would know where I am, where the books are, and that's the only thing that makes sense to me."

"Okay. You're going to have to examine both books in search of something like that. Trackers can be extremely small, by the way. Don't think Air Tag size – think pencil eraser size and even smaller."

"Small enough to be in a bookbinding," Sarah said.

"You're going to have to be the one to examine them and see what you can find," he said. She nodded in agreement and he continued, "Tell me what you need to examine them without damaging the books."

"Before I do that, what should I do about Collins?" she asked. "He thinks I'm arriving in Illinois today."

"I'm going to give you a burner phone, something untraceable. Text him, let him know somebody tried to mug you at the airport. That you're safe but bruised and shaken up, but you'll be in touch with him in the morning." As he spoke, Liam texted Rick about that disposable phone.

"Do you think Collins sent that guy to steal a book he already purchased?" Sarah was clearly trying to make sense of what had happened, and was coming up short.

Liam gave up on trying to maintain any distance from her. He held her hand within his own. "I don't know yet, but we're going to figure it out."

Even as he assured her of that, Liam was thinking through the possibilities. With the bidding irregularities Collins had demanded of

Sarah, why would he be trying to steal his own property by sending someone after her? He didn't even have possession of the books yet, but had he managed to already insure them? Since Sarah was Collins' agent and the books were in her possession, was that just as good for insurance purposes?

Liam went to book auctions sometimes, but he was no expert about them. He knew how to make sure an item had a condition report, and the info that went with that. He understood that if he won, he had to pay the winning "hammer price" plus a "buyer's premium" that usually cost him an additional 20% of his winning bid. He wasn't a big enough or frequent enough bidder to use an agent that could bid on his behalf.

Liam hated how worried Sarah looked, and he wanted nothing more than to resolve these problems for her. Liam couldn't figure out why he was so personally invested in this woman and what was going on with her. It wasn't simply because she was beautiful; he'd known plenty of beautiful women in his life. There was just something about her... The feeling was similar to that reliable instinct he had about imminent danger. Similar, but so different. He couldn't quite find the words to describe it.

But this wasn't the time to write or recite poetry in his head.

Right now, he needed to be decisive.

He reached out to gently trace around the bandage on the side of her head. She didn't flinch or pull away. "Do you need to rest a while?"

"No. I couldn't sleep if I tried, and it's still afternoon even though it feels like it's been a long day," Sarah said.

"We never did get to eat this morning in the rush to get to the airport, or in that food court at the airport. I don't know if anyone cooked today, but I'm going to order in whatever we feel like having. What sounds good? Chinese food, Italian, Greek, something else?"

Liam felt like he was having the same conversation they'd had a couple of hours ago in the airport food court.

"Chinese maybe?" she shrugged.

He stood, gently encouraging her to come with him. "Let's go by the break room and grab a menu. I'll have to send a group text to see if anybody here right now wants anything." Liam tilted his head closer to Sarah's, like he was telling her a huge secret. "The guys are like big babies if you leave them out when it comes to food, and the ladies can be pretty ferocious about it, too."

Chapter 20

Sarah

Later, after a plate of chicken with broccoli and an egg roll, Sarah was facing her next challenge. The conference room table was covered in a special type of cloth that Liam told her was used when they dealt with evidence and things they had to examine carefully. He didn't explain what type of evidence he was talking about, and she didn't ask because she wasn't sure she wanted to know.

She felt like a surgeon.

To her right were neatly laid out an array of implements – white gloves, small flashlights, tweezers in different sizes, thin scalpels, various adhesives, magnifying glasses, and other things she didn't even recognize. There were also a pile of fiber free cloths, and a hand-held device that she knew could be used to gently remove dust from electronics, probably equally good at removing dust or debris from books.

To her left was the square box made of who knew what. It was some thick, heavy duty material, and in it Liam had placed the gift bag from the auction house. After closing and securing the lid, he'd explained that it was soundproof in case a tracker was present and also recording things, and that it would jam any kind of signal a tracker might be emitting. Sarah just nodded her understanding. She didn't bother commenting about how this wasn't a Jason Bourne film, and hiding a tracker in a book like that would be exceedingly difficult as well as totally unlikely.

Dax and Mason stood along the far wall, discussing something in voices too low for her to hear clearly. Both had their arms crossed like it was required of them. Callie was setting up a small video camera on a tripod aimed at the table in front of Sarah. A shiver of awareness tickled Sarah's spine then, and she knew Liam had walked into the room even though she couldn't see the doorway behind her. Before she could turn around, he gently touched her shoulder. She was glad it wasn't the same shoulder the man at the airport had bruised. Even though it still hurt, she'd avoided mentioning that to Liam.

He took a position close to her at the table, and she watched him make eye contact with each of the others in the room. Liam gestured at the table. "Sarah, are you ready to get started so we can see what we can find out?"

He held up a flat black wand. "Shall we start with this?"

Sarah nodded and spoke to the others in the room. "As I told you all previously, we don't need to wear gloves to prevent damage to the item. If we find something today, I won't touch that particular object itself without gloves."

"Should I go ahead now?" Sarah asked Liam. This had all seemed like such a fuss right up until this minute. Now she was being hit with an overabundance of nerves.

Sarah withdrew the first book from its careful auction-house wrapping. She set it on the table in front of Liam. Dax and Mason moved a little closer as Liam methodically examined it with the sensor. There was silence. No tracking device detected. Nothing detected. He shut it off while he waited for her to present the second book.

Sarah reached into the bag again and unwrapped the second

book. Within the outer protective packaging, this one also had an old cover that Sarah maneuvered with extra care.

The scanner in Liam's hand sounded within seconds of when he turned it on again. He silently locked eyes with her, and then looked around at each of his colleagues. Liam touched a finger to his lips in the universal sign for "Quiet." He shut off the device he was still holding and slipped it onto the table then gestured for Sarah to proceed.

She set the book of Shelley's poetry on the table and stared at it like the book was something she'd never seen before. Sarah frowned. It really was, wasn't it? She'd never seen a book that contained a tracking device. Why would somebody put one inside a book, especially inside an old and rare volume?

Liam touched her arm lightly.

Sarah flinched, her head swiveling in his direction, catching herself just before she spoke. Silence. Right. They'd agreed before checking that if the presence of a tracker was detected, no one would speak around it until it was examined and somehow dealt with. She'd thought she could stay quiet with no problem, but now it chafed. As usual, she had a lot to say. Liam gave her a thumbs up sign, silently encouraging her to proceed.

As Sarah had reminded them earlier, she wasn't a restoration expert or anything like that. Yes, she knew how books were supposed to look, what details about materials and binding processes indicated age and contributed to value, a lot of details like that. But she never disassembled such a valuable piece.

Sarah ran her bare fingertips over every inch of the cover, back cover, and spine of the Shelley book. She opened the volume and examined the inside of both covers. How could somebody put a tracker in this book without it being easily discovered?

It wasn't a stiffened cloth cover; those hadn't become popular until the mid-19th century. Even as she asked herself the question, she already knew the answer; it had to be within the rounded spine.

The publication date for this book was listed as 1830, which certainly would've made it much easier for whoever planted the tracker.

Right up until the late 1820s, books published in England used tight-back binding, where the binding was fully attached to the spine. But at the very end of the 1820s, English publishers began using the hollow-back style popular in France and a few other countries. It was a style that didn't attach the spine of the cover to the spine of the text-block pages, allowing for a slight, half crescent-shaped gap between the two parts.

Sarah grabbed a small flashlight from the implements and switched it on. She focused the thin beam of light down into that gap. It was still too shadowed within to see anything.

After again scrutinizing the various items on the table, she turned to Liam. Sarah held up the book in one hand and pointed at the slim gap space with the other. She tried to pantomime using a plunger or a stick. Understanding lit his eyes and he held up a single finger, indicating he'd be back in a minute.

He rushed from the room. Sarah repeated her motions to the others still with her in the conference room. Even as they all nodded their own understanding, she wondered if it could really be that simple. After all, if someone dropped a tiny tracker in that space, what would prevent it from simply falling out when the book was turned in different directions and transported?

The silence in the room was broken only by faint sounds from the central air conditioning.

Dax finally spoke. "Sarah, we *will* get to the bottom of this."

She appreciated his reassurance, and wished she shared that level of confidence.

Liam reappeared, moving as quietly as usual. He crouched next to her chair and spoke at a level that was barely audible. "What do you think?"

He presented her with two items, one a clear plastic rod that was barely thicker than a filament, and the other a slim length of metal. Sarah took the plastic one from him. She wiped it down with a lint free cloth. Very carefully, she inserted it into the space between the pages and the cover. She tried to keep her hands steady and push it straight down the middle. Within seconds it emerged from the other side. Sarah shifted her hands and drew it out the other end.

How was that possible? There was nowhere else in the book something could be hidden. Nowhere she could think of, at least. Sarah studied the thin, slightly flattened gap again. She switched to the metal, turning it slightly in her hand. Then she went back to the plastic one; the metal could potentially do more damage.

Sarah lined the plastic one up with one edge of the gap and slid it down all the way until it peeked out the other side. Nothing. She moved it up a little bit on the side wall of the gap space and pressed it through again. And again, nothing. She knew everyone's eyes were on her – or at least on her hands and the book. Sarah tried again. Nothing.

But then, on the next pass through, there was a slight glitch as the rod passed through the space. There was a faint click when the plastic came into contact with something within the channel.

Trying to stay calm in case it was nothing of any importance, Sarah drew the implement out and pushed it through again more firmly. The end of the plastic hit the obstacle again. When she did it another time she pushed it through harder, and with more speed.

A tiny, flat silver disc made an equally small clatter as it hit the table. Sarah froze. She looked to Liam. He nodded at her, silently confirming what she found was indeed a tracker of some kind. He signaled to Mason, who approached while pulling on thin black gloves of his own.

"I got it." Mason swept the device off the table with his right hand and cupped it in his left. He left without saying anything to her, or to anyone else in the room.

Liam anticipated the question Sarah was about to ask. "He'll see if he can get any part of a fingerprint off that and then destroy it."

"But it's been here for at least a couple of days, so whoever put it there knows where I am. Where the book is." She stopped and corrected herself. "Where both books are, right?"

"The vehicle we were in contains a device that blocks any tracker not authorized by us. This building does the same. So you don't have to worry about that, Sarah," Liam said. "By being very quiet around it, we were just using an excess of caution."

Well, that was somewhat comforting at least.

The big questions remained, though. Who had put that in the book? When? And why? Did Collins know about it, and did it have something to do with his purpose in demanding she meet him in Illinois?

Chapter 21

Liam

The one thing he knew for damn sure was that this was about much more than one 19th-century book of poetry.

Liam sat forward in a chair in Dax's office, hands braced just above his knees. He and Dax listened as Mason reported what he'd already expected. "No fingerprints, no markings, and high quality." Mason said. "Not something you pick up at a local gadget shop."

"Where is it now?" Dax asked.

"I put it back, as we discussed," Mason said. "Sarah is reading the Shelley volume down on the computer cave, where there are jamming devices. When moved anywhere outside that space, the books are to be kept in a box that contains another jammer."

"This doesn't make sense," Liam said, and not for the first time. "There was no tracker in the other book, so this is about the Shelley volume. Sarah's client significantly overpaid for it. He wants her to bring it to him in another state, something he didn't ask her to do the three other times she worked for him. That guy who grabbed her at the airport had to be monitoring the tracker."

He scrubbed a hand through his hair like it would make the answer rise to the surface of his brain.

"First, I was thinking money laundering, but Collins could have had the book shipped to him by the auction house. And even though he overpaid by a lot, it was nowhere near a big enough amount to launder anything significant."

He'd already discussed that with Sarah, and they were in agreement that the one book didn't make sense in that regard. Collins would have to be over bidding on hundreds of items to legitimize significant amounts of money gained from illegal transactions.

Liam continued, "Simple theft doesn't make sense either. It's a great book, but not worth attempting what would be a felony theft – and right in the middle of a major metropolitan airport with lots of security."

"Then what are you thinking?" Dax prompted him.

Liam couldn't sit still anymore. He jumped up, started pacing the way Dax usually did when trying to figure something out. Why was that book so damn important? Liam stopped in the middle of his circuit around the large room and faced the other two men.

"It's something about that particular copy of the book. Collins overpaid because he couldn't risk somebody else getting their hands on it instead of him. He didn't want to even risk something happening if the auction company shipped it to him."

"You think someone else knows what is so important about it, and that's who tried to steal it," Mason said.

Liam nodded. "Exactly. Not necessarily somebody working with Collins, but someone else knows why the book is more valuable than just being a rare book."

"What could somebody hide in an old book?" Dax wondered out loud. "I'm sure the auction house would have paged through it, right? So, there wouldn't be anything stuck between the pages."

"Yes," Liam agreed. He braced his hands on his hips. "I have to discuss this with Sarah again."

Less than 10 minutes later, Liam found Sarah where Mason had said she was– in a subbasement level computer room. Rick was in charge of tech for Infinite Security, a serious role with heavy responsibilities that seemed at odds with his All-American, "beachcomber" style. But the man had a mind like a steel trap.

Rick acknowledged him from across the room then pointed toward the small tables in a far corner of the long room. Liam indicated his thanks with a lift of his chin and headed in that direction. Sarah was deeply engrossed in what she was reading. Even in profile, she was stunning.

Before he could speak, she looked up into his eyes.

"I'm glad you're here," Sarah said. "I have an idea of what might be going on. It's far-fetched, I admit, but I haven't been able to think of anything else more reasonable."

Liam grabbed a chair across from her and carried it over to her side. "Okay. What are you thinking?"

"Obviously, somebody really wants this particular book," she said, indicating the volume in her hand. "Enough that Collins was willing to substantially overpay, somebody put a tracker in it, and either *that* somebody or somebody else tried to steal it."

"Agreed. I just went over those points in a meeting upstairs," Liam said.

"Since something about it is clearly more important or more valuable than the book itself, something else has to be hidden inside it. There's nothing else in the hollow space around the spine where we found the tracker." She tapped the pen in her right hand against a small notebook that lay open on the table next to the laptop. "Even though the auction house would've checked the pages, I just went through it myself, and there's nothing tucked between them." Liam waited for Sarah to make her point, because it was obvious that she had one.

"Liam, since there's nothing in the book that we can find, it has to be something within the words of the book. Something easily overlooked. Something that looks like part of the book, but isn't."

She was brimming with excitement, and he felt like an idiot because he wasn't following her train of thought.

"Is this a riddle? Something that looks like part of the book, but isn't part of the book..."

"Sounds like one, right?" Sarah grabbed his hand. "What if something is hidden inside but was made to look like a regular page?"

Chapter 22

Sarah

As terrible as the last three days had been (except for meeting Liam), Sarah was finally feeling excited about *something* to do with the book she'd acquired for Edward Collins. She was certain that somebody had managed to add some kind of material to the pages that made up the volume. Otherwise, there'd be no reason for a tracker. The book wasn't so valuable it would necessitate something like that, and messing with it would actually lessen its value.

Who would've done such a thing? When?

As usual, the auction house had made public, in the catalog, the identity of the seller. The name, Veronica Cross, was one Sarah recognized immediately as being a woman known for buying, collecting, and selling books and antiquities. Not every seller was known or familiar, of course, but some were known to be reputable. Mrs. Cross was one of the respectable ones.

Within whatever it was that had been added, there had to be something important – something valuable to Collins or someone else in the know. Did that mean the tracker was added after Mrs. Cross transferred the book to the auction house? Sarah shared those thoughts with those in the room, and added, "Putting in a tracker defaces the book. I can't even imagine a real collector, like Mrs. Cross, doing such a thing. The auction house never would've done it. They wouldn't have auctioned the book off that way."

Liam agreed with her. "It's a trustworthy auction house. They'd never put it on the block with that without full disclosure." He put both hands behind his neck, lacing his fingers together. "I can't figure out why somebody would want to track that particular book."

The answer to that question was obvious to Sarah, even if it was a vague answer. "The only thing that makes sense to me is that something was inserted into this copy of the Shelley book, and it's something important to Collins."

"How could someone accomplish that?" Liam asked. "Something like that would be tough to pull off."

Sarah confirmed his thinking. "If a page was added, someone had to take apart the binding and reassemble it meticulously. Otherwise, auction house experts would know something was wrong."

"Accomplishing that kind of deception would require knowledge about 19th-century bookbinding and time to make the changes well enough for the book to pass inspection at the auction house," Liam said, tipping his head back to look at the ceiling while he thought about it. After a full minute of silence, he straightened up again and fixed his gaze on Sarah. "And if someone inserted the tracking device before the auction, how would that make it through all the quality and authenticity checks?"

"Good question," she said. "And whoever did it would've needed uninterrupted access to the volume for a length of time, which seems unlikely." Sarah leaned closer to him. "But I think someone with the right preparation might be able to sort of insert an additional page by literally gluing it into the binding from the inside or cutting the page a little smaller than the rest and adhering it to another page."

"Like piggybacking it?" He clarified that he was understanding her point. Sarah could see he was thinking seriously about her speculation.

"Yes," Sarah said. "It would still take skill, but it might be able to be done without really being noticeable."

"I guess the only way to know is to look," Liam said wryly.

"If that's what was done, it had to be done really well. Impeccably. I think the only way to look is to sit down and read through every page, making sure that the language on one page leads logically into the next," Sarah said.

"You're right. That's what you're doing now? Would you like to continue, or shall I?" Liam asked. "It wouldn't be a hardship for me. You know I was going to bid on the book."

"I never did ask why you wanted the book. I mean, you can get the contents in a trade paperback for $10 or so," Sarah said. "Why be willing to spend thousands?"

"Do you ask all your clients that question?" Liam deflected her question.

"No, I don't ask that question of all my clients." Sarah shrugged. "I know in advance that many of them simply enjoy being able to have rare books in their collections. Like a status thing or particular social connections. Some people do collect for other reasons, of course, like aesthetics. I'm wondering about *you*. Is it the thrill of the hunt? The competitive challenge?"

"I once read it described as 'a gentle form of madness', and maybe that's what it is for me," Liam said. "I think I appreciate the precision of words that poetry requires. The craftsmanship people display in choosing words that perfectly convey whatever their purpose in writing."

"You collect all types of poetry?" Sarah asked.

"No." He shook his head. "I read widely, but only collect 19th-century. I see by your expression that you're going to ask why. Aren't you?"

"Is there an answer to why?"

It was Liam's turn to shrug. "It just calls to me. It's hard to explain." Something in his expression changed. Became even more serious. "Why is someone deeply attracted to one person and not another? They could both be beautiful people, objectively, but one makes your blood run hotter and your breath come faster, yet the other leaves you cold."

Sarah was certain he wasn't speaking hypothetically now. Was she out of her mind to think he was talking about her? About the undeniable attraction between them that had burned so brightly in his hotel room three mornings ago?

"You guys making any progress?" Rick's voice snapped Sarah out of her reverie and had her twisted in her chair to see him. She hadn't even heard the door open.

"Don't you know how to knock?" Liam commented. "Sarah didn't hear your left sneaker squeak and announce you."

Did Liam really hear the computer guys sneaker?

Instead of asking him that, she answered Rick's question.

"We have what I think is a good idea." Sarah looked between the two men. "I just have to quickly read a book."

"I think I should read the other one cover to cover, also," Liam said. "Even though you didn't find anything in the spine of that one, we should check it out the same way."

"Okay," Sarah said. "He didn't give me strange bidding instructions on that one, so I was thinking it was just to dilute any focus on the first. You're right, though, it does make sense to do that."

Liam gave her a smile that lit her up inside. "Come on then, Sarah, let's find a cozy place to kick back and read a while." He smirked at the tall blonde guy who looked like he'd forgotten where he parked his surfboard. "We'll vacate the computer cave."

Chapter 23

Liam

The changed page Sarah found a couple of hours later was surprisingly well-crafted, even though they hadn't known that if something like it existed, it would be well-done. The page itself wasn't literally changed and replaced by another page; it was the original page, still in place, but with sequences of numbers written in word form and seemingly random letters having replaced some original text. Examining the book for auction purposes wouldn't have revealed the changes to anyone. It was only noticeable if one read the text, line by line and word by word.

Liam had found no anomalies in the other book. He and Sarah, along with Dax, Mason, Rick, and Callie occupied the conference room in the tech area in the subbasement. They were staring at the spot where Rick's computer projected the altered page on the wall. Next to that, in a split screen, the sequences were rewritten in numerical form.

"Account numbers." Three voices spoke almost simultaneously.

"They don't look domestic," Callie commented. She tilted her head to the side as she studied the image. "More likely something offshore."

"Ideas about where?" Dax asked. Liam knew the head of Infinite Security would typically ask for others' theories before sharing his own. The guy never wanted to prevent people from coming up with their own ideas.

"Could be Switzerland or Cayman Islands." Callie sounded confident.

From her body language, Liam could see that Sarah was paying close attention to the conversation. He wasn't surprised when she asked Callie another question. "How did you narrow it down like that?"

Callie turned to face Sarah more directly. "Different countries utilize account numbers of differing lengths, structured combinations of letters and numbers, some use hyphens, some don't, things like that."

Callie's greatest strength on the team was her skills in tech and code breaking. She pointed at the numbers displayed on the wall. "In Switzerland and in the Caymans, account numbers typically have one letter followed by 20 digits. Makes them highly secured."

Sarah hesitated, then pointed out the obvious discrepancy. "But the sequences in the book are a jumble of numbers and letters. It's not at all like you describe, except for the total number of characters."

"Whoever created this set up another layer of protection." Instead of appearing aggravated, Callie's eyes were wide, her features animated like she was excited. It was a look Liam had seen on her many times.

Callie said, "We have to untangle a cipher to convert the number to a letter and the letters to numbers."

Sarah's dismay would be easy to recognize, even to a novice in understanding body language; her shoulders slumped, she exhaled sharply, and her eyes closed for longer than a normal blink.

When she spoke, her question was logical. "How are you guys going to figure this out? There are so many things we don't know."

Liam was searching for something encouraging he could say to

Sarah without giving her false hope. He moved his chair closer to her and grasped her hand where it rested on the tabletop.

What was the point of trying to pretend there wasn't anything between them?

Rick stepped into the conversation again. "I'm running the code sequences through a program I created years ago to look for patterns, see if they match to sequencing styles in any particular area," Rick said. His fingers on his computer keyboard barely slowed down as he spoke.

When he paused, Callie had more to say. "While another computer program works on figuring out any cipher, I'll also be looking at it the old-fashioned way, working it through with pen and paper."

Sarah posed another question. "I understand what a cipher is, at least in general terms. With this, though, how would it work? I don't think I'm understanding that part."

"In this case, a cipher would be like a key to understanding a map. It would tell anyone who understood it how to read the lines and sequences."

Callie moved closer to Sarah and put a piece of paper down on the table in front of her. Writing quickly, Infinite's resident code breaker wrote down a mix of letters and numbers. "These are just to make it kind of real in front of you. I wrote down 20 characters. If we can't come up with a clear code swap, then we know there's probably a cipher involved. A cipher could be something like substituting letters or numbers for different letters and numbers. Think of every A actually being a Z, every B being a Y, stuff like that. It's not going to be something so simple and straightforward, but that's the broad idea."

Sarah stared down at the paper.

"I can't wait for you guys to figure this out before I speak to Collins," Sarah said. "He can cause problems with my career if he complains to the auction house that I'm not turning over his acquisitions. Something like that would really damage my reputation."

It was obvious that the thought of that distressed her tremendously.

"It's hard enough for a woman to get respect in this field," Sarah said. "If I have to overcome bad feedback and complaints about my work, it'll scare off potential clients." She pushed her glasses up further onto the bridge of her nose. "I can't afford to lose income."

Her obvious distress tore at Liam's heart. He spoke slowly as he thought about what she'd said. He knew she made valid points. Although he knew about her father's situation, he didn't know details about the extent of her financial obligations. Her concerns about damaging her earning power were undoubtedly sincere.

You should look into that. She doesn't have to know it's because you want to help her. No, if you want to know about those things, you should ask her.

Great. Now he was arguing with himself.

Hard on the heels of his self-recriminations, Liam had an idea. One he knew was a solid idea. It would keep the meeting under their control, minimize the presence of any bystanders, yet be public enough that Collins wouldn't want to start trouble and attract attention – if starting trouble was part of his intentions.

"We can arrange for you to meet with Collins here on Long Island. There are a few communities where most of the businesses are closed on Saturdays. That could buy us three days. We can be set up before Collins gets there to make sure you're safe."

Liam looked at the ceiling like he was picturing how things would play out. "Meanwhile, if the code isn't deciphered by then, the team will keep looking for the meaning of the altered page. We've already documented everything about the book. Photograph and videotape it."

"He wanted her to meet him out of state. How is she going to convince him otherwise?" Mason playing the devil's advocate, like he so often did.

"Sarah, you're going to need to play the damsel in distress and make Collins believe you're afraid to travel with the books because of what happened at the airport," Liam said. "You need him to either let you ship them or meet you locally. Or even simply within driving distance. Then we can control logistics and security."

She was clever and capable, and he had no doubt she could pull it off to make this guy believe her.

"It's not like I'm terrified or something," she pointed out. "Yeah, I'm nervous about the oddness of everything having to do with this situation, but it's nothing I can't handle."

Her gaze was steady on him. Sarah certainly had been tougher and more resilient at the airport than he had expected. She'd fought back ferociously against her attacker. Instead of even acknowledging her own injuries, she'd put on a brave face and dealt with the authorities there, then in the car with him she didn't even speak of those things or of her pain. Instead, Sarah maintained her focus on her responsibilities.

Her presence, so near to him, always charged in the air in a way he could feel but couldn't see. It was like the static electricity in the air before a lightning strike.

"What if he can't come to New York now or soon?" Sarah seemed to be giving his idea serious consideration.

"It's not a long flight from Illinois to here. He wants the books, and he'll figure out how to make it happen," Dax said.

"He's probably anxious to get his hands on those codes," Liam said.

"I need my commission from the sales," Sarah said. "I can't have him refusing to pay because he says I didn't deliver the books."

"He's going to receive the books. He didn't tell you why it wasn't good enough to let the auction house arrange secure delivery." Liam repeated what they had already discussed multiple times. "The paperwork you both signed leaves that up to his discretion, but that doesn't mean the guy gets to change it at his whim."

"From his perspective, it does mean that," she said. "I can't risk him not paying me."

"As long as he gets the books, why would he not pay you what he owes you?" Liam countered.

"I can't take the chance," Sarah insisted. "And before you tell me I could sue him, I can't afford to do that, to hire a lawyer, and get tied up in a court."

Liam caught Dax's eyes, hoping his friend and employer would be on the same page as him. If not, he'd pay any legal bill for Sarah.

Dax cleared his throat, drawing everybody's attention. "Sarah, I know Liam explained to you that we offer our services to a certain percentage of people *pro bono*, which is how we are handling your case. That includes providing any legal services connected to what's going on. We have attorneys on staff, and on retainer when needed."

Sarah looked back at Liam, and he read the surprise in her expression.

She turned back to Dax. "I – I didn't realize that. Thank you for explaining." Her eyes shifted down to the table in front of her. "That's a huge thing, of course. But I also have to protect my professional reputation because my career is crucial. A wealthy client who speaks ill of me can do a lot of damage." She glanced quickly around the room. "The community of people who bid on rare books is surprisingly small. The number of people who hire someone like me to handle their bidding is even smaller."

Sarah tapped out a soft staccato rhythm on the conference room table with her fingernails and nibbled at her bottom lip. He'd seen her in action at the auction house. There, she'd been calm and cool under pressure. About this, though, she was nervous, and not even trying to hide it. Liam wanted to fix it for her, but he couldn't run roughshod over her decisions about something so important to her career.

She ignored everyone else in the room and looked only at him. "I trust you. If you believe your plan is the best way to handle this, then let's do it."

Liam nodded. "We have a lot of planning to do."

The typically taciturn Mason chimed in, his comment a sincerely encouraging one. "We are good at planning, you know. Particularly on the fly."

"Yes," Liam agreed, a chin lift directed at his colleague acknowledging his appreciation of the backup.

His next words were purely for Sarah. "After we make a solid plan, we excel at changing, adapting, and spontaneously handling anything that happens. We will see you through this, no matter what."

Chapter 24

Liam

Liam escorted Sarah to her room. After the first few steps along the way, he reached for her hand. He wasn't certain how she was feeling or what kind of mood she was really in, but his instinct was to touch her. Not only did she accept his touch, she entwined her fingers with his.

"How are you feeling?" he asked. "Need pain meds?"

"No. I'm stiff, but not too bad," Sarah said. "I still think I should've called Collins today."

"I get that. Doing it tomorrow is strategically better because it drives home the fact that what happened today affected you badly. That might make him more likely to go along with the meet-up being here in New York."

They reached the elevator on the floor, and he tapped the button to call it.

"It's just one floor. Why don't we take the stairs?" she said.

"This isn't a high-rise. The elevator won't take long." Liam squeezed her hand. "After everything today, don't push yourself."

"One flight of stairs isn't exactly pushing myself," Sarah said dryly. "It might even help the stiffness."

He wished she'd stop using words like "stiff" and "stiffness", both of which described the condition he battled whenever she was close to him. Like a damn teenager.

"Callum said you should take it easy, so please humor me," he said.

The arrival of the elevator was a welcome one because it put an end to the debate. He and Sarah stood shoulder to shoulder inside it, and exited in barely a minute. Hands still clasped, they walked down the familiar hallway leading to her door.

"Are you coming in?" Sarah looked at him with a warmth in her eyes that let him know that the invitation may have included a little more than that. He was reminded of those first moments when they met; she wasn't a woman afraid to go after what she wanted.

"Much as I want to, and I *really do* want to, you had a brutal day. Callum said you should get some rest, and I need to coordinate plans for tomorrow."

He reached out and opened the door. Sarah stepped into the room and immediately turned around. Liam drew her close and felt her arms slide around his waist. She leaned the uninjured side of her head on his chest.

"Can I help you check the bandages?" he asked. "If you don't want painkillers, can I get you anything else?"

"Not now." Sarah sighed. "I hate to admit it, but I'm actually tired. I'm going to try and get some sleep."

Liam tried to think of anything else she might need. The mini fridge in the room was fully stocked, like it would be in a luxury hotel – without all the liquor. There might be a couple of single-serving wine bottles, but most of the beverages would be nonalcoholic. He wasn't sure what snacks would be included, but he knew there would be a good assortment.

Without any good reason to stall further, he said, "Okay. I have to catch up with a couple of the guys about tomorrow. My room is close by, further down the hall. Call me if you need me and I'll be here as fast as humanly possible."

Liam wanted to physically comfort her somehow. Hold her. Rub her back. But there was a risk of hurting her, of irritating the cuts, scrapes, and bruises that marred her skin, and he couldn't risk it. *Wouldn't* risk hurting her more.

"I don't understand what Collins is doing, or what he has to do with all this," she said, her words slightly muffled against his shirt. "I know I'm repeating myself, but I can't stop thinking about it."

"I don't understand it either, and I don't really care. Right now, all I care about is ending your involvement with him."

She nodded her agreement, then pulled slightly away from him. Her eyes were searching his, looking for something, and her cheeks flushed gently when she found it.

All day, he'd wanted to kiss her. Not in a fleeting, chaste way, but the way his pounding pulse insisted they both wanted. Yeah, it'd been a long and stressful day. They deserved...

And then Sarah was gripping his shoulders and kissing him. Her lips were soft, her mouth was warm, her taste beyond delicious. Liam pulled her closer, part of his brain reminding him to go easy because she was hurting. The kiss was wild but his hands were gentle, all paying tribute to this woman who fascinated him like no other.

When their mouths eased apart, her eyes were closed. He cupped her cheek in his hand, caressing it with his thumb. "Please rest."

Sarah opened her eyes, blinked, and whispered, "I'll try."

After she closed and locked the door, Liam walked away. He hadn't been able to resist kissing her right there in the hallway. It didn't matter that someone might see them. It didn't matter that the kiss would probably be caught on the security camera at the end of the hall.

Hell, now that he thought about it, there were cameras in the conference rooms. If any of his teammates didn't realize there was something between him and Sarah, then they needed to brush up on their skills for interpreting body language.

Liam jogged down the stairs one flight back to the floor below. Near where he exited on the floor, he reached his destination.

Several of the upper tier guys had their own office spaces within the mansion. Rick had an office on the same floor as the others, but had also taken over a smaller one on the basement level where tech and surveillance was based. Ethan's office was further down from Rick's, adjoining a large room set aside for disguises and related items. Some of the other guys were doubled up. In fact, Liam could hear the soft murmur of voices coming from the office Derek and Brandon shared, diagonally across the hall.

At the end of the hall, his office was almost directly across from Mason's, which was his destination.

"Got a minute?" he asked Mason when he stopped in the other man's open doorway.

"Sure." Mason waved him in and Liam shut the door behind him. He dropped into the chair across from Mason's desk.

Mason wasn't one to make idle conversation. Or chitchat. So his next words weren't surprising. "What's up?"

"I've got a bad feeling about tomorrow."

"Why?"

"I don't know why. When do we ever know why?"

He knew Mason understood the importance of those gut feelings. Almost everyone at Infinite had at some point served in the military or law enforcement. They all took things like battlefield intuition and the vague warnings that instinct sometimes generated as real and serious things.

In the military, you usually couldn't change or delay an op because your gut told you something wasn't right. But the private sector was different.

Mason swiveled his chair a couple inches toward the left then a couple inches toward the right. He repeated the action a few times, studying Liam while he did so. "Can you pin it down at all?"

"Meaning?"

"Are you feeling janky about the buyer? The tracker situation? The delivery?"

"All of the above."

Mason made a harsh sound somewhere between a derisive snort and a snicker.

Liam shook his head in response. "Not even joking. Too many things don't make sense." He leaned his forearms on his legs, pressing into them.

He continued, "If Collins is involved in some kind of criminal activity, why use old books, rare books, and deface them, and then take the major risk of transferring them to somebody else at auction? I can't figure out how that's worth taking a chance that somebody else will get their hands on it."

"I figure that's the reason for the tracker," Mason said.

"A tracker enables whoever placed it to know where the book is," Liam agreed. "But it doesn't guarantee that the wrong person won't get ahold of the book." He shifted and leaned back against the padded chair. "Why not just pass the book to the intended recipient another way? A simpler way."

"Like in a coffee shop, or at a restaurant."

"Or in a park. Or by fake courier," he added. "There are so many possibilities that would be less risky and more direct than an auction."

"I think we touched on this briefly the first day, but how would the auction house staff not notice the tracker or the page that was tampered with? They've got to have people who scrutinize stuff that gets put for auction. They got to make sure things are authentic, or they can't sell them, right?"

"Yeah, the auction house puts its reputation on the line if they don't disclose everything that needs to be disclosed about an item. That means someone on the inside was in on this, or the tampering took place after the auction concluded."

"Not likely this was the first time, then."

"No. Not likely at all," Liam agreed. "I don't even give a damn about all that. I mean, if Dax agrees we can try to unravel whatever we find, but my primary concern is getting Sarah's connection with this guy finished."

Chapter 25

Sarah

Sarah looked down at the "burner phone" on the conference room table in front of her.

How was it possible that she was in a situation crazy enough that she needed to use an untraceable phone number? She'd pursued a career in a field most people thought of as stuffy and boring, exciting only to book collectors or super fans of the occasional celebrity author. Yet for the last few days, she'd felt as if she was stuck inside a mystery novel. Hopefully it wasn't going to turn out to be a murder mystery.

She'd gone over the plan multiple times with Liam, then reviewed it again with his team.

It made sense. It was simple and straightforward. But she was still nervous.

"Let me know when you're ready to make the call," Liam said.

When Sarah first met him at the auction house she'd been impressed by his good looks, and then by his personality. Then she was impressed by how he made her feel when he touched her – and even when he didn't. His presence made her shiver, like a feather with its barely-there touch skimming over her skin and creating chills.

After that, she had been just as impressed by his kindness and competence, and his determination to help her and keep her safe. With Liam sitting next to her, she could do this.

"I'm ready," she said. Under the table, he placed his hand on her leg and squeezed gently in silent support. His warm hand lingered there, the roughened skin of his thumb caressing the smooth skin above her knee. It was comforting and arousing all at the same time.

Most importantly, Sarah understood the message his silent touch was sending her.

She wasn't dealing with this alone. Whatever "this" was, he had her back. And, incredibly, so did his whole security team.

Sarah put the phone on speaker and dialed Collins' number, which was written on a piece of paper on the table next to the phone so she wouldn't have to search for phone contacts for it.

The line rang once. Twice. Then the ringing stopped.

"Who is it?" Collins demanded. His voice was easy to recognize, with its clipped, short tones and nasal quality.

"It's Sarah Prescott, Mr. Collins," she said.

Before she could continue, he snapped at her, "You're supposed to be in Naperville, Ms. Prescott. Where are you? Where are my books?"

She didn't have to pretend to be angry and upset. "Mr. Collins, I tried to go to you. I was viciously attacked and injured while I was at the airport." Sarah didn't have to fake her distress. The lingering pain from her cuts, scrapes, and bruises was all too real. "I value you as a client, but I'm not going to put myself at risk like that again. I could've been killed!"

She swallowed hard, then took a deep breath, trying to calm herself and remain professional.

"You're all right, aren't you? You're talking to me," Collins countered. "I need those books. Were they damaged?"

What an ass! He didn't ask a single question about her injuries, or for details about what happened. All he cared about were his books.

"The books are fine," Sarah fought the urge to curse at him and disconnect the call. Collins couldn't even fake giving a damn about what happened to her.

Why was she in this business at all, dealing with narcissistic people who only cared about themselves, about their own –

The touch of Liam's big, warm hand on her forearm brought her out of her own furious thoughts. Sarah looked from his hand to his face, finding calm support in his expression.

"You got this. Stick to the plan." Liam's words were nearly inaudible, but he exaggerated the movement of his mouth to make reading his lips simple enough.

Stick to the plan.

Sarah nodded at him and said to Collins, "It wasn't in our agreement that I would *personally* deliver them. I tried to go along with your unexpected demand, and I told you what happened at the airport yesterday."

She let her anger put steel in her voice when she gave her client his options. "I can either meet you in the suburbs of New York City or go back to the auction house and request that they ship the books to you. Which do you prefer, Mr. Collins?"

Through the speakerphone, everyone in the room could hear Collins cursing under his breath. He finally said, "Fine. Either my associate or myself will meet with you tomorrow."

Her shock at his answer jolted through her. Wasn't he in Illinois? If the flight had gone as planned, would she have ended up in Naperville only to find out that he was in New York?

Liam signaled that she should stay calm.

He partially rose in his chair, enough to reach a piece of paper on the table and pull it closer to. Using a pen lying near his phone, he scrawled *Remember –2 days – Saturday!*

"Tomorrow is no good," Sarah said aloud to Collins.

Liam had stressed to her the importance of making the meeting take place on Saturday in the late morning or early afternoon. Sarah felt the weight of everyone in the room looking at her.

"Your books are completely safe. I promise you that, but I'll need time to get them from the vault." She looked at Liam and shrugged, making that part up as she went along. Sarah also added, "Plus, I need time to heal a little more from the injuries I got yesterday." *Injuries that you don't even care about.* "Saturday, in the later part of the morning or the early afternoon would be fine."

Without waiting for Collins to agree, she looked at the small piece of paper in front of her on which Liam had written the address. The desired meeting place was a strip mall in a neighborhood where almost every store closed from sundown on Friday until sundown on Saturday, out of respect for the religious practices of most area residents.

"I'll meet you in the parking lot there. I'll give you the books, you can transfer my commission, and we can both be on our respective ways." It could, and should, be as simple as that.

The team had chosen the location with care. It would give Liam a high place of overwatch, places for team members to monitor the hand-off from a distance, and it would also dramatically reduce the chance of other people stumbling onto the meeting.

"I or my associate will meet with you, Ms. Prescott," Collins said. "You realize it's risky to meet in a parking lot with my valuable property?" Sarah could hear the anger that fueled his words. "Until you put them in my hands, those books are your responsibility. You better be taking it seriously."

"I've quite literally shed blood to protect your *valuable property*," she said, not caring if he could hear the anger in *her* voice.

Sarah really didn't appreciate his attitude, or the fact that he was impugning the seriousness with which she took the responsibilities of her job. It wasn't her fault he'd decided to suddenly forgo having the books delivered to him via auction house arrangements.

Sarah struggled to keep her tone as professional as possible. "It's an extremely safe neighborhood, Mr. Collins. Plus, nobody will know what the books are, if anybody happens to see them at all, which is extremely unlikely."

Collins made his displeasure clear, but in the end, he begrudgingly agreed to the place and general time. Then he added, "This is ridiculous. With what I'm paying you, you should be willing to go anywhere I tell you to go. "

"I very much appreciate your trust in me, Mr. Collins. You're one of my most valued clients." Sarah rolled her eyes at her own blatant lie, but she tried to keep her voice sincere. "However, as a professional in my field, I have a lot of demands on my time, which is part of the reason that last-minute changes are so difficult."

Sarah looked to Liam, not sure what she should say next. He put a finger to his lips, indicating she should wait. It was tough to do, but Sarah stayed silent.

Finally, Collins spoke. "Fine. You better hope there are no issues, Ms. Prescott, because I'll be holding you responsible. Personally."

"Are you threatening me, Mr. Collins?" Sarah's hands fisted on the table. It was a rhetorical question, because she had no doubt that he was doing precisely that.

"Do I need to? Are you doing things with my books that you shouldn't be doing?"

What the hell would I be doing with his books?

Sarah exerted the self-control that had gotten her through so many tough times and ignored his strange additional commentary. She instead asked, "How will I know whether to expect you or your associate?"

"I'll text you a time that works for us," was all Collins said before he disconnected the call without saying goodbye. She knew that if he could've slammed the phone down, he would have – a definite disadvantage of touchscreen technology.

Sarah pressed the button to disconnect the phone on her end. She stared at the phone for a minute before looking up at Liam and then around the room at the others. "He agreed more easily than I expected," she said.

"He needs that book," Liam said.

"I really want to know what those numbers are," Sarah admitted.

From the head of the table Dax told her, "We agree, and we're going to keep looking into it." He stood. "You and Liam should see if you can figure anything else out from the auction angle." Dax nodded at Mason and Rick. "Rick, keep working on what we discussed. Figuring out those codes can tell us a lot. Mason, you're with me. Let's start planning the hand-off."

The three of them quickly and quietly left the room. Dax had his head down, typing out a rapid text on his phone. Mason sent a chin lift in their direction, which Liam returned in kind. Rick had an ever-present laptop tucked under one arm and he nodded his goodbye.

Liam followed the others to the door. Sarah was surprised (and disappointed) that he was also leaving, and without a word to her about... anything.

The man has a lot of things to do to deal with your problems, plus whatever else he's working on. You're lucky he's given as much attention as he has.

Instead of leaving, though, he closed the door behind his colleagues and immediately turned to face her again. His body looked physically relaxed, but that aura of strength and control that he wore so naturally was there, as usual. Liam's facial expression, that was another matter. His jaw was set, brow furrowed, lips compressed into a tight line. Either he had something difficult to say, or there was something weighing heavily on his mind.

"By the end of the day tomorrow, we'll have gone through a detailed plan for the meet up with Collins or whoever he sends in his place," Liam said. "No matter what that guy is up to, you'll be safe."

As he spoke, Liam returned to the table until he stood barely three inches from her.

His confident words were reassuring, as was his steady gaze. Sarah trusted him. Completely. The calendar said she didn't know him for long, but her heart said she'd known him forever.

Chapter 26

Liam

Finally alone again with Sarah, Liam tried to decide how to address the issues bothering him most. It was obvious that Edward Collins knew damn well what was hidden within the pages of the Shelley book. They hadn't figured out the details on those offshore account numbers yet, but no one had those types of accounts without there being a fuck ton of money involved. A fuck ton of *illegal* money.

There had to be more than rare books involved. To warrant the kind of money typically put into offshore accounts, there was something much bigger involved. Something big enough to have this guy and whoever was working with him take the risks of running a book that had been tampered with through a reputable auction house.

How the hell did Collins pull that off, anyway?

If the guy just wanted a nice, legitimate buyer's agent to innocently handle his less than innocent acquisitions, why not treat Sarah with respect? Who wouldn't exhibit some compassion to a person working on their behalf that was physically attacked while in the process of conducting that work?

It was also obvious that Edward Collins was a condescending, insensitive prick. It had taken a massive amount of effort for Liam to maintain even the façade of calm professionalism while Sarah was on that call.

When he was near Sarah, he wanted to pick up where they left off in his hotel room the day they met, but that had to take a backseat to this dangerous situation. They had to deal with Collins – and ensure Sarah's safety.

Liam stepped closer to her.

She didn't move away, just stared back at him. God, she was beautiful.

Sarah's hair flowed down her back and around her shoulders like a cocoa river with those fascinating variations of auburn and blonde streaks running through it. Behind her delicate eyeglasses, her eyes were sparkling, but also serious. Intelligent. Even though she wasn't smiling, her lips were still lush and inviting. Liam didn't miss the fact that her feet in those black, high-heeled shoes were planted firmly on the thick carpet, her stance and posture strong and confident. Like she was.

"I appreciate all your help, Liam. I know I've told you that, but I really feel like I need to say it again," she said.

"You don't need to say it again. But thanks."

They had such an immediate connection when they met at the auction house. Did she think he always got quickly intimate with women he met? He didn't think she behaved that way with men indiscriminately. Didn't think it was routine for her to slide effortlessly into third base with guys she just met. It was sort of insulting that she might be thinking that about him.

Don't even analyze the fact that she has you thinking in language a teenager would use.

He needed to get his mind off her lips.

"Everyone on the team will have their assignments," he said. "We'll communicate and coordinate throughout the op and get this handled."

"I haven't asked you much about Infinite except on the drive here," Sarah said. "Are you all former military?"

He paused and thought about how to reply before he finally said, "Most of us. There are some people formerly with alphabet agencies, or who are just the best at what they do."

Liam hoped she understood that he couldn't be much more specific, but figured he better spell it out in case it wasn't clear. "The cases we handle are almost all highly confidential, so I can't give details. I'm not trying to be big or elusive. That's just the way it is."

"I get that," she said and actually laughed. "When Jillian had me sign all those nondisclosure forms, that was the big clue."

"Yeah, she handles the piles of paperwork that go along with what we do. It gets complicated."

For someone whose ability to focus and concentrate was a huge part of his skill set, Liam was having an embarrassingly difficult time *not* thinking about how much he wanted his mouth on hers. *On her everything.*

Liam noticed that her gaze kept drifting to his mouth. Was she thinking thoughts similar to his own?

Conversation between them stalled. Tension, the delicious kind born of attraction, climbed. Yes, he'd been physically attracted to plenty of women before, but not like this.

He had to speak, needed to break the sexually charged silence that was growing and intensifying like a tangible thing. Liam cast about in uncharacteristically distracted brain for something reasonable to say, but Sarah beat him to it.

"Do you think they'll make progress with the number codes?" she finally asked, her voice slightly husky now. It was a perfectly appropriate question, and a perfectly reasonable one.

Liam managed to answer. "Yes."

No one on the team had figured out what the number sequences in the Shelley book corresponded with. It was frustrating, but truthfully, Liam didn't care about it all that much. Not on a personal level. There was always another jackass or criminal out there wreaking havoc. For all he cared, Collins could take whatever he was up to and make someone else crazy with figuring out his game.

Normally, he was determined to right wrongs, to stop criminals of all types and remove their ability to do harm. Why was he more worried about protecting Sarah than about figuring out what Collins was up to?

One of them had moved closer to the other. Both of them, maybe. The coconut body wash she'd used had teased his senses the whole time they'd been seated at the conference table. Now it seemed stronger than before, adding to the sensory overload her mere presence already caused.

"That's good," she murmured, looking at his mouth again.

Sarah needed to get the books to Collins and be done with this. Liam was all about bringing down bad guys. And yeah, this Collins guy was obviously involved in some illegal crap, but whatever that happened to be was nowhere near as important as getting her free of her connection to him. Which meant getting the books to Collins and completing the transaction.

Liam had a plan.

Keep Sarah safe. Build their connection. Explore what was between them.

Hold her. Kiss her.

Kiss her.

Between one breath and the next Liam went from wanting to kiss Sarah to holding her in his arms. He slid the fingers of one hand in her hair, securely cupped her head, and moved the fingers of his other hand to curl around her waist. Nothing had ever felt so good as having her tightly pressed against him. Her softness was the perfect counterpoint to the harder planes of his body. The soft fragrance of her body wash, her perfume, and her essence created a scent that he'd never be able to resist or forget.

He nuzzled her jawline close to her left ear, the silky waves of her hair caressing his face. It was as if she was stroking him everywhere.

"I'm going to kiss you," Liam said. He wouldn't if she denied him, although he wasn't quite asking permission.

Sarah's fingers gripped his shirt sleeve in one hand and his bicep in the other. Her reply was shared on an exhale of "Yes", a breathy sound so unlike her usual, confident tone. He found her cool confidence incredibly sexy, and this alternate version of her equally hot.

Liam pulled back just enough to see her lift her mouth as her eyelashes fluttered down and she somehow managed to get even closer to him.

Their mouths met in a moment of mutual claiming that didn't have the charming lilt of romantic poetry, but was instead a dramatic burst of timeless music. His heart beat in time to their frantic dance of hungry lips and tangling tongues and nipping teeth. The low, needy sound that escaped from her was met by the deeper rumble of his own.

The need to breathe forced their mouths to part.

Liam smoothed one hand cautiously up and down her back, acutely aware that she was sore from the airport attack. He eased his hand forward, over the silky soft shirt that didn't come close to being as enticing as her bare skin, and caressed her arm.

She kissed him again, and he enjoyed that she was willing to go after what she wanted. Even as he kissed her back, Liam recognized that the part of her personality that enabled her to do so was also responsible for her refusal to yield to allowing someone else to deliver the books.

"What is it?" Her words were mumbled against his mouth. "What's wrong?" Sarah pulled back a bit further, no doubt to get a better look at his face.

Liam considered telling her it was nothing, then quickly discarded that idea. He didn't want to lie to her, not unless keeping her safe made it necessary.

"Why are you so determined to do whatever your client wants about delivery?" When she immediately pulled away, Liam grabbed her hand. He was careful to not be rough about it – he didn't want to scare her or be overbearing right now. But he also didn't want her to run away from the conversation.

Why was the commission so important that she couldn't bear even a slight delay in receiving it if the guy was a huge asshole and stalled paying? Infinite Security would even provide her with legal support, as he'd told her. As Dax had also told her.

Was it really just about her father? If so, why didn't she tell him about that situation?

He and the Infinite team had a solid plan in the works, even though it had to be put together quickly. That uncomfortable feeling in his gut still remained, and he couldn't ignore it. The feeling that told him they were missing something. Or that trouble was coming. It was a feeling he'd had before, and it never steered him wrong.

He tried again to change Sarah's mind about letting him deliver the books. "Collins said he might send someone in his place to take the books, Sarah. There's no reason I can't deliver the books in *your* place."

"Thanks again for the offer, but no, not happening," she said immediately. Too quickly for her to have given his words any serious thought. Frustrating woman.

"Why not?" Liam kept his response short, trying to hide his frustration.

"This is my job. My client." Sarah faced him with hands planted firmly on the curve of her hips. "I was willing to go out of state to complete this transaction. I think I can manage to go 20-ish miles from here to Cedarhurst."

"Going out of state to complete the transaction wasn't such a good idea, was it?" Liam blew out a harsh breath. "Why take a chance on having another huge problem? On being attacked again? My God, you still have the bruises from what happened at the airport."

"We don't even have information about who that was," she reminded him. "It could've been a random thing. There's not a huge amount of crime at the airport, but it happens."

"You know it wasn't random." Why was she intentionally being so foolish about this? "From what you said, that guy was very specific. He wanted the books."

Sarah averted her gaze, took in a breath deeper than his big exhale, and then she looked back at him. "All I have to do is give him the books. I told you already, I can't risk my reputation in this field. I have to deliver and get a signature as proof. That's it."

"I can do it on your behalf," he insisted. "He wants the merchandise, not you."

"No." Sarah wouldn't yield. "Look, Liam, I'm grateful for your help and the help of your team. Your plan will keep me safe no matter what. But I have to be the one who closes this deal." She wasn't trying to hide the note of pleading in her voice. "I have to keep my word, and not give him any excuse to delay paying me. The commission will cover all of my bills for a few months. It's vitally important."

"I get that." He really did.

Sarah was smart. Well-spoken and professional. She also shouldered a lot of responsibility in her personal life, evidently solely responsibility for her father's well-being. He didn't have a right to make decisions for her, and he knew he was acting like some overprotective Neanderthal.

But that didn't mean he was wrong.

"Collins is up to no good. We can all see that, including you. I understand you're in a tough position with him right now, but I don't want to see you put yourself unnecessarily at risk, Sarah." He ran his hands through his hair again. "You mean too much to me already."

"You and your team planned this delivery," she pointed out. "You chose the location and set the time. It's supposed to be smooth and quick, right?"

"That's what we expect. But there's always risk in every op. Always."

"At the heart of it, this isn't a typical op of yours, Liam. It's an eccentric auction buyer. All I want to do is finish earning my commission and put this client behind me." Sarah shook her head, her hair swaying slightly with the motion. "Believe me, I won't be doing business with him again."

Liam was relieved to hear it, but it wasn't enough.

Sarah reached up to put a hand on his cheek.

"I understand you believe it's a risk, Liam, but you don't get to decide what risks I take. It's my career, and I do well at it. I must. I'm responsible for my dad, and I need that money for him. He has medical issues. Expensive issues."

Liam hesitated. Should he tell her that he'd known that? At this juncture, it didn't feel right to tell her that they'd had to investigate *her* and her associates, in an effort to make sure she was on the up-and-up.

"You have to give the money to him?" Liam decided to see if she'd share anything more. "Does he have outstanding debts?"

Sarah remained facing him, but her eyes focused on a point over his left shoulder instead of on his face.

"Kind of," she said. "It's not from anything nefarious or something like that. It's all medical."

She wasn't being very forthcoming, but she wasn't lying, either. Liam decided to shelve that part of the conversation. For now, at least.

Instead, he repeated his earlier point. "Collins told you he might have someone stand in for him at the meeting place. What's the harm in having someone stand in for you? "

Her fists were planted on her hips. "We are assuming Collins is up to something, but we don't have proof of that. Not really. I didn't alert the police because there's nothing to really accuse him of, is there? So, he is still just a client and I have to get the books to him."

"Yeah, I get that. But we both know there's more to it than that."

"Seems to be, yes."

He was surprised she admitted even that much.

"So you just want to forget about what happened at the airport?"

"No. Of course not. I don't trust Collins, at all. But you and your team say you can keep me safe, right?"

He nodded. "Yes, but keeping you away from the handoff would be even safer."

"I have to see it through so I can get paid and put this behind me." She was resolute on this, and he was at a loss.

Chapter 27

Liam

The basic plan was simple.

A sniper positioned on a roof for overwatch of the area. An operator positioned at the bus stop on the corner before the parking lot.

An additional man would be stationed in the main floor lobby of the small office building within the strip mall. The building would be closed, but they'd still be able to access it. That person would also prevent anyone working in the building from walking unawares into the parking lot during the hand-off.

Two team members would be positioned in a vehicle parked on the street just past the parking lot entrance. They'd keep an eye out for vehicles slowing to enter the lot, and they'd watch for potential innocent bystanders.

Sarah would arrive at the location four minutes after the appointed time. Her driver would keep her secure in the vehicle and negotiate the physical hand-off of the books. Transaction completed, Sarah and her driver depart.

They'd run it through alternate scenarios. They had emergency plans about how to exit with Sarah if necessary.

Liam studied the whiteboard with the scrawled schematics of the location. He looked down at the blowup of the map in front of him on the table.

It would be a standard six-man team. Dax, Mason, Jack, Derek, Jace, and him. From Sarah's arrival until her departure would ideally take less than 10 minutes.

He only had one significant change to make.

"I'll be in the car with Sarah. No offense, Jack." Liam didn't want Jack thinking he didn't trust him, but he'd be a hell of a lot more at ease with this if he himself provided Sarah's personal protection.

"I prefer you on overwatch." Dax tapped a spot on the diagram. "From the top of this portion of the building, you'll have range on the entire parking lot."

"Jack can handle it. He's as qualified and experienced as I am."

"I'm aware," Dax said.

Of course he was aware. Dax had recruited just about everyone at Infinite, even those people recommended to him by others. He knew their skill sets thoroughly.

Liam wasn't ready to yield on this. "I need to be positioned closer to her for this."

He needed to be close enough to keep her safe. Given the situation, that meant being up close to the situation, not on top of a building. Even with a sniper rifle in his hands.

Everything Infinite undertook was essentially a team mission. Somebody always had your six. And somebody was always in charge. That somebody wasn't always Dax, but since he was in charge of the organization itself, his knowledge (and experience) carried considerable weight.

The silence between them dragged on.

Liam wasn't going to cave on this. They weren't dealing with a combat situation with government oversight, or other officials and suits to answer to.

If Liam thought someone else could do a better job as Sarah's escort, he'd absolutely yield that position. But he didn't, so he wouldn't.

Apparently, Dax finally recognized and accepted that. Still, he held Liam's gaze when he said, "You're Alpha 1 on this, so it's your call." Dax's mouth was tight when he said it. He glanced down at the schematic again. "Positions?"

"Jack on overwatch. You in the building lobby. Mason at the bus stop. Derek and Jace in the car." Liam tapped each spot as he called them out.

After another round of position-specific discussions, the group disbanded, leaving Liam alone in the room with Dax. Instead of waiting for the other man to speak, Liam said, "Thanks for that."

Dax didn't bother pretending not to understand. "I know you realize that closer isn't always better."

Liam *did* know that. Being too close to a case, to someone you were guarding, to an issue being handled, or anything else of great importance, could make you focus on the wrong thing. It could skew your judgment. Fuck with your priorities.

"I've known Sarah less than a week. I'm not too close."

Instead of responding to that statement, Dax asked, "Can Sarah handle a gun? Does she have any self-defense training?"

"No to the first question. And she says she has some basic self-defense training from a course she took at a local library a few years ago, and a series of classes given at a gym she belonged to."

Liam knew Dax's wife, Tia, had gone through extremely brief lessons in both things when she'd been embroiled in a search for her missing sister some time back. In fact, he'd accidentally walked in on them in the gym during a personal training session that had become *extremely* personal. He'd tried to mentally obliterate that awkward memory.

Liam asked, "Did the crash courses help Tia at all?"

Dax rubbed a hand over his jaw. "The firearms lesson wasn't particularly useful. But I think the self-defense lesson had some benefits."

Liam barely stopped himself from asking if Dax meant that *he* benefited or that *she* did. The laugh might help his tension for a second, but Dax definitely wouldn't appreciate it. And he didn't want his friend to think he was being disrespectful.

He settled for saying, "I'll go over a few things with her."

Chapter 28

Liam

"**S**elf-defense?" Sarah repeated after Liam. "Like I told you, I do have some experience with that."

She'd answered her bedroom door barefoot, hair down, but still wearing her pencil skirt and silk blouse, with her glasses perched upon her small nose. Sarah was a juxtaposition of casual and elegant, perfectly combined. So beautiful.

"I know. You did tell me that," he said. "I think it might be a good idea to brush up on that since you said it's been a while."

She took two steps closer to where he stood just inside the bedroom door. "You know you don't have to make an excuse to put your hands on my body."

This more relaxed, slightly risqué Sarah brought him back to the first few moments after they'd met at the auction house. She was confident. Flirtatious in a way that was sexy and enticing, not vapid. Not a wallflower, but not vulgar, either.

Sarah was captivating in a way that ignited him.

Liam stepped to the side so she could close the door if she wanted to. He didn't want to make her feel trapped or presume anything. But hearing those words out of her mouth was unexpected, and unexpectedly hot.

She slipped past him to do exactly that – closed the door. Locked it.

When Sarah turned back to him, she raised her hands and put them flat against his chest. Liam had fully intended to discuss self-defense with her. Have her demonstrate what she knew and give her some tips about breaking holds and getting away from an assailant. He had no intention of getting even closer to her, of fanning the flames that burned between them and letting the fire become even more of a distraction.

And then his lips slanted over hers, and he was tugging up her skirt so there was room to guide her leg up around his own. He deepened the kiss, his tongue finding hers.

Liam slid one hand up the column of her neck, and traced the other up her rib cage until his thumb caressed the underside of her breast.

Sarah made a needy sound low in her throat. "I need to get this off. Please."

"I don't have long," he told her. "We're in the final planning stage. They'll be looking for me, and I have to be there."

"I understand." She pressed a kiss to the underside of his jaw. "I'll take you for as long as I can right now."

He released her long enough to tug her blouse up over her head and toss it to the side. Her breasts heaved up and down as he studied her, appreciating the way her cocoa lace bra contrasted with the golden tones of her lightly tanned skin. He'd never seen nor imagined ladies' undergarments in that color before, but it was perfect for her. On her.

Sarah carefully reached behind her back and unclipped her bra. The straps relaxed, and she shrugged them off her shoulders, then slid them down her arms and tossed it in the direction where he'd thrown her shirt.

Liam cupped her jaw, his eyes now burning into hers. "I want you so damn much, Sarah. It's not a good time, though. I need to be focused. *We* need to be focused."

"I'm just giving him the books," she said. "Do you truly think it's so dangerous?"

"There are a lot of unknowns about this guy, about who put the codes in that book, about why he's so insistent on getting it from you personally, about whether he's connected to the assault at the airport. Unknowns are dangerous. So *this* is dangerous."

"*This* as in the meeting with him or *this* as in between us?

"Both," he admitted.

The pull between them was so strong, it was like a sensual tether between their bodies, binding them together with the vibration of need.

Liam succumbed to the effortless allure of her mouth again, kissing her softly, gently, then deeper. A wild clash of giving and taking, hunger and gluttony. He guided her the half-dozen steps to the bed, sat her down upon the edge of it, and knelt before her.

Liam's gaze drifted from her incredible hazel eyes down to her full breasts with their pretty pink nipples, back up to her delicate collarbones, the graceful column of her neck, her kiss-swollen lips, then back to her eyes. He didn't try to hide the hunger he felt for her.

"I want my mouth on you." Liam told her. "Unless that's not what you want?"

He didn't want to pressure her. Could he possibly be reading her signals all wrong?

"I want *you*, Liam," Sarah said, her voice soft and husky, but clear and steady. "I want to share everything with you."

"We don't have time for *everything* right now."

"How much time *do* we have?"

"Nowhere near enough, especially for our *first* time." He narrowed his eyes at her. "Our first time isn't going to be a fast and frenzied fuck. You deserve to be worshiped and savored."

Liam leaned forward and captured her mouth again. He kissed

her and coaxed her to lay back upon the bed. While he cupped one breast and trailed his mouth down her neck to a nipple that strained toward his mouth, he worked his other hand underneath her waist, in search of the zipper to her skirt. When he didn't find one, his fingers searched again.

He felt her smile beneath his lips and pulled his head back slightly. "A little help here?"

Sarah tugged his hand to her right hip. "There."

Liam watched his own fingers grasp the zipper tab and slide it down over the curve of her hip until it reached the end of the track. Using both hands, he gently pulled her skirt down, revealing more golden, fragrant skin. Liam tossed the discarded clothing over by the nightstand. He didn't see where it landed, exactly, because he was so intently focused on the scrap of cocoa satin and lace shielding her sex.

He inhaled the intoxicating scent of her, letting her overwhelm him with painful anticipation. In that moment she was bared to his eyes, to his touch, to the ravages of his questing mouth. Her hips undulated in a desperate attempt to get closer still, and her hands clutched the bedclothes at her sides when she couldn't; he was already surrounding her with his lips and tracing her with his tongue, nibbling with his teeth, conducting a symphony of pleasure.

Sarah's breath stuttered and she called out his name in a voice he intended to hear again.

"Liam! Oh, yes, Liam!"

Her pleasure flooded his mouth so sweetly, so beautifully, he heard bells ringing.

And they didn't stop ringing.

"Liam, your phone." Sarah's voice was still suffused with the aftereffects of her release.

"Dammit." Liam muttered under his breath as he leaned over to grab it off the nightstand, keeping one hand on her leg and then her arm, trying to maintain their physical connection.

It was Dax. Of course.

Liam sent a quick text, then directed his attention back to Sarah. "I've got to go back." He kissed her quickly. "See if you can get rest while I'm gone."

Chapter 29

Sarah

Liam never made it back to her side the night before. He and his team all wore serious expressions as they spoke in hushed tones before breaking off from one another. They all departed headquarters before she and Liam. Sarah received several nods of acknowledgment, but no one spoke to her and no one cracked even the smallest smile.

Why make such a big deal about a simple transaction?

She just needed to hand over the books and leave. It wasn't like this was a negotiation or something complicated.

"How are you doing?" Liam asked. "Tell me the truth, not what you think I want to hear."

"Good... I think." Sarah fidgeted with the bag on her lap that contained the books. It wasn't heavy, which she knew from carrying it around so much since receiving it at the auction house. Stress made it feel weightier than it was.

"This should be a fast transaction," he reassured her. "We're almost there already."

Lost in her own thoughts, she'd barely paid attention to the drive. In the last village they'd driven through, and now this one, there was some pedestrian traffic and parked cars, but not many vehicles on the road.

There were a lot of stores on both sides of the main street. Nearly all of them were closed. Most would open after sunset today, in keeping with traditional religious practices of a majority of the local residents.

Liam flipped on the right turn signal and turned into a parking lot at the end of a long row of stores. Within that parking field, another few business storefronts lined the right side. Sarah could see only three cars in the lot, each parked in different areas.

She craned her neck to look around more thoroughly, and to scrutinize the storefronts more closely. A dry cleaner. A laundromat. A real estate office. A little café. And a two-story office. Nothing flashy. Nothing open for business. At the far end of the lot, there seemed to be what might've been railroad tracks.

"There's no one here," Sarah said. She thought the others from Infinite were supposed to be there already. *Wasn't that the plan?*

"Jack is on overwatch already," Liam said. "Everyone else is also in place. We're just waiting on your client."

She nodded, trying to see Jack on top of one of the low buildings. She couldn't. She didn't notice anyone, anywhere.

Sarah squared her shoulders. It was going to be fine. There was no threat against *her*; like she'd pointed out to Liam. She was just making a delivery of property a client had purchased. The attack at the airport had to have been random, just awkward timing.

A little voice in her head counted the thought instantly. *What about the doctored page in the book your client made you overpay for?*

Sarah shook her head to admonish herself. Collins didn't have the book yet, so he could not have messed with anything. And it wasn't illegal to be odd.

"Has Collins reach out to you yet?" Liam asked. He adjusted the earpiece she knew he wore to keep in contact with his team.

"No, nothing," Sarah said.

It was a good reminder of that item's presence, and the fact that others would hear her if she kissed him like she wanted to do, or sought more reassurance for her nerves. After all, Liam wasn't her boyfriend. He was a caring and protective guy who was willing to help her. So what if they had amazing physical chemistry between them? That was all it was.

Several more minutes passed in silence.

"Copy that." Liam was obviously responding to someone talking to him through his ear. He shifted his attention to Sarah. "Black Escalade about to turn into the lot."

Sarah thought out loud. "Maybe it isn't Collins?"

Liam said, "About to find out."

They watched as the late-model luxury SUV pulled into the parking lot. The driver of the vehicle drove further into the lot than Jace had. They positioned the vehicle to point in the direction from which it had entered. Doing so also had the newcomer facing Sarah and Liam.

"What do I do?" Sarah was getting increasingly nervous. Was Collins in that car? Or had he sent somebody else?

"Follow my lead right now, and then we'll take it from there," Liam said.

"Are you going to drive closer to them?"

"No." Liam unlocked his door. "I'm going to stand up and call out to them. I'll open your window a crack so you can hear, but you stay locked in the car until I open your door."

Before Sarah could think it through and decide if she had any argument, he was already out of the car. He clicked his key fob to lock it.

Liam moved to the front of the vehicle and loudly called out, "Collins?"

She watched as a man larger than she remembered Edward Collins being stepped out of the Escalade. He was dark-haired whereas Collins had been blonde – although hair color could be easily changed.

"Who are you? Where's Prescott?" the man shouted back.

"I'm her friend," Liam said. "Who are you?"

Another car door opened behind the other driver. Sarah recognized her client when he appeared. She'd only met him once before. He was as tall and slim as she recalled. That other meeting had been in wintertime, when they'd both been wearing bulky layers of clothing to protect against the cold.

Today, though, the overwhelming heat had Collins in shirt-sleeves, pressed chinos, and deck shoes. The summer clothing revealed that his thin frame was amply muscled, and he had a colorful sleeve of tattoos stretching down his right arm all the way to his wrist. When he spoke, his distinctive voice was laden with irritation.

"Consider him my friend that keeps me safe," Collins said. "Seems like Sarah has a lot of *friends*, too," he sneered. "Does she have my property?"

"She does. I'll bring it over to you," Liam said.

Even from a distance Sarah could see Collins' eyes narrow. "No. I take delivery from her, as agreed in our contract."

"Just a minute," Liam said.

Liam backed up to the SUV he and Sarah had arrived in, keeping Collins and his bodyguard "friend" in his field of vision. When he reached a position where he was in line with Sarah's window, he turned his head slightly in her direction.

"That the right guy?" Liam confirmed.

"Yes. I'll just give him the books, and we can be done with this," Sarah said.

"We can have you stand here, next to the door, and I'll give him the books."

"Liam, he's not a menace. The books belong to him. He may not even know one has been altered, remember?"

"The status of his knowledge doesn't matter. There's no reason he can't accept them from my hand."

"Look, he wants to be a stickler about delivery being as stipulated in the contract. It'll take a few seconds, and I'll be done with him."

Sarah tugged up the inside handle of the door, but Liam was leaning against the metal so it wouldn't open. "Liam."

"I'll be right next to you," he said. "Remember, you're not alone. We have eyes on you at all times."

"Let's just get this over with," she said.

Sarah allowed Liam to open her door and she stepped down out of the vehicle. She held the bag with the two books tightly to her chest and walked quickly over to where Collins remained by his car.

Trying to not be obvious about it, she attempted to see who was in the vehicle Collins had exited. Even as close as she was, the window tint was too dark for her to be able to make out more than shadows. Were those shadows more people?

She looked to Liam, who was focused intently on Collins. Had he observed the other shadows in Collins' vehicle? He probably had, she reassured herself. And who knew what the others had observed?

She should have worn an earpiece like the rest of the team had. She'd tried one, but when several of the men carried on a conversation to simulate the type of thing she might hear through it, Sarah immediately realized it was distracting and confusing to have all that going on in her ear while she simultaneously tried to do something else. Liam had been comforting and reassuring about how it was normal to need to adapt to dealing with an earpiece in an active situation.

Now, feeling so out of the loop wasn't comfortable or reassuring. Not that anything about the situation was either of those things... but still.

"Good to see you, Mr. Collins," Sarah said when she was close enough to him.

"I don't appreciate the delay," he responded. "But I'm glad you met with me today." Collins glanced around with a disgusted look on his face. "Even if you did pick a ridiculous place for it."

Of course he thought that any place he didn't personally frequent was ridiculous. Sarah decided to not even reply to his comment, or the fact that he said nothing about the attack on her at the airport.

Instead of commenting on that, she held the small gift bag out toward him. "Here are both books, along with the documentation from the auction house."

"Give them to me one at a time," Collins instructed her.

Sarah struggled to remain patient and professional despite his irritating tone of voice. She didn't want to put the bag down on his car, so instead she awkwardly maneuvered it so she could access the contents. The sound of car doors opening was a momentary distraction from her task. Two men emerged from the rear doors of his vehicle, both men fitting movie stereotypes of big-screen bad guys.

Why are you surprised? You knew there were others in that truck.

Sarah forced her focus back to the task at hand. With the bag now opened and the top layer of tissue pushed aside, she perversely decided not to give him what she was sure he wanted most, the one with the strange codes first. She handed him the other one instead.

Collins barely glanced at it before handing it off to one of his bodyguards. "The other one."

She carefully withdrew the Shelley volume from the bag and handed it to him in the wrapping with which the auction house had protected it. He tore the protective wrapping off and roughly removed the centuries-old silk cover. Collins hurriedly flipped through the pages.

Sarah couldn't stop herself. "You're going to damage it!"

"Mind your business," he snapped at her.

"What did you want the book for if you're not going to handle it with respect?" Sarah couldn't keep a lid on her anger. She thought of the tracker in its spine, and the despoiled page. "Didn't you risk enough damage already?"

"What I do with my property is none of your damn business," Collins glared at her. "You didn't take perfect care of it, did you? What did you do to it, Sarah?" He gave up all pretense of being polite. "Nosy bitch."

The sound of an approaching train in the distance momentarily distracted her. Liam put a hand on her arm. "Leave him the bag and let's go."

Collins signaled to his bodyguard, who lunged at Sarah.

"Get to the car!" Liam shouted. He tightened his grip on Sarah's and pulled her away from the group.

A loud popping sound made her involuntarily flinch. There was the smell of fireworks, but clearly it wasn't that. Almost instantaneously, she knew.

Gunshot.

Liam stumbled back, still holding tight to Sarah's arm. She saw the blood running down his arm.

Someone *shot Liam?*

Where is his team?

One of the men with Collins tackled Liam to the ground. The impact tore his hand away from her arm and that made Sarah stumble again. Before she could orient herself and regain her balance, she was hauled over the shoulder of a man accompanying Collins, and he was running. Her midsection bounced painfully against his shoulder.

She added her voice to the din of others she heard yelling. "Put me down!"

Sarah struggled to lift her head despite the awkward position. She tried to pummel her captors' back, his head, but it was way more difficult than it sounded in books.

She tried yelling again, but it was hard to draw a deep breath with her abdomen compressed over his shoulder. With the shallow breaths she could take, Sarah continued to yell for help, and for her captor to release her.

Sounds of fighting, of punches connecting with their targets was unmistakable. Sarah heard several more shots. She couldn't look around to see what was happening.

She wanted to look for Liam, but fear of what she'd find stopped her.

"Shut up," her abductor snapped at her, racing around the corner at the far end of the parking lot. The background noises were changing. Sounds of machinery, the odor of diesel fuel, the whistling release of air brakes maybe?

The sound of Collins' voice startled her. "Hurry the fuck up!"

Until Sarah heard his voice, she hadn't realized Collins was running along with them. He and the man carrying her rushed up a short staircase and from the increased volume of the sounds, she knew they were getting on a train.

"Keep your mouth shut or your Gold Coast friends are going to die at the same time you do." Collins issued the threat as casually as if he were ordering a cup of coffee.

How did he know Infinite Security was headquartered on the North Shore... The Gold Coast of Long Island? How did he know anything about them at all? Had he recognized Liam somehow?

"Hold the doors!" He called out the request to someone, as if nothing untoward was happening. And then added to his bodyguard in an equally conversational tone, "We don't have to run anymore to catch the train. Put her down." Collins looked at her blandly. "Behave yourself or somebody will die."

He sounded nonchalant, but Sarah had no doubt he was serious.

The railroad conductor was standing on the platform, the short sleeves of his blue, summer uniform shirt crisply pressed. The perfect creases remained defined, even in the summer humidity. The badge with his ID number declared his last name was Vaughn.

Sarah's mind raced in those few moments before she knew they'd board the train. How did she grab his attention, maybe make him remember her?

"So few people at the station today, Conductor Vaughn," she said, making a point of using his name.

The train whistle blew shrilly, and Collins gripped her arm. "We better get on board." And then he was pulling her onto the train car.

Where was Liam?

Chapter 30

Liam

In the nearly deserted parking lot, Liam pressed the wadded cloth against his upper arm. The bullet had grazed him, shredding some skin and leaving a burn trail, but there'd be no lasting damage. His fistfight with Collins' two bodyguards had left him with battered knuckles and, from the feel of it all, an array of cuts and blooming bruises. Nothing major. It was the only good luck he'd had today.

That, and the fact that they'd captured one of the bodyguards before he could jump in a vehicle with his companion and escape. The other guy hadn't hesitated even a moment before taking off alone.

The unconscious thug was still out cold in the backseat of Jack's vehicle. He'd be moved momentarily to one of the holding cells Infinite maintained in a small building on the premises. From the outside, it looked like a storage place for bags of soil, fertilizer, and gardening equipment. An outsider wouldn't know there was more to it than that.

"How did we not know about the damn train station?" Liam shouted the question at himself more than anyone else.

Mason was on his phone, either searching or scrolling for information. "There's only a few train stops south of here."

"If they get off at Inwood, it's a short drive to Kennedy Airport," Liam was already jogging toward his vehicle. "That's got to be where he's taking her. Charlie Mike at JFK."

He left his earpiece on and knew the others would as well after he declared he was going to *continue mission.*

"How could Collins time it perfectly enough to catch a flight before we could catch him?" Jace said, right at Liam's heels. "I'll drive, man."

"He couldn't." Liam wrenched open the door. "Has to be a private plane."

Through his ear piece he could still hear the other guys on his team getting into their vehicles. Jack let them know he was heading back to headquarters with their detainee, while Jace put Liam's SUV in gear and turned it around. "Want to head to the airport?"

"Yeah." Liam looked at him. "You know the back way?" There was a quicker way to go than GPS would offer.

"Rockaway Boulevard, right?" Jace confirmed as he tore out of the parking field.

"Yeah." Liam switched his focus to the others on the team, who were also on the way to the airport. "Someone loop Rick or Callie in. Confirm location of the private plane terminal. I know we've used it before, but we can't waste a second looking for it." Liam's mind was racing. "Have them hack the most recent flight plans filed."

"Alpha 3, on it already," Mason said.

Jace drove as fast as he dared, making a sharp right onto Broadway again. With scarcely any afternoon traffic in the area today, it was only minutes later that they were making the necessary terms to get to Rockaway Boulevard. There was a lot more traffic there.

Liam dug around under the front passenger seat for the small first-aid kit all Infinite Security vehicles carried there. The big one would be in the back of the SUV, but the contents of the small one would be enough for his purposes.

He hissed through his teeth at the sting of the disinfectant wipe cleaning the area the bullet had grazed him and wiping the blood off his arm as best he could. Then he slapped a large adhesive bandage over it, pressing down the edges. It was more than good enough.

"Terminal 4," Mason shared with them all over comms.

"Roger." Liam strategized out loud. "We can't descend on the entrance with three vehicles like this."

Each vehicle carried a couple of state and federal premise authorizations, but if they arrived en masse there would be too many questions to deal with before they could try to intercept Collins.

Pulling the relevant access documents out of the glove compartment, Liam shoved them to the front of the dashboard. There would still be questions, but at least they were visible. That should dissuade anybody from shooting at them without asking questions first. International airports were ultimately federal property and security around the aircraft would be anything but slack.

Liam gritted his teeth in frustration until they got to Boundary Road, the rear entrance to the back of the airport, where the maintenance buildings and other support functions were based.

He'd never felt like this before, the rage and fear twisting together in a maelstrom of painful intensity. Liam consciously shoved it down, down, down. He was going to get Sarah back and Collins was going to pay. It didn't matter what demands other crimes were – because obviously he was involved in *something* – putting Sarah through this was going to be what ultimately brought him down.

The plan was that while Liam and Jace would go in the back way to the terminal and the tarmac, the other two vehicles would wind around to the nearest side entrance. All the areas would be busy, but at least a little less congested than the main.

Through his ear piece, Liam listened to Dax on the phone with someone he managed to reach at the airport, a contact Infinite had near the top of the on-site Command Center. Although the other side of the conversation was muffled enough to be indistinct, Liam could hear Dax clearly.

"A woman's life may be at stake... –"

"Edward Collins... –"

"Private plane... –"

"Yes. I do."

After another several minutes of clipped conversation with whoever was on the other end of the line, Dax addressed Liam directly. "They know you're heading in through the cargo area. If he can get the word out fast enough, Caputo will have his people try to delay the aircraft if it can be identified and if it hasn't taken off yet."

Too many ifs.

Liam bit back that comment. "Roger that."

At the first security checkpoint, the entrance to the cargo area, it was immediately obvious that Caputo had been true to his word. A stocky security officer at the gate with a sidearm strapped to his belt greeted them. The man's ID badge identified him as Steve Harkness. "Infinite?"

"Yeah. I'm Connelly," Liam said, producing his own ID. "We gotta hurry."

"Understood." The fellow gestured to a small, open vehicle similar to an oversized golf cart, that already had another officer behind the wheel. "We'll provide an escort to the back of the gate at Terminal 4."

The roar of jet engines was almost deafening. Strong odors of jet fuel and oil were heavy in the air. They evoked visceral memories of previous ops, in both the military and the private sector.

Another security officer ran up to those leading the way for Liam and Jace. As the new guy conferred with the one in the passenger seat, he was shaking his head. Liam jumped out of the SUV and had taken only two steps when Harkness did the same.

"Private plane heading for Florida took off less than five minutes ago," Harkness said. "In the time it took to pinpoint the plane, it was too late to stop it."

Whatever else the officer said was drowned out by Liam's pulse pounding in his ears and the self-recriminations shouting in his brain.

Chapter 31

Liam

Less than an hour later, the men who'd been at the botched book hand-off and the airport were gathered in Dax's office. Rick and Callie joined them there.

"Recap what we know," Liam demanded of everyone.

He was afraid for Sarah and furious at himself. What should've been a straightforward, simple op to hand over damn books had gone sideways. FUBAR. That slimy son of a bitch had his hands on Sarah.

Rick jumped in immediately. "The sequences of numbers definitely fit with patterns of accounts in the Cayman Islands," he said.

It was what they'd suspected, but it was still startling to hear it confirmed.

"So somebody's messed with that book to convey secret account numbers?"

The way Dax asked it, the question wasn't really a question– it sounded more like he was processing the information out loud. Stating it for everyone.

"Evidently." Rick confirmed it succinctly. "Whatever Collins is up to, it makes more sense now that he was desperate to get his hands on the money stashed there."

Liam kept pacing. He couldn't keep still the way he usually would when absorbing information or strategizing.

"How the fuck didn't I think about the train line? I know the Far Rockaway line goes through Cedarhurst."

Arms crossed over his chest, Mason leaned his upper back against one wall of the office. "We all know that. The train line wasn't on our map of the shopping plaza." He shook his head, obviously disgusted with himself, too. "None of us thought of it. Maybe not surprising, what with the short timeline."

Mason never made excuses for anything, so Liam knew the comments were intended to try and lessen the guilt he was feeling. It didn't work.

Dax gripped the back of his neck in his own obvious frustration. "We let the fact that it's nearby and a somewhat familiar area, a safe area, convince us that we didn't need to squeeze in on-site reconnaissance." He dropped his hand to the desk in front of him. "This isn't on you, Liam. Any one of us should've thought of this."

Another well-meaning but useless attempt to lessen Liam's own frustration. Guilt. Anger.

Mason added another thought. "Even if we had checked out everything about the line, I don't think we would've thought Collins would jump on a train to exit the scene."

Liam wasn't ready for that level-headed logic. He looked around at his team and said, "All that matters is finding Sarah and getting her back. Safely. Why the hell does he want *her* anyway? He's got the damn book."

Liam's mind kept jumping from one point to another. Collins had the books now. Why kidnap Sarah? "He got his codes. That doesn't involve her."

"We don't know his end game because we don't know what he's up to," Dax said, stating the obvious.

Liam started thinking out loud again. "Intentionally paying more than you have to for something to win an auction isn't a crime unless the person behind the bidding is money-laundering, and it's something that can be proven."

Liam tipped his head back to look at the ceiling, like an answer was going to be written there. "We don't have any indication of that. There's no way to know definitively who put the device in the book," Liam pointed out. "At least not right now. Even if we find that out, it wouldn't necessarily be a crime."

And if it was a crime, it sure wouldn't be a major one.

Silence reigned in Dax's office.

Mason cleared his throat, but didn't say anything. Liam looked over at him quizzically. The big guy slowly shifted his gaze from Dax over to Liam before he said,

"Look, Liam, I get that there's some kind of something between you and this woman, but you can't really know –"

"She's not involved. Not the way you're implying. She isn't involved, except as a legit buyer's agent." Liam spoke with his jaw clenched tightly.

He reminded himself that Mason was being devil's advocate again. That he was doing his job, not being an ass.

"Why was she so quick to trust you, anyway?" Mason asked. "You said you met her for the first time at the book auction, right?"

"That's right. I don't know why she trusted me, but it's a damn good thing she did."

"Not if she's in on this with Collins."

"If she was in it with him, why the hell would she involve me at all?" Liam was having trouble controlling his temper, which was unlike him. "You want to believe she's in collusion with him, and staged her own abduction? Faked everything with that book? Had them attack and shoot live ammo?" His fists clenched at his sides.

Mason's answer was a question of his own. "Gives her plausible deniability, doesn't it?"

"For *what?*" Liam wanted to take a swing at his own colleague, but that wasn't going to help Sarah. "I was the one who approached *her*, not the other way around."

Hadn't he told them that? Liam was certain he'd told Dax when he called him from the auction house.

His own eyes shifted to Dax. "You didn't mention that to them?"

Dax didn't confirm or deny. "If you trust this woman, we need to get back on track here."

Jace stepped into the breach. "From where we were, there were only three stops left going south," he said. "Did they get off at Woodmere or Inwood? We know it wasn't Far Rockaway, or they wouldn't have gotten to the airport so quick."

Liam took a few steps away from the part of the office where the group had clustered. He stared out the office window that looked out over the gardens behind the house, and the Long Island sound beyond. The sun reflected brightly off the water and the white sails on some of the boats that had dropped anchor off the coast. It was usually a peaceful, picturesque tableau. He'd wanted to take Sarah sailing out there.

Damn it, he was *still* going to take her sailing.

He wasn't going to let her die because of him, like Kelsey did.

Liam hadn't wanted to leave the airport, desperate to find some kind of lead. Without a warrant, or any proof of exigent circumstances, airport officials wouldn't disclose the private plane's destination; they would've held the flight a few minutes to enable emergency conversation and make sure nobody was aboard against their will. But that was it.

The argument at the airport wasted valuable time, and Liam had quickly realized they'd have more equipment and better technology to help them find clues if they returned to headquarters. There they could access more information, and use their own private transport so they could travel with weapons and other critical equipment.

Arguing with his own team was also a waste of valuable time.

"He's probably taking her to Illinois," Liam said, turning towards his teammates. "Where he wanted her to meet him. Naperville."

Dax picked up his phone from where he'd left it on his desk. "I alerted our main flight crew from the car. I'll update them while you guys gather everything and the research on Collins."

Liam looked to Rick. "Any progress getting the flight plan for Collins' plane?"

Shaking his head, Rick said, "We're still working on it."

Liam nodded. There was nothing to say. He knew that breaking into secure info took time, and Rick or Callie would let them know as soon as they had more intel. Still, he'd had to ask.

The work Infinite did – the dangerous *and* the more mundane assignments – all required information gathering, research, strategy development, and plenty of "boring" stuff. The adrenaline driven efforts accounted for a small percentage of the time they invested in everything. But that boring stuff was usually why they succeeded.

There were a lot of things to figure out, but they'd do it.

Get your mind off the train tracks.

He hadn't even noticed the tracks were there, on the other side of the fence, at the far end of the parking lot. They weren't elevated at all, and the part of the fence visible from the parking lot hadn't been marked.

The Cedarhurst Station itself was a block away from the meeting spot, and the possible existence of a closer track access point hadn't occurred to any of them.

He'd only experienced this level of distress, felt this useless and incompetent, once before. Kelsey died as a result of his failure last time.

That, too, had been a situation where if any single minute unfolded differently, then *everything* would've ended differently. For years Liam had tormented himself about how he could've called her sooner, kept her on the phone longer, surprised her at work to take her out for coffee or for dinner the way he had originally intended.

How if he wasn't so caught up in what he was doing, she would still be alive.

So many ways the timeline could have been changed by fifteen or twenty seconds, and she wouldn't have been in that intersection.

Now, some thirteen years later, he was unexpectedly falling just as hard for another incredible woman, and he'd fucked up again. Except this time, an innocent woman wasn't going to pay the price for his incompetence.

Chapter 32

Sarah

"Not a sound," Collins' underling, Ronnie, warned her again, his stale breath hot against her ear.

He'd already warned her a half-dozen times that if she fought or made a scene, he'd shoot the nearest bystander. Sarah couldn't risk getting someone else hurt, some stranger just innocently going about their day. She stayed quiet, didn't even make eye contact with anyone, afraid this maniac would perceive that as attracting attention.

After just a few minutes on the train, they'd disembarked at Inwood Station, and she had been rushed into an awaiting Town Car with slightly tinted windows. Seated between Collins and Ronnie, she had no delusions that she could somehow get out of those confines and out of the moving car itself.

"Where are we going?" she demanded to know, with a bravado she didn't feel.

"Shut up," Ronnie hissed.

"Ms. Prescott is our guest, Ronnie. Show some respect." Collins issued the extremely mild rebuke while he toyed with the auction house gift bag, where he held it balanced on his knee.

Sarah consciously held her limbs in tightly, not wanting to inadvertently touch either man. The air conditioning in the car wasn't working well. The odor of stale cigarettes and sweat were oppressive.

She wondered if the uniformed driver was somebody from a car service or employed by Collins himself. Sarah couldn't really see him through the privacy screen that had already been in place when she was pushed into the car.

"Don't bother. He works for me." Collins made the statement mildly. Had he noticed her trying to find an angle at which she could see something upfront – or was he making a logical assumption that she was trying to figure out if she might find someone to be an ally in this car?

Sarah was ready to demand to know where they were going, when she started actually paying attention to the passing surroundings. It looked vaguely familiar and... then it clicked in her memory. This was the back way into Kennedy Airport, through the cargo and maintenance areas. Years ago, she'd worked for an aviation maintenance company based in the back section of the airport. When traffic on the Belt Parkway was bad, she'd frequently take the back roads into the airport.

There was nothing else of significance on this route. They were obviously catching a flight.

Where was Collins taking her? Why?

Illinois? Or somewhere else?

As the car wended its way through the back streets and passed through security for the cargo areas, the fear twisting Sarah's stomach continued to grow. They went through more security, the driver getting out of the car at one point and handing something to a guard.

After a certain point, there were very few regular vehicles in sight. Port Authority transport vehicles passed by; maintenance trucks passed. Multiple aircraft, with workers clustered around them, were on the ground not too far away.

All those people, and she could not get anyone's attention even if she tried because she couldn't reach a door and the windows were darkened just enough.

"Let me explain what's going to happen now, Ms. Prescott." Collins spoke as casually as if they were chatting over dinner. "We are getting on a private aircraft. Our way has been smoothed for a speedy departure. If you make a fuss or make a scene, Ronnie here will punish someone at random. The blood, metaphorically of course, will be on your hands and on your head."

Ronnie fisted his hands on his knees, opening and closing his fingers. "Give me any reason at all to show you what he means."

She made the mistake of turning her head enough to see more clearly. His expression of gleeful anticipation was sickening. She was wondering if Collins was serious in his threat, but one look at Ronnie convinced her that he was. There was no way Ronnie had acting skills enough to fake that kind of malevolence.

Collins resumed, "You are going to act naturally, smile and nod when appropriate, and be a model guest and passenger progressing through the airport. Do you understand that, Ms. Prescott?"

They were maneuvering on a road that led to the side of a terminal. The driver stopped the car near a sign for Private Aircraft. He scurried around to Collins' door at the rear of the vehicle.

"Remember." Collins said the single word as the driver opened his door. After he exited, bag in hand, the driver extended a gloved hand to Sarah. She thought vaguely how crazy it was that the man was wearing gloves in such heat and humidity, but apparently if that's what Collins wanted, his employee obeyed.

"Stay next to me," Collins said, pointing to where he wanted her.

Sarah fought the urge to tell him she wasn't a dog to be ordered around, but then she reminded herself it was better not to bait him when there was so much she didn't know about what was happening.

Ronnie fell into step on her other side, close enough that she could feel his arm occasionally brushing hers. Sarah tried to hold herself away from him, which pressed her against Collins' arm.

They were escorted through a private security access point. The driver had followed with several suitcases, all of which were summarily checked in and whisked away.

Through a wall of windows, Sarah could see several private planes lined up. There was activity around two of them. She wondered which they were going to board, and she fought the panic rising in her throat.

"I need to use the restroom before we board," she said to Collins.

"No." His reply was brusque.

She wasn't going to be dissuaded so easily. "I'm a nervous flyer, and I need to use the restroom. Do you have anything for travel sickness?"

Sarah didn't have to put any effort into sounding stressed. It wasn't that she was actually a nervous flyer or prone to travel sickness; she was freaking out about getting on a plane and going who knew where for who knew what reason.

"You can use the restroom on the plane," he said. "I'll get you something for motion sickness. Don't need you puking all over my beautiful aircraft."

She had to ask him straight out before this went any further. "I don't understand this. You have the books." Her voice rose. "Why are you taking me with you?"

"I will explain when we get there," Collins said. He gestured to Ronnie, who came closer. Collins whispered in the other man's ear, and they both watched the burly man approach a hostess in the lounge where they were waiting.

"There has to be some kind of misunderstanding," Sarah said with increasing desperation. "I had to give you the books, and that's done. You didn't even look at them both, but they are the ones you wanted to win, and I won them for you."

Finally, he looked directly at her. His pale blue eyes were cold and dispassionate. "Are you worried about leaving your father?"

What did he know about her father? How did he know anything about her father? Sarah stared at him, her panic skyrocketing until her heart rate felt dangerously fast.

"My father?" She repeated the words as if he could've said something else, despite knowing he hadn't.

"Yes. George Prescott. Your father." Collins spoke as casually as if he was talking about the weather. "I understand his condition is stable, though unchanged." He tapped two fingers on his free hand against his chin as if deep in thought. "I hope that doesn't change for the worse anytime soon. I've heard that head injuries can always be unpredictable."

Sarah couldn't find the words to reply. How did he know about her father? And about his injury?

Before she could put words together to ask him those questions, he spoke again.

"Don't worry. Lisa is such a good Certified Nursing Assistant; you can be confident she'll keep a close eye on him. Her little gambling problem doesn't have an effect on her skills at work."

The fear that gripped Sarah was more chilling than anything she'd felt before. Lisa was one of her favorite people at Highland. The cheerful healthcare worker was someone her father responded well to, and Sarah trusted with his care. Was Collins actually intimating that Lisa was on his payroll? How did he know of her at all, let alone that the woman had a gambling problem. Or was he making that up?

Chapter 33

Sarah

"Sit." Ronnie ordered, his heavy hand clamping down on her shoulder to shove her into a seat in the last section of the airplane. He seated himself across from her. A nasty smirk twisted his face. "I'm almost sorry you're behaving so well."

She wanted to curse at him but consciously fought the impulse. The more they believed she was compliant, the better it had to be for her. Right?

Sarah could see Collins at the front of the aircraft talking to an older man in a captain's uniform who had welcomed them aboard alongside a cabin stewardess. The captain had a dignified but friendly appearance and air about him. Maybe she could somehow speak to him, tell him she was being kidnapped. Slip him or the attendant a note of some kind...

As she watched, Collins reached out and clapped the captain on the shoulder in a friendly sort of way, then strode towards where she and Ronnie were seated. Collins leaned over slightly and braced a hand on the top of her seat.

"That's Captain Ortiz. Excellent pilot. He's got a wife and three children. The oldest, I believe, is about 13. It would be a shame if something terrible befell him. Or maybe one of his kids."

Sarah understood very clearly what he wasn't saying. She didn't know if she should respond at all, or what to say. Her hesitation wasn't noticed because he wasn't done yet.

"I know you met Melissa when we came on board. She's also an excellent employee. I pay her very well and she appreciates what that allows her to provide for her eight-year-old son. She's a single mom. That's such a difficult thing, isn't it?" He straightened up to his full height.

"She's divorced. Wasn't widowed like your dad. It would be a shame if anything happened to either or both of them, wouldn't it?"

While he spoke in a frighteningly conversational tone, Sarah had been watching Melissa make her way through the cabin toward them. Did the airplane crew have any idea that their employer wasn't a good or even decent guy?

She hadn't realized it. Why would they?

Collins turned to the woman in her modest uniform and sensible shoes. He smiled at her like he hadn't just intimated that Melissa and/or her son could pay a heavy price if Sarah didn't cooperate with him.

Melissa favored them all in turn with a friendly smile. "Captain Ortiz wanted me to inform you all that we've been given the go-ahead to leave the gate area and take our position on the runway. Will you kindly take your seats and secure your seatbelts? I'll then review the safety protocols with you."

"Thank you, Melissa," Collins said. "I have some work to do so I'm going to take a seat on the other side for now. If you'll excuse me." He inclined his head to them in a show of politeness and selected a seat in a grouping forward from them and across the main aisle.

Sarah fumbled with the seatbelt, stress and her nerves making her fingers uncooperative. Without looking directly at Ronnie, she could see that he was snapping his own belt into place.

The plane started to move slowly as it was towed away from the gate. Melissa held up a laminated safety guide and started running through an abbreviated version of safety procedures Sarah had heard on commercial flights. Evacuation, crash landings, and who knew what else. She spoke smoothly, and clearly had done it many times before. Sarah couldn't pay attention. She was too busy thinking about all that Collins had said and *not* said in the last few minutes.

How did Collins know anything about her father, or about her upbringing by him after her mother died? Now he'd threatened the lives of the flight crew and their families.

The way he spoke was so nonchalant, so casual. Sarah debated with herself whether or not he was bluffing. She darted a furtive glance in his direction. Collins was on his phone, his eyebrows pulled together as he spoke to someone with an intensity she could glean from his body language.

With what was hidden within the Shelley volume, she had to go on the assumption that he was telling the truth because he had a lot at stake. But *he* didn't know that *she* knew about that – or did he?

There were too many questions bouncing around inside her head. None of the potential answers she could think of were good ones. For the next several hours, Sarah sat stiffly in what was undoubtedly a comfortable seat, but she couldn't appreciate it at all. All she could think about were the questions running through her mind on an endless loop.

Obviously, Collins had investigated her. That was understandable when he was entrusting her to carry out costly business transactions on his behalf. That's what auctions ultimately were – business transactions. When she'd agreed to take him on as a client, he'd had to provide her with certified financial statements showing he could pay for items she bid on for him. It was business, nothing personal.

Everything he'd talked about today was personal. The way he made his threats – and that's what they clearly were – was casual, couched in nonthreatening words that still managed to make the underlying threats perfectly clear.

Sarah turned her head to look out the window at the peaceful sky above the clouds. Right now the storm was roiling inside her, not outside the aircraft.

Neither she nor the people at Infinite had thought that Collins was a danger to *her*. Well, Liam had expressed concern about that, but it didn't make sense to her at the time so she'd argued against that theory. She should've listened to him and not insisted she knew best.

Stupid, stupid, stupid. She'd been so ridiculously stupid to ignore Liam's instincts.

Now she had to hope that somehow Liam and his team would be able to find her, wherever she was going to end up. It was a bigger long-shot than winning the most anticipated, rarest lot at the most anticipated book auction in the world.

Chapter 34

Liam

"I don't understand this," Liam turned to Rick. "Could she have been separated from the trackers? Could they both be malfunctioning?"

"It's highly unlikely." Rick was confident as usual about the technology he'd provided. "Did you put them where you intended?"

"Yes. One in her left earring and the other in her right shoe," Liam said.

It had been difficult to hide them without Sarah knowing, but that unsettled feeling in his gut had made it necessary. He'd seen in the past how important tracking devices could be.

Dax stood next to him, also studying the image being projected on the wall. "Both trackers are together, and we're going to have to presume that they are with her."

"In the suburbs of Philadelphia, Pennsylvania," Liam said. "Nowhere near Florida. Or Illinois."

Mason stood nearby, also studying the image. "If it wasn't for those trackers, we'd be on a wild goose chase to the wrong state."

"What if Collins found the trackers and sent them to Pennsylvania as a decoy?" Jace theorized.

"Liam?" The tone of Dax's voice broke through the mental fog surrounding him.

The four other men and Callie were looking at him, some with different degrees of surprise, and Dax with understanding. He never spoke about Kelsey to anyone, leaving the past buried where it needed to be. No one knew how much it haunted him, except Dax, who knew the whole ugly story and respected Liam's desire to keep it private.

It didn't affect his work for Infinite, and it hadn't affected his military career. Yes, he'd lost brothers in arms and even a couple of colleagues at Infinite, but that was different. It hurt like hell, but they knew the risks and had willingly chosen a dangerous path in life.

Unlike Kelsey years ago. And unlike Sarah today.

"Repeat?" Liam requested. "I was thinking."

Liam suspected Dax understood what he'd *really* been thinking about and he appreciated that his boss simply repeated the question. No doubt Dax would bring that subject up in private later.

"How do you want to proceed?" Dax asked, still giving Liam the opportunity to guide this mission.

"We go to where the trackers lead us, continually monitoring them. Revisit the deep dive on Collins. Keep looking for why he wanted her in Naperville." Hands on hips, Liam kept staring at the two dots moving on the monitor. "We keep trying to learn more about all the numbers and cipher in the book. It's all connected." He shifted his gaze back to Dax. "I'm going to Pennsylvania."

Dax nodded. "There has to be a reason he picked Illinois to begin with, and then changed it."

"Maybe he always intended to bring her to Pennsylvania," Liam said.

"I've still been working on the number codes and the cipher," Callie said. "I think I'm close."

"They aren't all account numbers?" Liam was looking for confirmation of their previous thoughts.

Callie agreed. "Two are, but not all of them."

"Any gut instincts about what additional info is being obscured by the cipher?"

"I don't know enough about the guy or the situation to speculate on that," Callie said.

"Some of the criminal networks Collins has links to are out of Chicago, Pittsburgh, and Miami," Rick said.

"How wide are this guy's connections?" Liam muttered. "Sarah told me she did due diligence and didn't find any issues."

"I'm not surprised," Rick said. "We didn't either on the first go round."

Mason spoke up again. "Any common links between Collins' shady connections?"

"There are probably some we still haven't pinpointed yet," Rick said. "I put two more guys on digital investigation." He looked at Dax. "That's what I wanted to originally meet with you about today. You might want to have boots on the ground in a couple of those places if this is a priority."

Before Dax could answer, Liam bit out, "Damn right, it's a priority. My boots are going to Pittsburgh, tonight."

"We didn't PACE properly and the mess in Cedarhurst happened as a result," Dax said.

There was a good reason for PACE planning, and Liam had survived a slew of dangerous missions because of it. Having primary, alternate, contingency, and emergency plans in place mitigated the risk of operational failure.

Mason looked up from where he was typing into his phone. "The company jet is currently at MacArthur, right?"

"Yeah. Ethan got back in the middle of the night."

"Flight time from MacArthur to Pittsburgh is slightly less than an hour."

Dax was already sending a message of his own. "I told our pilot we need to be wheels up as soon as he can assemble a crew and file a plan."

Liam looked to Mason. "I can go alone, but I'd prefer backup."

Still texting, Dax spoke up before Mason could reply. "We're both going with you. I'll sort out who's heading to the other cities. Grab your go- bag and think about how you want to play this."

Liam agreed, "Will do." He looked between Callie and Rick and back again. "Somebody pull together some info on where Sarah is right now. Then we need somebody continually monitoring her location." He ran both hands through his hair again, pulling on it in his own frustration. "I'm going to get some notes Sarah had in her room."

As he hurried down the hall from the meeting room, he heard the low rumble of multiple voices sorting out immediate plans.

His own voice was low but determined. "Hang in there, Sarah. I'll be there soon."

Chapter 35

Sarah

Again in the rear row of a vehicle, Sarah fought the urge to scream in frustration. Before they'd disembarked from the plane, and under Collins' watchful gaze, Ronnie had blindfolded her. Melissa and Captain Ortiz had bid them goodbye in friendly voices, as if having a blindfolded passenger get off the plane was not at all unusual.

That in itself was frightening. Did Collins regularly transport blindfolded women across the country? Around the world?

They hadn't been in the air for very long. Certainly not the four or so hours a flight to Illinois would've taken, nor even the couple of hours it would've taken to get to Florida, which was what she thought she'd heard somebody say when they were boarding. They were somewhere else, unless her perception of time was seriously messed up. At this point, anything was possible.

Somebody – it seemed to be Collins – secured her seatbelt.

"I'm very pleased with your behavior, Ms. Prescott. Kindly remain quiet and cooperative and we can keep this simple and civil."

"What is *this*? I don't understand," Sarah snapped. The situation definitely was dangerous. Good God, they were threatening people!

But she was desperately trying to stay calm. "I gave you the books, as per our contract. Why are you doing whatever you're doing with me?"

"You're going to understand very soon." Collins told her in a tone of voice an adult might use when dealing with a child. "Now, no more."

Sarah could feel Ronnie pressing harder against her side. He made a noise that could have been a warning, a threat, or humor about her situation. Whatever his intent, it was undeniably aggressive. With Collins so close on her other side, there was nowhere to go.

She was *not* going to panic. Liam was going to find her. She didn't know how he was going to, but she had to have faith in him.

Liam is going to find me. That quickly became the refrain she repeated in her mind over and over again. *Liam is going to find me.*

There was no conversation between the men on both sides of her. The heavy silence in the vehicle magnified the weight of the nerves that twisted her stomach. Sarah couldn't hear turn signals even though the vehicle turned left, then right, then right again, then left, each turn separated by straightaways of different lengths. Eventually, she couldn't keep track of the turns anymore because she had to focus on not hyperventilating. On not panicking.

When the vehicle stopped after a particularly sharp turn, relief flooded through her, but then a split second later fear charged in on its heels. Sarah heard a car door open and quickly slam closed. Then long minutes of silence before the doors to both sides of her opened. The men were getting out.

Had they brought her somewhere to hurt her?

Why would Collins want to hurt her?

Sarah fought mightily against the tears that surged behind her closed eyelids. They stung.

What was going to happen to her dad if she died?

No one would know what happened to her.

What would happen while people figured it out?

How long would it take before the police and court system figured out that she disappeared?

The authorities would know, Sarah reassured herself. Liam would make sure of that. Her father was the beneficiary of her life insurance policy, and that would cover his care for some years.

Would her dad even know she was gone?

Was Lisa, a CNA she liked and trusted, involved in this whole thing?

Liam would look for her; Sarah knew that. If Collins hurt or killed her, or if he never found her, would he blame himself?

She hoped her father wouldn't suffer the pain of knowing, and that Liam wouldn't hold himself responsible.

"Come on, Ms. Prescott." Collins spoke, but from the roughness of the hands that yanked Sarah across the seat and to the car door, she knew it was Ronnie pulling her out. Her ankles were twisting because he didn't give her time to get her legs out of the car before he was trying to pull her upright.

"Stop! You're going to break my ankles!"

"Idiot!" Collins said sharply. The word was accompanied by the sound of what had to be a punch landing on what she assumed was Ronnie, who released her hand.

"Get out of the way." Collins sounded disgusted. Sarah heard Ronnie mumble some sort of apology.

"Are you okay?" Collins asked.

She told herself he wouldn't care if his plan was to hurt her. Would he?

Sarah tried to compose herself best she could. "I think so. Can you take the blindfold off, please?"

She wanted to reach for it herself but knew that would only ratchet up the tension level.

"Soon," Collins said. "Take my hand, and we'll go inside."

Sarah couldn't hear any particular sounds, so wherever it was that they were going to "go inside" was quiet.

Much as she didn't want to, she had no choice but to let him hold her hand to escort her into whatever building was at their location.

"There is a handrail on your left," Collins said, "and six stairs in front of you."

Carefully, Sarah reached out to her left side and was rewarded with the feel of a metal railing. Wrought iron, maybe? Whatever it was, it was pleasantly cool to the touch. She awkwardly shuffled her right foot forward to locate the step then began her climb, feeling for safe placement of her feet. She mentally counted the stairs as she trod them.

"Stop." Collins commanded her and she had no choice but to obey; she didn't want to stumble or fall.

There were several noises Sarah couldn't quite identify and then the unmistakable sound of a door opening. Sarah's heart pounded so fast her chest hurt. She was walking blindfolded into an unknown building; she didn't know where, and she didn't know why, but she was with someone she *knew* was up to no good. She'd been afraid but on some sort of autopilot during this whole ordeal, foolishly sure everything would be okay, because why would Mr. Collins want to hurt her?

That naïve certainty vanished like a puff of smoke. Her knees gave way, and she crumpled to the ground.

Chapter 36

Liam

"**M**atteo is waiting for us at the airport," Dax said. "He'll drive because he knows the area better."

"When do we land?" Liam wanted to verify that nothing thus far had changed again without him being aware.

The updated knowledge they'd received when Rick accessed the flight log – the one that had been amended in-flight – had been critical in guiding them to Pennsylvania. Specifically, to Pittsburgh.

"12 minutes."

Liam continued studying the blueprint of the house where the trackers he'd placed on Sarah continued transmitting. Brantford Woods, a suburb of Pittsburgh with large homes and high property values. Not the kind of place anyone would expect to find a guy with murky connections hiding out with a woman he'd kidnapped.

"We're agreed then. The initial plan is for brief surveillance of the property, and heat signature recon. If we can determine where in the building Sarah is being held, I access the room from the ground, secure her, plant listening devices anywhere they might be helpful, and get the hell out with her."

Mason nodded. "Alternate plan, we go in the back entrance closest to where we think she is. Secure her, skip the listening devices, and exfil fast."

"Contingency, I climb up to the roof and drop down from it to her window or balcony, or the closest one to it. If no alarm is raised, secure Sarah, set devices, and get out." Liam recited it quickly.

Dax crossed his arms again. "Emergency plan, will go right in whichever door seems closest to Sarah, and get her out." He made eye contact with both of them. "No casualties unless we have no choice."

They were going in without local police support. Not ideal, but it was a lot quicker if things went smoothly. Better to ask forgiveness than permission, and all that.

"What are we missing? Based on his associates, we suspect Collins is involved with the drug trade. He's possibly laundering money through auctions, but that wouldn't clean big numbers for him, so maybe not. But why is he involving Sarah in whatever he's got going on? Everything points to her always being on the up and up."

"He wants her skills," Dax said. "It's the only thing that makes sense."

Liam had also come to that conclusion a while ago. "Sarah understands more about old and rare books than how they are valued. She knows facts about how they were made, the materials used, the trends at different places and times in history."

"Don't most experts have that kind of understanding?"

While replying, Liam pulled another area map in front of him. "From what I've learned, no, not necessarily. You can look up basic valuations in guides and reference materials. Even I do that. She has a deeper comprehension of how books were made and why they were crafted the way they were at different times and in different places."

He backed up from where he'd been bent over the table at the rear of the plane and twisted at the waist, stretching his back. "At least that means Collins needs to keep Sarah safe. But she's got to be scared out of her mind."

Dax's phone buzzed in his pocket, and he stepped away to answer it. It was an important benefit of flying private, not commercial – along with the ability to discuss confidential matters, and transport things that would never be allowed on a commercial flight.

Tom, the attendant for this short flight to Pittsburgh, quietly notified Liam and then Dax that they needed to prepare for landing. Liam quickly secured the papers he had spread across the table. He took a seat across from Dax and put on his seatbelt.

"That was Rick," Dax said. "They hacked into enough security camera footage to verify Sarah and Collins arrived at JFK Airport from the Inwood train station. The bodyguard that escaped arrived soon after them." He tapped the cell phone in his hand against his knee. "They also were able to verify that a private plane from JFK landed at Pittsburgh International after a direct flight."

Exactly as they'd suspected. "Ownership of the plane?"

"Callie is still peeling back shell companies. It's been thoroughly buried."

"Did the guys get anything out of the bodyguard we detained?" Liam hadn't received an update about that. Not that he really expected a guy who was probably just muscle to know much about Collins or the operation, but you never knew for sure.

"Not yet," Dax said.

They weren't going to work the guy over too much. Whoever he was, he'd be tied up and kept in uncomfortable conditions, probably punched a few times and hopefully frightened enough to tell them something that would be useful. Then he'd be turned over to the local authorities, along with whatever info could be divulged.

Liam stared out the window as the lights of the airport became more and more defined when the aircraft made its final approach and the pilot positioned it for landing. The engine sounds changed again with the next phase. The ground sped towards them. There was a slight bounce when the wheels touched down.

The three men unclasped their seatbelts and stood almost simultaneously.

Dax said, "I get the urgency, Liam. You know I do. We're not far. Let's just stick with the plans."

"I know. Believe me, I know."

No matter what Dax said, Liam intended to have his hands on Sarah within the next couple of hours. And once he did, he wasn't letting go.

Chapter 37

Sarah

Sarah woke up on a stiff leather couch. The first thing she noticed was that the blindfold was gone. She moved slightly, trying to assess her situation. She wasn't tied in any way. She was barefoot but otherwise fully dressed. Sarah sensed that she wasn't alone in the room but hesitated to look around, hesitant to draw attention to herself. From the bad body odor she detected, Ronnie was there somewhere.

He probably took her shoes so she wouldn't be tempted to run. Not that she'd have a clue where to go if she even managed to get outside. It was summertime though, so the ground wouldn't be frozen or even cold, and cuts from rocks would probably be much better than whatever Collins wanted from her.

As if her thoughts of him had reached out and touched him, Collins spoke from somewhere in the room. "I know you are awake, Ms. Prescott. Your breathing changed the moment you woke up."

There was no point in pretending otherwise, Sarah decided. She sat up cautiously.

Collins stood by a bookshelf across the surprisingly large room. His happy expression was startling. When she'd seen him before he'd been serious, and at the train station he'd been brusque. Was he so pleased he'd successfully kidnapped her?

"You fainted. Are you ill?" he wanted to know.

"I'm not. Maybe everything just caught up with me." Sarah hated that she'd shown such weakness in front of Collins and whoever was with him.

"You're going to eat and drink something," Collins ordered. "Soon, you can sleep for a while."

"That's not necessary." She didn't want him thinking he could tell her what to do. Never mind that in her current situation he could do exactly that. Sarah thought for sure he'd point that out, but he didn't.

Instead, he gestured at the two chairs positioned in front of the cold fireplace. "Sit."

Sarah hesitated and he repeated himself, louder this time. "Sit down, Sarah. Now."

Her first instinct was to argue with him – about the kidnapping, the books, his attitude, his nerve in talking to her the way he was – but the little voice of self-preservation shouted in the recesses of her mind. "Shut up and do it, Sarah!"

So she did.

In the silence that followed she heard the rustle of Ronnie's clothing as he shifted his position. A clock ticked loudly, the sound a rarity in the digital age. Sarah didn't recognize the book in Collins' hands. She did note that it wasn't one she'd won for him.

Collins closed his book and made a show of replacing it on the shelf behind him. He turned to face her and she got the feeling that he was moving dramatically, as if setting the scene.

"You have been chosen, Sarah." He said it dramatically, like it was a big deal.

Sarah knew her expression had to reflect her confusion, and she didn't care. She had no idea what the hell he was talking about. "Chosen?" she repeated.

"Yes. You will be working directly for me."

"I do that already," Sarah pointed out. It didn't seem like a good time to tell him that she'd never work for him again. She didn't want to risk agitating him, especially with Ronnie in the room, Collins had backup, and she had no one.

"Don't act stupid," he said sharply, and took a single step toward her. Collins stopped himself and raised his hand in the universal sign language signal for someone else to stop as well. He must've been signaling Ronnie.

"I'm just confused." Sarah laced her fingers together to hide their trembling.

"Obviously. You used to work for me sometimes. Now you work for me all the time."

She didn't know how to handle this strange conversation, so she decided to be as professional and reasonable as possible. "Mr. Collins, your auction participation won't be enough to support me."

"I'm not explaining clearly enough. Being my agent will only be part of your responsibilities." His pleasant expression changed, and his friendly demeanor vanished every bit as quickly. "I know you found what was hidden in a book you acquired for me. Don't even pretend otherwise."

Sarah wanted to demand to know why he thought he knew that, but almost immediately against it; he was right, so why antagonize him? She remained silent.

"I'm also sure you found the reason I needed that book. You're going to replicate that work in other books."

"I don't understand –." Before she could finish the sentence, Collins backhanded her so fast she didn't even see him move before she felt the impact. Her head bounced back into the right side panel of the chair and her hand came up to cradle her face.

"Shut up! Look what you made me do!" Collins glowered at her. "Don't play stupid with me. Do not do that." He took two steps back. "When we figured out who you were with, I could have had you killed, you know. You owe me for convincing the Boss that you are still perfect for filling the vacancy on our crew." Another smile brightened his expression. "She died, you know. Got greedy, that one. You won't be that stupid, will you? Not when you need to protect your dear daddy right?"

The fear that twisted Sarah's gut made her forget about the pain in her face. She didn't know what to say, but Collins kept talking, so she didn't need to say anything at all.

"Oh yes, I know all about Gerald Prescott and his unfortunate situation. Don't worry, if you do your new job, he'll be just fine."

Her mind wanted to fixate on the horror of his words, but Sarah forced herself to ask, "What do you want me to do?"

"You're going to insert information I give you into books. You're going to bid on things for me, and represent me in outright sales negotiations. You're going to do whatever I tell you to do, Sarah, with a smile and appreciation for the fact that I am allowing you and your father to live."

How had she never noticed that this man was crazy? That he wasn't some quirky or eccentric rich man, but legitimately out of his mind?

"Why me?" She had to know.

"Why you." Collins rephrased the question. Picked up his glass off the mantle and swirled the ice cubes like he was giving her question thorough consideration. "So many reasons. All you need to know is that I saw you. I hired you and you were good at your job. Your background check confirmed you are perfect for me in every way." He lifted his glass and finished what was at the bottom of it. "That's what you need to know right now. You do as you're told, and you'll be okay." He gestured at her with the glass, the ice cubes rattling inside. "You obey me and no one else. Remember that."

Ronnie cleared his throat behind her. Collins added dismissively, "And obey Ronnie when I'm not around and he gives you orders on my behalf."

Chapter 38

Sarah

Collins kept a hold of Sarah's hand but didn't speak. Their footsteps were loud and echoed slightly. He had Ronnie replace the blindfold before they left the room where she'd awakened. Was it a house foyer? An apartment?

There were more footsteps nearby. Heavy ones. More than one set.

Men's footsteps.

Collins suddenly stopped and released her hand, and Sarah stumbled.

"Ronnie will take you upstairs and show you to your room. He'll bring you food. You can take off your blindfold once you are inside. You will stay in that room until you're invited out of it. Do you understand?"

"Why am I here? Where is here?" Sarah tried to keep her voice level, when all she really wanted to do was scream at him. "I don't understand any of this."

"I told you enough already, and I'll explain further in due time," Collins said. "Don't give Ronnie any trouble, and he won't hurt you."

Before she could even process that order with its threat and warning, Ronnie was pushing her forward. "Move it."

From behind her, she heard Collins. "There are handrails on both sides of the staircase. 14 steps."

The first several were awkward, then Sarah felt a little more stable. She held tightly to the banister on her right. It was cold and smooth beneath her palm.

"Don't trip," Ronnie whispered. "It's a long fall to the bottom."

Sarah didn't reply to him. He was trying to make her more nervous than she already was, and she wasn't going to give him the satisfaction of knowing that he had. She tried to focus on counting the steps, hoping that Collins had given her an accurate number. Was number fourteen going to be the last step before the landing, or the landing itself?

Uncertain, she explored more thoroughly with her foot before shifting her weight over and up. Her fingers told her the banister was ending, so she tried to concentrate on what had to be the landing.

"Would have been more fun if he hadn't told you the number." Ronnie actually sounded disappointed that she hadn't fallen. "Turn right and walk until I tell you to stop."

"Are there obstacles to look out for?" Was he seriously expecting her to find a way down the hall she couldn't see, with no guidance at all?

"I guess you're going to find out, aren't you?"

Sarah gritted her teeth but didn't bother answering him. The floor beneath her had some give, and her footsteps made no sound, so it had to be carpeted. She took small steps. Put one hand out in front of her and one to the side, trying to feel for a wall to guide her.

What was the point of replacing the blindfold? She didn't know where they were. Not what city, not what state, not what building. Was Collins afraid she'd recognize something somehow, or was he just messing with her?

"Stop."

She halted midstep and turned to look toward Ronnie. Sarah felt his arm brushed against her and heard the sound of the door opening. There was a clicking noise, and she heard the bottom of the door swish against carpeting.

With a small shove that made her stumble into the doorframe, Ronnie said, "Get in there."

Was he ever anything but nasty?

Sarah hesitated, wishing she could look into the room before she stepped over the threshold. Ronnie shoved her harder between the shoulder blades, and she tripped forward into the room. Wearing the blindfold, it was hard to catch her balance to right herself.

She was still wavering when she reached up and ripped off the blindfold. Even after wearing it for a relatively short time, she had to blink rapidly to clear her vision as best she could.

"Hey, I didn't say you could do that!" Ronnie snapped at her.

"Mr. Collins said I could take it off when I got to my room. Isn't that where we are?"

"Know it all bitch." Ronnie sneered. "Don't even try to leave this room."

He took two steps back and pulled the door shut with a bang. Sarah threw herself at it, grabbing for the doorknob.

"What about my eyeglasses?" she shouted.

There was an audible click as the door was locked from the outside, and then she heard the sound of the chain being secured.

Seriously? There was a chain lock in the hallway to secure the door?

Had that been installed especially for her, or did Edward Collins make a habit of locking people in this house?

Sarah turned and checked out the room she'd been locked into, desperate for something she could use to free herself, or defend herself if necessary.

She still didn't know what Collins was up to, but it obviously wasn't something good. Something safe. You didn't kidnap someone if you had good intentions. And that Ronnie was giving off plenty of vibes that he wanted to get violent with her. At that thought, her whole body felt chilled.

Behind long white draperies with a swirling gray and blue design was a small balcony, but the doors that led onto it were securely locked. *What else did you expect?* From what she could see past that small balcony, she was at the rear of a house.

She primarily used her eyeglasses for reading or up close work, but it would've been nice to have them on her right now. Having that would help her be certain she wasn't missing anything. There was a good distance to the tree line, and she glimpsed black fencing beyond them.

The room with its pale blue walls contained a full-sized bed of white wood made up with a gray and white coverlet and a couple of blue pillow shams. To its left was a single white nightstand with one empty drawer. A blue armchair was shoved into the corner just past and across from the bed. The coordinating footrest in front of it was hinged on one side, but when she opened it, it only contained a small lap blanket. A narrow closet behind a white door contained a half-dozen empty hangers. There was nothing else. Not even a mass-market picture above the bed, or a lamp, or a dresser for clothing, or a mirror.

There was another wall space in the room that was curiously devoid of anything. No furniture, no decoration, no anything. It might've been her imagination, but the paint was slightly shadowed there, like it'd been filled in at a different time and almost matched perfectly – but didn't.

The attached bathroom was equally bare, with a curtained shower, toilet, and sink. There was no cabinetry, just a few shelves on one wall that were bare except for some basic toiletries, a stack of dark gray towels, and a few extra rolls of toilet paper.

She'd emerged from the bathroom after looking it over one more time when she heard heavy footsteps in the hallway. Sarah froze between the armchair and the bed. The heavy tread sounded more in keeping with Ronnie than with Collins. Or maybe there were other people in the house? It was the thought that worried her even more.

The knock on the door was sharp and accompanied by Ronnie's voice and the sound of the key in the lock. "Open up."

Sarah's first instinct was to refuse, but what was the point? She turned the handle and immediately knew what he wanted, because he was standing there with a couple of bags from a fast-food chain clutched in one hand and a sixpack of water bottles in the other. Ronnie shoved it all at her, and she had no choice but to grab everything.

"Mr. Collins wants you to eat. He'll meet with you at 8 o'clock tomorrow morning."

"What am I supposed to do until then? Why can't he meet with me now and tell me what's going on?"

Ronnie reached for the handle to pull the door closed. "I'm not here to give you answers. He said he'll talk to you again tomorrow."

"Can I have my phone? A book to read? Something to do to pass the time?"

He yanked the door shut without answering her, and she heard him lock it. Heard the chain lock.

"Idiot." Sarah chided herself for wasting her own time.

She set the bags and the water bottles on the table against the wall. Much as she wished it didn't, the smell of whatever was in the bags convinced her to open them. Sitting on top of the contents of the larger bag were her eyeglasses, looking undamaged, crammed in among an assortment of other things. She grabbed them along with a paper napkin from the bag, and cleaned the lenses as best she could. Sarah slipped them on and breathed a sigh of relief. Seeing clearly always made her feel like she was thinking more clearly.

Her attention returned to the contents of the bag she'd opened: chicken nuggets, hamburger, fries, and more napkins. The smaller bag contained an individual apple pie, a couple of dipping sauces, and ketchup packets. She grabbed several French fries at one time and shoved them in her mouth. They weren't hot, but they weren't cold, either, and that was perfectly fine.

It also meant that wherever she was being kept was in an area populated enough to have at least one fast food restaurant.

Was she really supposed to sit here for who knew how many hours and stare at the four walls and the ceiling. It couldn't be later than... maybe 6 o'clock?

Sarah separated a bottle of water from the pack. She took it and the food bags over to the comfortable-looking chair in the corner.

She used her foot to maneuver the foot rest closer to the chair, then sat down heavily and she tried to keep from dropping anything. Sarah twisted open the cap on the water bottle, cracking the plastic seal. She took a big swallow directly from the bottle.

This morning, she been too keyed up to eat breakfast despite Liam's urging, and now she was so hungry her stomach was growling. Sarah set the bags of food on the floor and spread two of the napkins on her lap. Next, she set up the box of chicken nuggets, appreciating that it was a box of 10 pieces, not six. She carefully positioned the container of fries alongside the nuggets and opened both dipping sauces. Not what she would've chosen, but she was still ridiculously excited to have any food at all.

Amazing how circumstances affected perspective.

If anyone was with her, she'd probably be embarrassed by how fast she demolished the food, but Sarah was alone.

After Sarah finished eating, she made the executive decision to save the burger and the apple pie for later. She crammed the garbage into the larger of the bags and took it with her into the bathroom in search of a garbage pail. While in there, Sarah attended to her other needs and washed her hands.

Back in the bedroom, Sarah spent too long pacing the relatively small area. All it did was make her more agitated. Frustrated, she returned to the comfortable chair instead of flopping down on the bed.

She rested her head against the cushion behind it and debated with herself about getting up to turn on the ceiling light. She was tired enough to maybe nod for a little bit and the sun would be setting and then the room would get dark. Sarah's eyes drifted shut as the adrenaline that fueled the day finally waned. She could turn on the light in a few minutes.

* * *

The voices woke her up.

Men's voices. They were muffled, but she could hear them. Sarah blinked the sleep from her eyes and sat up in the chair where she'd fallen asleep. She gently stretched her stiff neck.

Where were they? What did they want? Was she in danger?

Sarah stood up and stepped around the footstool on her way to the locked door. She listened carefully. She went so far as to physically touch her ear to the wood. Nothing.

Had she been dreaming? No, she heard men talking. She was sure she had.

Sarah walked back to the chair and sat down again. She could still hear the voices, arguing now, more loudly.

Instead of standing up, she slid off the chair and down onto her knees, pushing the foot rest aside. Leaning forward, she pressed her cheek to the carpet and peered under the chair. Right there was a rectangular metal grate of some kind. Sarah frowned at it. A heat register?

Her heart rate accelerated again, this time with excitement. It was summertime, and the heat wasn't in use within the bedrooms of the house, so that part of the system was quiet. Quiet enough to let her hear through to whatever room where the men were speaking.

"She's not going to go for it." The unfamiliar voice was strident and sounded so certain. "Taking her was stupid."

"I know what I'm doing." That was Collins. She was sure of it. "She'll cooperate."

"I'm getting tired of telling you this. She's a Girl Scout. By the book." The other man was getting louder. There was a loud noise; something shattered.

"Watch it!" Collins snapped in a voice full of anger. "I'm getting tired of telling you that I know what I'm doing."

"You really think that Miss Prim and Proper is going to simply obey you because you offer her a cut? You're delusional."

Collins made a sound that she would later describe as a humorless laugh. "Prescott is going to do it because her precious father dies if she doesn't."

The other man responded but it sounded like he moved further away from wherever they'd been standing. Even so, she heard Collins speak again. "Everything is in place..." Then he, too, faded out, like he was also moving away.

Sarah stayed frozen in place. She was desperate to hear more. Without a watch or her phone, she didn't know how much time passed, but the sun had set, and the sky had darkened considerably. It was past twilight.

Sarah pushed herself up to standing. She pushed the foot rest back into position and made sure the chair was also positioned as it was before.

She'd been dreading the meeting with Collins tomorrow but now she was also anxious for it to come. What did he want her to do?

Whatever it was, damn right she was going to do it if it kept her father safe.

What other choice did she have?

Chapter 39

Liam

The lack of external security at the stately house where Collins had brought Sarah was surprising. There were two guards patrolling the grounds in a regimented fashion, never changing up their routine even as hours passed. Mason had spotted three men leaving the property earlier, one of them Collins and another the guy who'd run from the New York parking lot with Sarah over his shoulder. Back at headquarters, the tech team were trying to identify the third man from the night vision images Matteo had captured.

Liam checked again that his weapons were secure. Double holsters, knife in his cargo pants and another in his right boot. Ammunition clips. Pocket full of zip ties. Flash bang grenades. Assorted other tools of the trade. From what they'd discerned, there were only three heat signatures indicating people within the mansion at the current time. Two of them were moving around the first floor in repetitive patterns. One was upstairs, staying within a relatively small area. It wasn't difficult to discern that the first two were guards, and the individual upstairs was Sarah.

Not for long.

"Going up," Liam said as quietly as possible.

As he found his first hand and foot holds, he heard Dax in his earpiece. "Roger."

Liam scaled the blooming tree close to the rear of the house with an ease that surprised him, even though he'd always been a decent climber. It was surprising that there would be a tree someone *could* climb, that was allowed to remain so close to the house. Foolish oversight.

When he reached the highest point in the tree to which he could climb, Liam assessed his position. The balcony of Sarah's room was a bit higher than ideal, and about at the end of his reach, but he had to make it work. As he positioned himself in the most optimal way, he was already planning the best way to exit the room she was in and descend to the ground but with her.

With the intense focus that typically served him so well, Liam slowed his breathing. He synchronized the timing of his jump and reach so it coordinated with a deep inhale. His fingers in their snug black gloves tightened on the balcony railing as he exhaled. Liam hung suspended there for a moment.

On the next inhale, Liam began to swing his legs from side to side, not a lot, only enough to give himself momentum to get himself into position to hook his right foot over the top edge of the railing. From there it was only another moment before he shoved his leg over enough to use it as a fulcrum to haul himself over the top and onto the balcony.

"On balcony," Liam muttered.

"Roger that," Dax said.

He heard Mason make a similar comment, but Liam was already focused on the double doors that led into the room beyond. The access doors were covered by some kind of curtains, thin enough that he could make out the vague shadows beyond but no details.

He advised the team of that succinctly while he tried both door handles. Locked, as expected. Liam tapped lightly on one door, listening closely. Silence, except for the usual 2 o'clock in the morning sounds.

He ran his fingers around the door framing on the off chance that a key was hidden there in case of emergencies. He also looked under the two flowerpots that bracketed doors, and looked through the top layer of the soil within them.

Nothing.

He also didn't see any indication that the door was alarmed. Not that it mattered, because Infinite had already jammed the signal to the alarm company.

Still in a crouched position, Liam moved back to the doors. He pulled a penlight from a pocket of his cargo pants and clicked it on, shining the narrow beam on the faceplate of the lock.

For the first time since Sarah had been taken, Liam smiled.

The lock securing the doors was an old-fashioned, simple style. Not at all what he would've expected. From the same pocket that had contained the penlight, he withdrew the slim fabric roll that contained his lock picking kit. With one slender tool in each hand, Liam needed mere moments to turn the upper mechanism, press down on the lower, and disengage the lock.

"I'm in." Liam rolled up the lock pick tools and shoved them in his pocket. He listened again for several heartbeats, then slowly opened one of the doors. The room was cool, the soft hum of the air conditioning unit working hard to keep it a comfortable temperature. He kept the penlight pointed toward the ground and raised it in increments to check out the perimeter of the space. It was a matter of seconds before he found Sarah asleep on the bed.

After shining the light in all the corners of the room, Liam approached her. There was no gentle way to wake her up and be sure she wouldn't scream.

Carefully coordinating his movements, Liam covered her mouth with his right hand and gently shook her with the left while whispering to her.

"Sarah, it's Liam. It's me. It's Liam. Be quiet."

Her eyes were open before he spoke. In the dim moonlight that filtered through the balcony doors, he could see the fear on her face.

"It's me, Sarah." he repeated.

Sarah kept her eyes on his face and nodded frantically. Liam removed his hand from her mouth and pulled her closer. He buried his face in her unbound hair, inhaling her scent, the warmth of her. Her arms came up to wind around his neck. Having her in his arms, it was like he could breathe again.

"Are you injured at all?" he asked. Just because he didn't see any injuries right now, didn't mean she was physically unharmed.

Her sweet voice reassured him, "I'm okay." Sarah hesitated. "Where are we?"

"Close to Pittsburgh, Pennsylvania." Liam didn't ask why she didn't know that. There wasn't time; they had to get the hell out of the house and off the property. "We'll talk when we're out of here."

Reluctantly, Liam pulled away and stood up. "We have to go. Right now. Where are your shoes?"

Sarah shook her head. "I can't leave."

Liam heard what she said, but the words didn't register.

"I don't understand," he said, trying to be patient although there was no time for that.

As if he'd heard Liam's thoughts, Dax spoke through comms. "You're in too long."

"Come on, Sarah; we've got to go." He took her hand in his own, trying to urge her out of the bed. "We can't waste time. We've got to go. Now."

"I overheard Collins talking to some other guy. He wants me to do something for him, otherwise..." Even in the low, silvery light, Liam could see the sheen of tears in her eyes. "Otherwise, he's going to kill my father."

"What the hell –."

Sarah interrupted him. "He told me a little today, but he was really vague about what he wants. He's going to meet with me again tomorrow. I guess that's today, already."

He held her forearms, speaking urgently. "And do what?"

"Tell me what he wants me to do, I think."

Liam touched his earpiece. "Dax, are you hearing this?"

"Affirmative," Dax said. "Can she tell you more?"

Liam was conscious of the seconds ticking by. He tried to stay calm. To not argue and agitate her further. "Where did you hear them talking?"

"Through the heat register in the floor. It's under the chair." Sarah pointed to a corner across the room where he could make out the outline of an armchair.

"Collins told this other person what exactly?"

"That he had work for me to do, for him, and he was sure I'd cooperate because otherwise he'd kill my father." She looked down at the blanket and then up at him again. "My dad was in a bad accident a few years ago and had a traumatic brain injury. Earlier, Collins mentioned one of the nursing assistants there, like he knows her. And he told this guy if I don't cooperate with him he's going to kill my dad."

Before Liam could reply, Sarah said, "I can't leave until I hear what he has to say and agree to help him."

"You don't know what he wants from you," Liam pointed out.

"I don't care what he wants," Sarah hissed. "I'll do whatever I have to do to protect my dad."

Liam wanted to kiss her, shake her, carry her out the door, down to the ground, and far away from Collins and whatever the hell was going on. Instead, he struggled to remain calm. Reasonable.

"I understand about your dad. We'll protect him. But you can't stay here."

"Collins wants me to do something for him, which means he's not going to kill me." Sarah's voice was low but she spoke with enough intensity that she might as well have been yelling at him. "I'm going to hear what he has to say and promise whatever I need to promise so I can keep my father safe."

Liam's mind spun with possibilities. Angles. Questions.

He asked urgently, "No one revealed any specifics to you yet? Made his threats to you yet? You overheard all that, right? What he did say to you was vague?"

"Yes," Sarah said.

"Okay. It's going to look like you were taken from here. Since Collins didn't make his threats to you, he can't hold that against you. And we'll put a protection detail on your dad round-the-clock."

She was shaking her head. "He's going to freak out if I vanish." Sarah clutched the fabric of his shirt in both her hands. "On the way here, he also threatened my boyfriend, meaning you. He knows about you, about your company, that you're helping me. No matter what you do, if I disappear he's going to know you pulled me out of here. It's a huge risk for too many people if I leave."

Despite the dim light, Liam saw Sarah's fear for her father, and for him, in her expressive eyes. Heard it in her voice. He felt it in the way she clutched at him.

He kept his voice calm. Steady. "I can't leave you here, honey. I can't take that chance. He's volatile, and we don't know what he's got going on, but we know it's illegal and undoubtedly dangerous."

Liam started reaching into different pants pockets. "Show me the heat register where you heard what you heard."

Sarah stood up and rushed across the room. She pushed the foot rest out of the way. "Right here."

Liam dropped to his knees next to her. He ran his gloved fingers around the decorative plate, then shined his penlight into it.

"Sarah, get your stuff together, and rearrange the bed to look like you're sleeping."

"Why?"

"If anyone opens the door to check on you, it could buy us time."

He pulled a small case from another pocket, and from that extracted a tiny listening device. With practiced ease he attached it to the inside of the heat register. He wasn't concerned about heat or cold potentially affecting the adhesive; it had been tested against extreme temperatures.

Liam stood and pushed the foot rest back into place. He turned toward Sarah, who was again by his side, shoes in hand.

"Do you have any of your hairclips? Hairpins?"

"On the bathroom counter. You want me to put my hair up?"

He was already on the way to retrieve them. Liam shoved most of the hairpins into his pocket. "We have to give them a way you could have picked the lock."

He didn't mention that she'd need to be experienced at doing it to succeed with a hairpin. That, or extremely lucky.

Liam snapped off the end of one hairpin and dropped it on the floor near the balcony door, like Sarah had been struggling to open the lock with it. Then he used another to scratch up the metal plate area around the lock.

"Are you sure you can keep my dad safe?" she asked.

Liam heard and understood the worry in her voice, but there was no way he was walking out of there without her.

"Yes. I'm going to make sure you're both safe, but we have to get out of here."

As if on cue, Dax spoke on comms again. "Get out of there. Tangos three and four just arrived and are pulling into the driveway."

"Two more men just arrived. We have to go," Liam said.

Liam took Sarah's hand and tugged her through the door and onto the balcony.

"Stay low, and against the building."

Maintaining a crouch of his own, Liam closed the door behind him and used the lock kit to secure it, then shoved the second hairpin into the lock from the outside. The goal was for it to look like she'd locked it behind her, and so no one from outside would see she'd opened it. Hopefully, it would also at least momentarily confuse anyone who opened the door to her room.

Despite his hurry, Liam took another moment to attach a second listening device under the edge of the balcony railing. Odds were it wouldn't pick up much of anything, but there was always a chance.

He typically didn't obsess over the mechanics of his descent when climbing, relying on years of instinct and experience. Now, though, he had to keep Sarah safe.

"Do you have any experience climbing?" Liam asked quietly, while peering over the rail and as far into the distance as he could see.

"Recreationally. Indoors."

"Okay." He held out his hand. "Give me your glasses."

She hesitated but did as he asked.

Between Sarah's high-heeled shoes and tight skirt, plus her less-than-perfect vision and inexperience, it would be safer if he carried her.

Digging into the larger pockets on his cargo pants, Liam produced a handful of carabiners and a length of rope. Working quickly, he started paring off and linking together sets of carabiners. He tied a long rappel rope down to a shorter rope with a knot that would come loose when they were free of it and it slackened. He'd whip it down and replace the carabiner, so they'd just have to leave it behind. But at least there wouldn't be a swaying rope dangling and calling attention to the balcony of Sarah's room.

"It's not a far distance. Once over the rail, we'll be on the ground in seconds."

He latched one black carabiner to the railing, then lifted the little table on the balcony and put it near the railing.

"Pulling you over the rail might be bumpy, but aside from that it'll be smooth and fast." Liam checked with Dax again to make sure it was still clear to move. Then he said to Sarah, "I'm going to sit on the rail. Stand on the table in front of me, and I'll tie a knot around you, secured to my waist. We pop over and go straight down. Then you follow my instructions." He raised an eyebrow at her. "Got it?"

All she said was, "Yes."

Liam couldn't miss how pale she was. He tried to make her smile. "I'm a sailor, remember? Good at tying knots."

Sarah gave him what appeared to be an attempt at a smile.

Liam looked around again. He said to his teammates on comms, "Coming down."

In seconds, he was sitting on the rail and pulling Sarah up onto the table. He ran the short rope around her waist and clipped it to his own. Instead of giving her a countdown, he told her to hold tight around his neck and hauled her over with him.

As soon as they were clear of the top of the rail, he released the holding clip and rocked back, sending them smoothly down to the ground. It was a minuscule drop compared to many he'd done in his life, but he didn't doubt Sarah would experience it differently. He snapped the rope above them, and the long one and the short one both cooperated by spiraling down to the ground nearby.

He pulled Sarah behind the closest tree.

"Alpha-1 on the ground." As he updated their status, Liam released the rope tethering Sarah to him. "You okay?"

After Sarah nodded, he told her, "Stay down."

Liam crouched down to run the few steps back toward the house. He grabbed the ropes, wound them, and stashed them in his pockets along with the carabiners and returned to Sarah's side. Next to her, shrouded in darkness beneath the tree, he continued to assess his surroundings.

"Tango positions?" he whispered to Dax and Mason.

"Four in house, two on grounds." Dax told him, "Monitoring guards." Another pause, then "Count off 40 and reverse entry."

"Roger that."

Chapter 40

Sarah

Despite her exhaustion, Sarah was sure her adrenaline and fear would keep her awake for hours more.

She was wrong.

When she and Liam slipped out a side entrance on the property of the house where Collins had brought her, a black SUV was waiting. They sat in the middle row, Dax and Mason behind them. A guy she'd never seen before was driving, another unfamiliar man beside him in the front passenger seat.

Sarah wanted to talk, to ask questions, but when she tried, Liam stopped her. "Let's wait until we're on the plane."

"When will that be?"

Liam was texting furiously on his phone. He didn't even pause when he answered. "Less than ten minutes."

She could hear Dax and Mason both speaking quietly in the backseat, although evidently not to one another because their voices were overlapping. There was an unmistakable sense of urgency in the vehicle, and she didn't know if it was only because they'd rescued her from Collins, or something more.

Did Liam really think she could simply sit on her hands and stay silent?

Sarah wasn't going to just keep her mouth shut and her hands folded in her lap. Much as she appreciated Liam's help – everyone's help – *she* was the one who had to ultimately deal with Collins. She was the one with a disabled parent to protect.

"Why do I need to wait? I want to know what's going on."

"Rick, Callie, and somebody else in research uncovered some information that we didn't know before."

"*What* information? Why do you have to be so vague?" She was so frustrated.

"Because we're trying to put pieces together. It's like a moving picture."

"I know you just rescued me from Collins, but I'm not some storybook damsel in distress. I need to know what's going on. This isn't just about me, it's about my dad's safety."

Sarah knew that everyone in the vehicle was listening, instead of focusing on what they themselves were doing. Let them – what did it matter?

"Matteo, ETA?" Liam called out, but his eyes remained focused on Sarah.

"Two minutes."

Gaze never wavering, Liam said to her, "We'll be at the airfield and on our plane in five minutes. I'll bring you up to date as soon as we're in the air."

* * *

Until the last day, she'd never been on a private plane in her entire life, and now she was in a second one less than twenty-four hours.

The plane Collins used had been luxurious, even to Sarah's untrained eye. This interior of the plane was turned out to feel more like a traveling office than a flying cocktail lounge.

Despite her fear and her need to know what was going on, her eyelids were heavier with every passing moment. Liam saw her ensconced comfortably in a dark leather seat and reassured her, "Give me two minutes with Dax, then I'll be back, and answer your questions. I promise."

Sarah wasn't sure when she'd fallen asleep, but she woke up startled when Liam was climbing outdoor stairs with her in his arms.

"Put me down," she demanded, wriggling to get free.

"Easy, Sarah," Liam said. "You're safe."

"And I can walk!"

He stopped and eased her into a standing position. When her feet hit the ground, Sarah stepped away from him.

"I've had enough of being picked up, hauled around, and treated like baggage. Where are we now?"

Her eyes took in the rear of the house. It was a sizable house with classic fieldstone and shingle construction. Liam had been about to ascend several stairs leading to a wooden deck illuminated by softly glowing lights nestled among the landscaping and affixed to the house.

Before Liam replied, Sarah added, "Who lives here?"

"For now, we do." Liam gestured to the stairs. "After you."

When she reached the back door, it opened for her, revealing Mason on the other side. He held the door open for her and Liam, then closed and bolted it behind them. Sarah heard the alarm beep a confirmation sound when Mason set it from a panel mounted on the wall next to the entrance.

Even though it was still morning, the air outside was heavy with humidity. In contrast, the huge, gleaming kitchen they now stood within was refreshingly cool. It was a study in black-and-white, with glass-front cabinets, polished chrome light fixtures, and cherry red accents. She couldn't imagine making a mess on those marble countertops, or splattering sauce on the Viking range top.

"Dax is setting up in the media room downstairs," Mason said.

"Let me know when he's ready," Liam said, then turned to Sarah. "Are you hungry? Thirsty?"

Her stomach was so knotted with tension that she knew she couldn't eat. "Thirsty, yes."

Mason walked out of the room and Liam opened the refrigerator door. The appliance looked like something out of *Kitchens & Baths* magazine, perfect for its surroundings.

Liam pulled two bottles of water from the refrigerator. He cracked the top open on one and handed it to her. They both drank in silence, until he said, "You need to sit in with us while we review the situation."

"Yes," she agreed. *Obviously.*

She thought that reply to herself but didn't say it out loud. This was about her, somehow, and not just about the book.

Liam moved closer to her and put his hand over hers on the top of the kitchen island. The concern she saw in his eyes was echoed in his voice.

"How are you holding up, Sarah?"

"I don't even know," she admitted. "Confused. Angry. Frustrated. Scared for my dad."

"I didn't get a chance to tell you, but we now have people stationed at Highland Hills. One at the outside entrance, another on his floor."

"There's more than one outside entrance. And more than one way to get on his floor."Yeah." Liam nodded. "We're getting more people in position, and there will be somebody assigned *in* his room."

"How are you going to manage that?" Sarah didn't even try to keep the anger out of her voice. "If any of you bothered speaking to me about it first, you'd at least understand how the place is run. What needs to be monitored most closely." Sarah threw both hands in the air, unable to control her frustration. "It's my father who's in danger here, and you guys didn't even talk to me about it."

Highland Hills was privately owned, but it was still overseen by state agencies. There were considerations about patient and resident privacy rights that had to be taken into account. People from Infinite Security couldn't just walk in there and grunt, cross their arms over their chests, and stare at everyone menacingly. Sarah started to open her mouth to tell him exactly that, but stopped when he leaned over far enough to press a gentle kiss to her forehead.

"I understand you're worried about it."

Liam reached for one of her hands and coaxed her closer to him, while still giving her the opportunity to move away from him.

She didn't.

His fingers intertwined with hers, Liam maintained his focus on her eyes. "While we were on the way here, I personally spoke to Cal Lewis, the head of security at Highland Hills. I explained enough for him to understand that we have serious concerns, that it won't be a permanent issue, and the additional measures we need to immediately provide. It's all good."

"And he just accepted whatever it is you told him? Took your word for it?" She'd met Mr. Lewis once or twice in passing. Her impression of him was that of a pleasant but serious businessman, not a particularly empathetic one despite the type of business he was in.

"His nephew, Xander, served with Ethan," Liam said. "They still keep in touch."

"Ethan, who I've heard about but haven't met yet?" Sarah tried to remember what she'd heard about him. "He's the disguise guy?"

"Yes. If we didn't have that way to make a connection, we would've figured out another one." Liam adjusted his hand slightly and rubbed his thumb back and forth over her own. "We're going to make sure your father is safe, no matter what."

Sarah couldn't help but lean a little closer to him. "Collins made it sound like one of dad's aides is on his payroll. She has access to him every day she's on the schedule."

"I remembered what you said. Lisa, right? Lisa Marie Reynolds?"

"Yes," Sarah confirmed. "She's always been so good with him, but now I don't know..." She paused. "How do you know her full name? I don't think I told you that."

Liam didn't comment on the latter part of her questions. He simply said,

"We're looking into her, but we're not taking any chances. For now, at least, scheduling has been shuffled to rearrange staffing, not just her so it won't look obvious that she's being kept away from your dad. Callie is doing deep dives on staff, especially those selected to interact with your dad."

Sarah tipped her forehead forward, to rest it on Liam's chest. She inhaled more deeply of his scent, letting it and his steady heartbeat calm her.

He and his colleagues seemed to be taking everything seriously. They were paying attention to the situation and taking steps she didn't even know were possible.

What would've happened if Liam hadn't been at that book auction? If she hadn't met him and pursued the powerful attraction she'd felt toward him?

The thought made her sick to her stomach.

Sarah couldn't stop the noise she made, something somewhere between a hiccup and a sob, an embarrassingly pathetic sound. She wasn't a weak person. She didn't crumble and cry. No, she confronted what life threw in her path and dealt with it head on.

Liam's arms came up around her, one grasping her hip, the other moving in a soothing pattern up and down her back. "You aren't in this alone. I've got your back, Sarah. We've got your back, whatever it takes."

He said it with such confidence that she couldn't *not* believe it.

Chapter 41

Liam

He wanted to kiss her. Hold her. Wrap himself around her until she knew she was safe and secure.

Liam was amazed at how intensely the light of her inner beauty shone through and beyond her beautiful exterior, the combination a one-two punch that metaphorically knocked him off his feet. His admiration for her was countered by how disgusted he was with himself for being unable to completely ignore his own baser instincts whenever she was near. Or he thought of her.

When they were in Pennsylvania, through the comms link, Dax had heard Sarah tell Liam that Collins knew about Infinite being involved with her. Before she and Liam had even exited the property, he'd ordered the Long Island headquarters of Infinite Security placed on lockdown. They didn't have time to figure out exactly what Collins and his associates knew before taking defensive action.

Infinite had multiple safehouses; Long Island, upstate New York, a few boroughs of New York City, California, and others scattered among various states between the two coasts. Some were actual houses. Others were apartments, townhouses, commercial buildings, and cottages. There was even a small, working ranch in the Midwest.

The network of them was wide enough that it necessitated a full-time staff member at headquarters whose primary responsibility was to handle the safehouses.

This particular safe house in New Jersey was located among other mid-sized estates where everyone was too focused on their own lives to pay much attention to anyone else. All well-to-do people who valued their privacy and having an expensive address.

The house from which they'd rescued Sarah was far more ostentatious than this one. It had also been more secluded, which had worked against Collins because his incompetent guards hadn't been able to monitor it well enough.

Which was really Collins' fault more than that of the guards. After all, he'd been the one to hire them, or assigned them to guard duty. What kind of incompetent criminal mastermind didn't arrange to guard his own property properly?

It was another reason to think the auction buyer wasn't the brains behind whatever the reason was to obtain the book with the altered page.

Liam's phone vibrated on the countertop with an incoming text. He glanced at it.

Dax was ready for them downstairs.

Liam scooped the phone up and shoved it in a side pocket of his cargo pants.

Sarah straightened her shoulders lifted her chin. "I'm ready."

Liam had only been to this house twice before, most recently nearly a year ago. He'd been part of the three-man team providing protection for a bad guy hiding from some other bad guys. It'd been three days of listening to a big, ugly dude whine and complain like a spoiled child because he didn't like the food, the sheets, the television channels, or anything else. Handing him off to government authorities at a local park had been a welcome relief. Still, he remembered the layout clearly.

Sarah followed him to the door that went down to the basement. He opened it, then gestured for her to precede him down the steps that led into the basement. Liam pulled the door shut behind him and followed her down. At the bottom of the steps she paused, not knowing which way to go.

"To your right," he told her.

The room to the right in the finished basement was set up like a miniature movie theater lobby, complete with framed movie posters, a popcorn machine on wheels, and a scaled down, glass topped candy counter. Both the popcorn machine and the candy counter were empty.

Mason was waiting for them in the red -curtained doorway to the area marked Theater 1. "We're linked up and ready."

Chapter 42

Sarah

The room had a movie theater style screen at one end that was currently displaying a variety of other screens within it, in a Zoom style format. Faces of people involved in the investigation of the case connected to her looked back; Rick, Callie, Jace, Derek, and even Jillian, each in their own square. Three other people she didn't recognize were also present, one man and two women.

Dax and Mason were in their own squares on screen, their images being projected from where they sat in the front row. That front row was broken up into two sets of two seats with an aisle between them. The men each had a small tray table of their own raised up out of the console between their respective chairs.

On the giant screen, the assemblage was impressive and almost overpowering.

Sarah felt Liam's hand at her back, guiding her toward the vacant front row seats.

She sank into the chair he indicated. Liam settled in next to her and pulled up his table. From his pants pocket he withdrew his phone, a small notebook, and a pencil.

Her eyes were drawn to the big screen in front of them. Eight people in other locations, plus the squares showing her, Dax, Mason, and of course, Liam. Sarah didn't know where the cameras showing the theater room were hidden, but she didn't have time to give it much thought because Dax started the meeting.

"There's a lot to cover and not much time. Liam remains in charge of this op, so he'll be taking point."

When Liam nodded in agreement with Dax's statement, Sarah felt the slight movement next to her, but saw it both peripherally and on screen. It was strange.

Liam said, "Before we begin, I'd like to introduce Sarah to Ethan." The good-looking, brown-haired, light-eyed man lifted a hand to greet her, while Liam continued, "Sarah, meet Bethany, who works with Rick and Callie, and Tia, a professional genealogist and investigative research expert."

Bethany said, "I'm glad to meet you, but I wish it was in better circumstances."

Tia chimed in, "I was going to say the same thing. I'm sorry I didn't get to meet you when you were at headquarters, Sarah."

Dax said, "Full disclosure, Tia is my wife."

After those brief niceties, Liam addressed Ethan. "Bring us up to speed on arrangements to protect Mr. Prescott."

"For anyone who didn't know, I recognized the name of the head of security at Highland Hills, Cal Lewis, because I know his son from way back. It was a stroke of luck that saved us a lot of time." Ethan leaned forward and clasped his hands together on the table in front of him. "I explained what I could share, and Cal was willing to work with us. There are Infinite personnel stationed at front and rear facility doors, the loading dock, and the staff entrance. Deliveries come through three of those doors and inspections will be overseen by our staff."

Sarah spoke up, because there was no time for feeling awkward. "There's an entrance off an inner courtyard where Highland nurses and aides bring residents out to take the air."

Ethan nodded at her in acknowledgment. "Yes. But that courtyard doesn't allow an exit from it anywhere except into the building. The gardeners access it the same way the staff does, from inside the building. They just do it when it's closed to the residents."

Liam asked, "What about the situation with the nurse Collins intimated was on the take from him?"

Rick said, "I'll answer that. The woman, Lisa, has been reassigned to a different area on another floor; this was done as part of a broader staff shuffle so it wouldn't stand out. Two new care aides were brought on to the staff, one of whom has been assigned to Mr. Prescott's room and the two rooms on either side, the other of which has the same assignment directly across the hall."

How is Dad dealing with the change? Does he like the new person? Is the new person qualified? She wanted to ask, but didn't want to sound like an ingrate when they clearly tried to cover so many pieces so quickly. It was actually amazing.

Before Sarah could ask her questions, Rick said, "Changes began last night, and some are in progress today. Your father's care is top priority for us, but everyone there matters. Although she won't know the reason behind the changes, Lisa will be helping with the transitions to make it easier for him and the others impacted. But she won't ever be alone with Mr. Prescott now, and neither will anyone else."

Sarah said, "This is such a big upheaval for everyone there. People must be angry and annoyed."

Ethan said, "Regarding the care staff, they are being told it's a pilot program on integrating new staff and keeping people more deeply involved in different areas of the facility. Our security staff are being treated as newly assigned to the facility. Some of the regular security staff remains on site, as usual."

"How did you guys accomplish this so quickly?" Sarah rubbed her temples with her fingertips, trying to take it all in.

"We do what we need to do," Dax said.

Conversation shifted to Bethany, who told them, "Since the beginning, when Rick brought me into this, I've been looking into staff who were assigned to work at the auction house in the department that handles rare books and related items."

In her hands she appeared to be shuffling pictures that had been taken of the doctored Percy Shelley book. "I read through the notes you guys made about what was done, how it appeared to be done, and so on. We researched how the books are handled when the auction house examines them, accepts them, and holds them for auction."

Bethany continued, "The only thing that makes any sense at all is that the tracker was inserted by someone at the auction house. I went through the list of people with access to the books and dug up whatever I could about them."

"Out of the people who fell into the pool of possibilities, only one, Daniel Milligan, has had substantial sums of money deposited in his bank accounts periodically over the last nine months."

"Define substantial," Liam said.

"$100,000 total each month, divided into four different accounts at four different banks."

"He thought that would fly under the radar," Liam theorized.

"Apparently," Bethany said wryly. "Not the sharpest knife in the drawer."

"Is David Milligan a name familiar to you?" Liam asked Sarah.

She shook her head. "No."

Bethany held up a photo in front of her camera. "Here's his picture."

Sarah immediately recognized the man in the photo ID. "Liam, that's the guy who was assisting at the auction where we met. He was standing next to the auctioneer who made the delay announcement. When things got started, he was involved in bringing out and setting up the lots next to be called."

"Correct," Liam agreed. "No doubt."

Still focused on the picture of David Milligan, Sarah spoke her thoughts out loud. "He might have planted the tracker, or changed the page, or both. Or allowed somebody else access to do those things." Another thought struck her. "Bethany, do you know how long Milligan has worked there?"

"Nearly five years." Bethany rearranged a couple of the pages in front of her. "I haven't had a chance to finish the research on him yet, but initially, at least, there were no screaming red flags in his personnel file."

"Gotta be something," Mason said. "Doubtful someone would approach a guy who's known not to break the rules and bring him into something that necessitates paying him so much money to participate. Or to at least turn a blind eye."

The next topic discussed was the increased security measures at Infinite headquarters and related matters. Everything was connected to this mess Sarah had found herself – and her father – involved in, but she was now finding it surprisingly difficult to pay attention to the details. The voices around her blurred together because of her chaotic thoughts.

Whatever was going on involved more people than she'd thought. More danger than she'd realized. More unanswered questions than she'd imagined.

She knew how to push forward when faced with overwhelming problems. How to make a logical list, check items off one at a time as they were completed, progress towards her goals.

But now, what was really the goal? It wasn't a singular goal anymore. It wasn't "win the auction" so she could "collect commission" and "pay bills." No, it was figure out what Collins wanted from her in addition to the books, what he was involved in that he wanted to drag her into, also.

Why he was so determined to get her to cooperate that he was willing to threaten and hurt – *kill* – her father, who had nothing to do with any of it. Why did Collins even know about her father?

Chapter 43

Sarah

Sarah couldn't stay in her seat anymore. She had to get up, move around, fight the panic that was rising in her throat.

"Sarah?" Liam said her name softly, leaning into her. "Talk to me."

"I'm sorry," was all she could manage before slipping from her chair and rushing out of the room.

Sarah heard Liam's voice somewhere behind her. She couldn't quite make out the words and she didn't really care.

There was nowhere to escape in this unfamiliar house, but she couldn't stay still. She couldn't be calm in a meeting when she knew for a fact now that her father's life was in danger, because of her. That her own life was in danger, and she had no idea why.

It was too much.

"Sarah, stop. Please." Liam's voice was close to her, and it registered in her brain just before a hand touched the back of her upper arm.

"Sarah." He repeated her name but didn't put a hand on her again.

She stopped at the foot of the stairs that led up out of the basement. "I'm sorry," she said. Her voice was so low that she barely heard it herself.

"Why?" Liam sounded perplexed. "There's nothing for you to be sorry about."

"You don't have to be nice about it, you know. But maybe you don't know, because we haven't known each other that long in the grand scheme of things." She curled her fingers tightly around the top of the post that marked the bottom of the staircase. "My screwup in accepting Collins as a client has put my dad and anyone around him in danger. I have inconvenienced everyone at the nursing home. This is taking up time and energy from your company that I cannot even afford to pay for. I still don't even know what the hell he wants from me. *Why me?*"

Liam didn't answer her right away; he opened his mouth like he was going to say something, and then snapped it shut again without a word. It was wrong to put him on the spot like that. She hadn't thought to make it sound like she thought he had the answers, so she added, "Those are just rhetorical questions, you know. There aren't actual answers to them. I know that. It's one of the few things I know about this."

"Let's go upstairs," Liam said. "We can't go outside right now. Not yet. But we can feel like we are."

"Okay," she agreed.

Liam led her upstairs to the first floor, then up another flight to the second. He held her hand, his slightly callused fingers warm and comforting. Together, they walked down the carpeted hallway to a set of double doors at the far end. He pushed them open with a small flourish.

Sarah was greeted by the sounds of gently running water, the tinkling of windchimes, and the fresh fragrance of delicate flowers. The room beyond those double doors was like something out of a storybook – or more likely, one of those home decorating magazines thick enough to be used as a door stop.

Sunlight filled the room from multiple picture windows,

caressing furniture fashioned of neutral fabrics and what appeared to be bamboo. In several areas, there were stained glass windows, sending jeweled light on everything the sunlight encroaching through them touched.

There was a stone fireplace in the center of the room, not with fire in its hearth, but instead filled with lush greenery and massive arrangements of dried flowers. More of the same traced paths up the stone to the vaulted ceiling.

Sarah had never seen anything like it.

"Special, right?" Liam commented.

"Amazing," she agreed. "Nothing I would've expected to find in a house." She approached one of the wide windows that filled three walls. Her vantage point looked out upon an expensive stretch of flat grass. Each window she looked out from as she circled the room had a similar view; green grass, the occasional sculpted bushes, and more grass. Tall, brick garden walls outlined the distant perimeter of the property.

"I've never seen a sunroom on a second floor," she said.

"It was done this way because it's safer. The walls outside are flat surfaces with no handholds or footholds, and there's no way to hook repelling cords over the edge of the roof, making the walls nearly impossible to climb."

He continued, "The windows are bulletproof and shatterproof. If we go into lockdown, armoring comes out of the tracks and covers them."

Until he pointed those details out, Sarah hadn't even noticed the narrow track that went around the perimeter of the room at window height.

"Someone put a lot of effort into this space," she said.

"It isn't easy being cooped up even when it's a life-and-death necessity."

She turned away from the window to face him. "I haven't done anything wrong, but I'm in prison. My father didn't do anything wrong, but he's in a prison caused by a hit-and-run driver, and his situation is now made even worse by Collins." Sarah shook her head sadly. "I didn't think things could get worse, but I was so wrong."

Liam moved away from the fireplace. She watched him take a half-dozen steps in her direction and stop. He jammed his hands into the pockets of his jeans.

"Life can be brutally unfair," he agreed. "I'm sorry."

"You've got nothing to be sorry for. If anything, I should be apologizing to you for dragging you into this."

"You didn't drag me anywhere," Liam said. "I won't fail you again."

"Again? You haven't failed me at all."

"You got snatched at the train station because I screwed up."

"No, that happened because Edward Collins is a snake. My bad judgment caused an opening for that to happen," she admitted.

"You're a good person, Sarah. You don't have experience dealing with scum like him. I do, and I shouldn't have let you be there."

"I'm a grown woman, Liam. I decided to not let you keep me away from delivering the books. That's on me, not you."

"I need you to listen to me about safety going forward," Liam said. "Even when you don't want to. Even when you think I'm overreacting."

"I'll try, but I can't promise that. There are too many variables for me to give a blanket promise."

Liam braced his hands against his hips and rocked back on his heels. "I'm not a caveman; I wouldn't ask you to listen to me if it wasn't important. Somebody important to me died because she wouldn't listen to me."

"What are you talking about, Liam? Who died?"

He blew out a harsh breath. "It's not something I talk about."

"You brought it up. Don't shut me out now."

They stood in the silence of the peaceful room, the quiet occasionally punctuated by the central air conditioning causing windchimes to sway and make their presence known.

"Kelsey was someone I dated. We had friends in common, dated casually a few times over a year or two. When I'd been out of the teams for about four months, and I was still recovering from injuries that caused me to leave the service, she and a few other friends came to see me." He rubbed the scarred side of his face with an open hand. "My injuries didn't bother her, and we started dating again."

Liam's eyes met hers, and then shifted slightly to a spot over her shoulder. "Kelsey had a habit of driving when she was upset. She said it helped her relax. But when she did that, her attention wasn't on the road. She called me. My physical therapy session was finished, and I was sitting on a park bench, feeling angry and sorry for myself. Sometimes I needed quiet time to work through things in my head."

"Kelsey called twice in a row, and I didn't answer. Twenty minutes later, after I shook things off, I called her back. It went to voicemail. I had the feeling I get when something isn't right." Liam's eyes snapped back to Sarah's. "Kelsey lost control of the car. Went off the road. Crashed into a tree at the bottom of the embankment. She died on impact."

Sarah cringed. "I'm so sorry." In his eyes she could see ... was it guilt? She added, "That's not your fault."

"If I'd answered the phone, it wouldn't have happened." He hesitated before continuing. "Until you, I never even considered taking a chance again."

"You can't know that answering the phone would have changed anything. You deserve to move on, to love and be loved."

"It's been long enough that I've dealt with her accident." Liam shrugged. "I've had to deal with death plenty of times in life because of my career. I get the unfairness of it, the randomness, that sometimes it's a matter of how the wind blows. The accuracy of a bullet or the trajectory of an explosive device. But I can't stand idly by while someone takes unnecessary risks without trying to intervene. Yet you want me to stand back and let you knowingly endanger yourself." He shook his head at her, his jaw set. "I can't."

Sarah spoke quietly. "I promise you I won't take unnecessary risks."

At least now she had a better understanding about why Liam was so protective. It wasn't just the way he was made; it was his life experiences. "I understand about the unfairness, the randomness. If my dad hadn't been in the intersection when he was... A few seconds earlier or later could've made all the difference."

A wind chime somewhere in this indoor oasis punctuated her statement. Now it was her who couldn't maintain eye contact. "I'm ashamed to admit that in the darkest moments, I wonder if it would've been better if he'd not survived at all."

She didn't know why she confessed that to him. That was a thought she'd never revealed to anyone else. It made her nauseous to acknowledge it at all.

"There's no shame in thinking that. I think it's understandable." Liam reached for her hands. "You love your dad. It hurts to see him no longer the man you knew him to be."

"Yes."

Sarah allowed him to draw her closer, closer, until she was snug within the circle of his arms and her head was on his shoulder. There was so much weight on her shoulders, it felt like she could barely stand up. In that moment, though, hidden away in a safe place within a safe house, it was suddenly lighter.

Chapter 44

Liam

Liam stood in the hallway of the safe house, hands braced on his hips, deciding what to do next. He wanted to go back upstairs, go to Sarah. Those stolen minutes hadn't been nearly enough. He'd thought the unique woodland room would make her feel less restricted; that's what it had been designed to do by whatever previous owner had created it. For Infinite, after the security modifications were made, it was a bonus for anyone who had to be hidden in the house.

His good intentions had certainly backfired, and now they'd both been through an emotional firestorm. As difficult as it had been to talk about Kelsey, it'd been the right choice. Hopefully, Sarah also felt better for sharing some of her pain regarding her father.

His watch confirmed what the waning sunshine already told him. It was late afternoon, even though the day had been a particularly long one for Sarah. She claimed to be fine, but her eyes told another story.

A message from Mason made Liam's decision for him.

"Media room. They broke the cipher."

* * *

Liam wanted to include Sarah in any breaking developments, but he knew better than that. Before sharing anything, he wanted to know the facts if possible.

He ran down the stairs two at a time. This time, the huge screen showed only Rick, Callie, and Bethany. Mason and Dax were in the same seats they'd occupied earlier.

"Cut to the chase."

"We isolated key phrases that broke down the rest of the cipher." Callie told him. "Whoever's running this is smuggling drugs, and other things, possibly even people."

Holy hell. He'd been expecting bad things, but hearing it spoken into life ...

Dax spoke up. "Jace and Derek are questioning the bodyguard again. As of five minutes ago he confirmed enough info to corroborate we are on the right track."

Liam sat down. Stood up again. Turned around to face the wall. Turned back to the screen. "Auctions don't move fast enough to make sense for an operation like that. Whoever's in charge knows the books are going to be on the auction block. They have to get their hands on them. Go after them. Get a buyer involved to create distance. Successfully get hands on them again." He shook his head. "Too complicated, too involved. Too many steps."

"If there's a framework in place, and the people involved know their roles, why couldn't it just become routine?" Bethany said. "I don't know much about auctions, but I think if you had a couple of teams of people executing what you need, you might be able to pull it off. The part with the books, that is."

"We have to grab Milligan," Liam said. "I saw the guy in person, at the auction house. Looks can be deceiving, but he didn't look like a tough guy. I didn't get those vibes from him. Not at all."

"We'll have to grab them without tipping anyone off." Dax shifted his attention to Rick. "Get Ethan up to speed on Milligan. He and Tia need to figure out a way to make the approach stat."

Rick said, "On it."

He vanished from the screen, mobile phone already at his ear.

Chapter 45

Sarah

Sarah wasn't back in her assigned room for more than 10 minutes before someone knocked on the door. She didn't bother asking who was on the other side. It was a safe house owned by Infinite Security, so the possibilities were distinctly limited.

Still, she was glad when she opened the door to find Liam on the other side. She stepped back from the opening so he could enter. His natural scent and his presence warmed the air-conditioned room.

Liam sat on the bed. "What do you know about the seller of the Percy Shelley volume?"

Why was he asking about this now? "We talked about this before."

"Yes, but we need to talk about it again."

She knew that. They needed to go over everything again and again. They had to try and make sense out of a situation that didn't make sense at all.

Sarah asked a question of her own. "Have they heard anything new from the microphone you left at that house? At Collins' house?"

"Not much. The initial anger when you were found to be missing, and some minor conversation between Collins and someone else we can't identify." Liam adjusted his position on the bed and leaned forward with his hands on his knees, stretching slightly. "I know it feels tedious, but we need to go back to the beginning, Sarah. When Collins hired you to represent him at the auction where we met, what exactly happened?"

"Like I told you, I worked for him before. Everything was simple, nothing strange, no problems."

"How did he make contact?"

"Always by email at first. Then sometimes by text, and occasionally a phone call. After our first meeting with your colleagues, I forwarded all those emails and texts to Rick."

"What happened after initial emails?"

"Other emails, texts, or telephone calls discussing bidding parameters. An email or two concluding the business, arranging delivery, that sort of thing."

"Who were the sellers of the lots Collins had you bid on for him before?"

"It's pretty tough to remember those details without my notes, Liam. I think the first one was some corporation. I do remember the second one, though, because the most recent was the same. Veronica Cross."

"What do you know about *her*?"

"I don't know her personally, just by reputation. It's not like we move in the same social circles or something. I did see her once at a fundraising event. She's a wealthy woman in her late 60s, and I remember her being very elegant. I heard she's a widow. Mrs. Cross is a big collector of books and art. Impeccable industry connections."

"She buys and sells? Or just sells?" Liam was sitting there looking relaxed, but his eyes and his focus were anything but that.

Sarah leaned a hip against the small desk against the wall across from the bed. "Well, she has to do both, I suppose, to acquire things to put up for auction, right? But I've only known her as a seller."

"Any idea where she lives?"

"Not really. I heard California, I think. But I don't know for sure. Like I said, it's not like I ever dealt with her personally."

"I get that." Liam stood up. "I'm going to talk to the bodyguard we have detained at headquarters. I don't expect to be gone long, but if you need anything you can reach out to anyone here."

"Detained." Sarah repeated the word slowly. "You're not the police, so how do you get away with that?" Another thought occurred to her. "Is "talk to" some kind of euphemism for torture?"

"This isn't a movie where we work people over in a cement-floored dungeon, Sarah. Part of what we do is investigative work."

She wanted to push for details, but didn't; she refused to give much thought to why. Instead, she asked, "Can I talk to my father? I mean, he won't say anything back to me, probably, but I can let him hear my voice."

"Absolutely. How about I ask Jillian to set that up for you?"

"Thank you." Sarah reached out to place both palms on his chest. "When are you leaving?"

"Soon." Liam raised his hands and covered hers, "It's a short flight, and I'll make as quick a turnaround as possible. I'll get in touch with Jillian while on the way, and she'll set up your call."

Chapter 46

Liam

Liam followed Mason into the side entrance of the estate that was home to Infinite Security headquarters. There was relatively minimal staff on the premises because of lockdown, and half of those there were armed, active security personnel.

Two guards from Infinite Security were stationed outside the small outbuilding beneath which Manuel Gutierrez was being held. Liam hadn't lied to Sarah; the guy wasn't in a kill room. Infinite skirted the lines a lot. Blurred them, too. But they weren't mercenaries who'd completely abandon all humanity for the sake of expediency alone. It was a fine line to walk, but they tried to stay on the more honorable side of it when possible.

They were greeted by an array of shovels and rakes, stacked bags of fertilizer, and more bags of potting soil. It was all very organized and expected.

Liam shoved aside a tall, heavy-duty supply cabinet to reveal some lengths of bungee cords, tiedowns, extension cords, ropes, and other things that could be used in gardening. He quickly pulled on one hook, twisted another, yanked on a third, and part of the wall slid open. Mason followed him into the dark alcove and then closed the wall behind them.

Two minutes later they were both down the roughly dug steps that led below ground. Beneath the primitive entrance, a couple of single bulb lights led the way down a narrow passage that contains three doors. The first two were open, both rooms empty. Mr. Gutierrez was secured in the third.

In the three days since Gutierrez had been captured at the parking lot meeting for the book delivery, he'd been sequestered here. The subterranean cell was maybe 10' x 12' in its entirety. It was a poured concrete box, with an ominous, round drain in the middle of the gently sloped floor.

The drain itself was stained with a substance that looked suspiciously like long-dried blood. Liam knew for a fact that more than one bad guy had shed blood in this room, but he also knew that no trace evidence would ever be left behind. The faux "blood" was nothing more than window dressing to help set the scene. If dark humor was your thing, the setting was almost laughable, straight out of a Mafia movie or the like.

Gutierrez' hands were cuffed together in his lap, and a long chain secured those cuffs to a steel ring embedded in the narrow stone bench on which he sat. He was barefoot. His ankles were separately secured, so he could sit, stand, and even stretch his legs.

Collins' bodyguard looked to be in his late 30s, maybe even in his early 40s. He was heavyset more than muscular. Liam remembered the satisfaction of punching him right in the mouth, and he appreciated the fact that the man's still-swollen bottom lip was split. It was a good match for his equally swollen nose. Gutierrez also had a black eye, a bruise on his forehead, and a cut on one cheek. From the scrapes on his knuckles, obviously Gutierrez had fought back against other Infinite operatives, not just with Liam in that parking field.

Liam was in a hurry to get back to Sarah, but this required his complete focus. Acutely aware that the silent Gutierrez was watching his every movement, Liam grabbed a flimsy folding chair from the corner of the cell. He swung it around into position across from the prisoner. Liam straddled the seat and rested his crossed arms casually on the top of the chair back.

"Ready to get out of here, Manuel?" Liam asked the question in a mild, conversational tone.

Gutierrez shifted his weight slightly on the bench. He didn't answer, just flexed his hands in his lap and tugged on the chain between them.

"We can end this quickly and get you on your way," Liam continued. "Right now, it's up to you. Don't be an idiot. You have a chance to leave this room in one piece. Still breathing."

Liam saw the other man's eyes snap to the stained drain. *Violence perceived is violence achieved.* It was an old maxim in interrogation techniques, and he'd witnessed the truth of it more than once in his career.

"You're just gonna let me go?" Gutierrez scoffed.

"All I want from you is information."

"I don't have information."

Liam struggled to keep his voice agreeable; he didn't want to put Gutierrez more on the defensive. Yet. "I'm sure your boss doesn't tell you everything. Lucky for you, I don't need to know everything."

Liam left it there, and let the silence do some talking for him.

Silence made people uncomfortable. It gave them a void beckoning for them to fill it. Gutierrez wouldn't know everything about whatever Collins was doing, but he'd know something of use.

Several minutes passed. Accustomed to silent hours spent awaiting the perfect shot, the time was nothing to Liam.

Gutierrez finally asked, "What you want to know?"

"Your boss. Edward Collins. Who does *he* work for?"

"Don't know."

"Think again." Liam clenched his fists on the top of the chair back.

Gutierrez followed the small movement with his eyes. "I do what I'm told, man. That's it."

"When we let you go, you know you're a dead man, right?" Liam smiled. "Is Collins going to believe you kept your mouth shut? Is his boss going to believe that?"

Liam stood up and violently shoved the chair away. It slammed into the concrete wall in a burst of sound. "You've got a one -time only chance to save your own ass."

"I don't know anything –."

"Who does he work for?"

"I don't know –."

"Such a loyal soldier, aren't you?" Liam sneered at him. "Ready and willing to die for Collins." He paused. "Cross is good. We're better."

Gutierrez couldn't hide his shock at the name drop. Liam laughed. "You thought I didn't know? That Cross is in charge?" He shook his head. "You really are an idiot."

"Smart enough to know not to open my mouth."

Liam mocked him. "Such a big man. Afraid of an old lady."

"I don't know about shipments, or any of that shit." Gutierrez was trying to jump up, as if he could go anywhere or get close enough to set hands on Liam.

Instead of commenting on that, Liam dropped another name. "You're not smart enough to deal with that. Milligan runs that part of the show." Shock was a hard human emotion to hide, and once again, Gutierrez failed to do it. Liam continued, "Yeah, we know about him, too."

"Ask *him* your questions, then."

"I'm asking *you*." Without letting him say another word, Liam demanded, "Why does Collins want Sarah Prescott?"

Silence again.

"Mason!" Liam shouted. His colleague leaned into the doorway.

"Need the cart, after all. And tell the guys they'll need more bleach."

While he was talking, Liam moved to the wall perpendicular to where Gutierrez was secured. He keyed a code into the digital lock of a red metal case mounted there and turned the hand-crank inside. The clanking of the gears it controlled sounded like something out of a medieval torture chamber. The process quickly tightened the master chain that ran through the series of links that made up the restraint system and immobilized the prisoner completely.

When Gutierrez realized what was happening, he tried to fight against the strength of the metal bindings. It couldn't be done.

The growing rumble of metal wheels on cement announced the return of Mason, shoving his small two-tiered cart in front of him. Jace was close behind. Instead of watching them, Liam kept his eyes on Gutierrez. Everything on the cart had been chosen for maximum effectiveness, psychologically and physically.

Shears, hammers, mallets, scalpels, pincers, pliers. Some had been used, and others were intentionally manipulated to look that way.

"I strapped him down." Liam didn't bother looking at Gutierrez when he gave that order. "I don't have time to get the other table or move him to a bigger space." He turned around with pliers in one hand. Rusted pliers. "Don't even have time to make this fun."

Liam looked at Gutierrez again. "We'll save the pliers and cutters for later. The pain from those will make you pass out too fast, and I don't want to bother reviving you over and over again today."

Their prisoner thrashed as best he could on the stone bench, but there wasn't enough slack to move more than a fraction of an inch in any direction.

It only took a few well-placed mallet strikes, and some more encouragement, before Gutierrez decided his silence wasn't worth the price. For all the money and effort put into transmitting covert information, Collins should have put more effort into higher-quality muscle.

Chapter 47

Liam

By the time Liam arrived back at the safe house with Mason, it was nearly four in the morning. While Mason had brought Dax up to speed by telephone during the flight, Liam was digging back through public auction records.

He believed that Gutierrez had been honest, but could a low-level gangster in physical pain, and not educated about auctions, possibly be a good source of information? Had he really paid attention to what went on around him while working for Collins, or did he blindly do what he was told to do?

The safe house was relatively dark and quiet when Liam walked through the back door, Mason on his heels. They were due in the media room downstairs at 0630 hours

Liam stood in the kitchen, once again deciding what to do.

"Grab some rack time," Mason advised, as if he'd heard Liam's dilemma. "Might not be a chance later."

"I know. I'll check on Sarah, then do that."

Mason reached out and clapped him on the shoulder. "Got it." He took a couple of long steps past Liam, then turned back slightly. "I know you've been through some hell, and Sarah seems okay, but protect yourself."

Liam frowned. Protect himself? From what? Was Mason talking about condoms like he was a teenager, or something else? If it was something else, what the hell?

Not sure what to say, Liam didn't say anything, and Mason went up the back stairs two at a time.

There was a covered bowl of fruit on the kitchen counter. Liam lifted the net dome and picked up an apple. The smooth red skin reflected the narrow overhead pendant light that illuminated a small portion of the room. He looked at the apple, but didn't really see it.

Whatever Mason had meant by that strange statement, he had it all wrong. Liam didn't need to protect himself, he needed to protect Sarah. He'd failed Kelsey by not being there when she needed him. He wasn't going to fail Sarah that way.

He was going to make sure she was extricated from this booked up situation, and when she was safe, he'd go on his way. Liam tossed the rest of the half-eaten apple in the garbage pail under the sink. He didn't bother washing his hands, just headed upstairs.

In the hallway outside the room Sarah was occupying, Liam hesitated. He wanted to check on her. He wanted that so badly he braced his hands against the door to block himself. He knew she was safe right now.

"Stafford's dead husband was high up in a Cartel. Colombian, I think. He got whacked in a sailing accident in the Caymans."

"So what?" Liam pressed. *"What's her real name, what was the husband's name?"*

Gutierrez didn't answer. Liam hit him again where a rib was probably already cracked. *"Cross isn't a Cartel name, is it, genius?"*

"Viuda Negra." *Gutierrez whispered the words with enough drama to befit a creepy late-night movie.* *"Black widow."*

"Her name."

"I don't know. I was told she's in charge. Her husband was her cover. Her shield."

Pablo de la Cruz. English translation of the last name? Cross.

Was it really so simple? Her identity right there in the open.

Could some white society woman really be in a power position within a Cartel? Even as he asked it of himself, Liam thought anything was possible. Even that.

"How do the auctions fit in?"

"I don't know, man. Something about the shipments."

"Sarah Prescott. Why does Collins want her?"

"All I know is that they needed to replace someone. That's all I know."

It took some more persuasion before Liam was confident Gutierrez had told him all he could. While he washed and changed into clean clothes upstairs in the outbuilding, Liam's mind worked the puzzle.

Collins wanted to recruit Sarah to replace someone in their organization. That fit perfectly with what little Collins had told her in Philadelphia.

But why Sarah?

Chapter 48

Sarah

She was trapped in a nightmare stuck on repeat. Sure, there were variations every day. Things like location changes. New York. Maybe Illinois. Maybe not Illinois. Pennsylvania. New Jersey. None of it making much sense.

"Everything is falling into place," Jillian reassured her. It had been quite the surprise when the other woman knocked on her bedroom door early this morning.

They were in a regular conference room in the basement this morning, instead of the high-tech media room. Bagels, muffins, a few pastries, and a bowl of fruit were spread down the middle of the table, like it was some ordinary gathering of accountants or marketing reps, instead of highly trained special operators and support staff tackling unfathomable problems.

"Coffee?" Jillian asked. "Or peppermint tea? Earl Gray?"

"Coffee is fine," Sarah said. She accepted the cup from the other woman.

"Bagel?" Jillian said next.

"Seriously?" Sarah didn't want to sound exasperated, but she was. "You got me up at 6 o'clock for a meeting. It's now almost 10 o'clock. What is going on, Jillian, and where is Liam?"

At 7 o'clock, Jillian had told her the morning meeting was delayed "briefly", and then nothing further. The woman was a pro at prevaricating.

Sarah's nerves were stretched thin. She'd seen Dax walk down the hall. Had heard the low rumble of Mason's voice. The two of them were meeting with others in the media room. Once, she thought she heard Liam's voice outside the door, but he never appeared. He also never replied when she texted or called him.

She was being excluded, even though whatever was going on had been centered around her.

"I want to know what's going on," Sarah said. She stood up and headed to the doorway. "I need to make sure my father is okay. I need to find out what the hell is going on, and I can't do that sitting in here with you and sipping tea."

She'd not known how quickly Jillian could move until that moment. She was standing between Sarah and the door before Sarah even reached it.

"They've been verifying information. Reaching out to confidential sources. Things like that." Jillian reached out a hand to stay her. "I can't let you go out there yet."

"Seriously?" Sarah was several inches taller than the other woman, and far from weak or frail. "You plan to physically stop me from leaving this room?"

"Don't let my appearance fool you," Jillian said. "I'm a lot tougher and stronger than you think I am."

Sarah snapped around at the sound of Liam's voice coming from the other side of the room. "Thanks for keeping Sarah company, but we are ready to move ahead."

He stood in a doorway that hadn't been there just two minutes earlier.

She stalked toward him. "I don't like being an afterthought, Liam. What is going on today?"

"You are anything *but* an afterthought," he said.

Chapter 49

Liam

Rick was known for being calm and easy-going, a personality that fit with his All-American, surfer-dude appearance. When he burst into the dining room where pizza boxes were spread across the table, he was anything but calm.

"Veronica Cross is attending a gala at the Waldorf-Astoria Hotel in Manhattan in four days."

Liam put down the plate he'd just picked up. "What gala? How do you know?"

"That useless listening device at Collins' house in Branford Woods finally became not so useless anymore." Rick grinned. "Sounds like it's going to be a formal, big money event full of legit and not so legit names."

Pushing past Rick to get into the room, Bethany told them, "It's part of a fundraiser for tri-state area food banks. They're raising money with the ticket prices, plus a silent auction."

"We can do something with this." Liam focused on the two computer experts. "Can you get me a ticket?"

"Callie is working on that right now," Rick said.

Sarah spoke up. "I'm going, too." Before Liam could object, she said, "Nobody will expect to see me there. As far as they're concerned, I've vanished."

Liam glowered. "For good reason." Collins and his crew had kidnapped her once, and now she wanted to waltz into a ballroom and present herself for the taking? Unbelievable.

Sarah faced him directly with hands on hips. "My dad is safer than ever right now. If I show up at this event, maybe Mrs. Cross, Collins, or someone with them will make a mistake. Something, anything that gives you an opening."

"They could just grab you and put an end to *you*," Liam said. "No."

The hands on her hips became fists. Sarah narrowed her eyes behind her eyeglasses. "You don't get to decide that for me, Liam."

It took effort, but he kept his voice calm. "I'm in charge of this, so yes, I *do* get to decide for you."

"I don't work for you, and I don't work for Infinite Security, so think again." Sarah took a step closer to him, like she was going to make a physical challenge. "I'm going."

Liam met her challenge with one of his own. "Not without a ticket, which you don't have."

She actually scoffed at him. "I don't need you to get me a ticket. I have lots of industry contacts. I'll figure it out myself."

Liam struggled to keep the reins on his temper. "And do what when you get there? You could get yourself killed."

Instead of answering his question, Sarah challenged him with her own. "How are you going to stop me? Will you "detain" me?"

He knew she was referring to Collins' man who they'd captured and were holding.

"How about a rational moment here?" Mason spoke up, a dispassionate voice of reason. "This is safest if approached logically. We make plans, get thorough diagrams and floor plans. Blueprints. Come up with a logical analysis of who should attend the event."

Liam heard very clearly what Mason wasn't saying – that Liam was allowing emotion to cloud his judgment. That, and the screw up at the Cedarhurst train station, were messing with his usual calm, tactical logic.

"Agreed," Liam said tightly.

It took several hours of planning, discussion, more planning, and more discussion, before Liam was satisfied that they had a solid plan of action with all contingencies in place. They would have a solid team from Infinite at the party, two as guests and two more in undercover roles. Rick would be stationed outside in a vehicle with a signal jammer to mess up other people's communications when necessary. Other personnel would be on the premises as well.

It was arranged fast, it wouldn't be perfect, but it might yield something helpful. And they would keep Sarah safe.

When Liam took her hand and they retreated to the woodland room, it welcomed them with peaceful quiet and soothing sounds.

He stopped in front of a double chair beneath the sculpted tree in the center of the room. "This okay?"

"It's perfect."

Chapter 50

Liam

Liam used the key Callie passed him when he'd entered the hotel through a rear entrance she'd opened for him. It was just as well the Waldorf-Astoria was booked solid, because it was better for them to arrive with the majority of the other guests to the fundraiser. It'd been difficult enough to secure appropriate accommodations at the Metropolitan Manor Suites.

He kept his face averted from the security cameras in the hallways and the elevator, maintaining a casual façade. His clothes were upscale but casual – designer jeans, polo shirt, loafers, and a New York Yankees baseball cap. When a couple joined him in the elevator, Liam kept his head bent to his phone. He ignored them, and they returned the favor. The elevator arrived at Sarah's floor – and he disregarded it, glad he had pressed more than one floor.

The man in front of him glanced over his shoulder. "This you?"

Liam looked up for a fraction of a second, keeping the scarred side of his face just slightly angled away. "Nope."

The guy went back to his conversation with the woman without another word to Liam. At the next stop at a floor Liam had picked, he exited the elevator and walked to the left. A few seconds later, after the elevator doors closed, he turned and headed for the stairwell at the far end of the corridor. Three flights up and he exited onto Sarah's floor.

Without hesitation, Liam went directly to the door of her suite and unlocked it with the key card. A rush of scented air hit him just before her soft body did. His hands flashed out to pull her more snugly into him, one hand on her neck, the other pressed against her back. His mouth found hers in a frenzy, and lips explored, tongues tasted, teeth nipped. Liam spun Sarah around and pressed her against the door that had swung shut behind him. With one hand he closed the security latch, and with the other he traced the side of her body from breast to hip and back again.

"You feel so good." He whispered as best he could, but the words emerged as more of a growl. "Are you alone?"

"No," she said in a husky voice that betrayed her own passion. "Callie is in one of the bedrooms."

"Damn." He kissed her again, unable not to. This time he felt the gentle tug as long fingers tangled in the hair at the nape of his neck. She knocked his baseball cap askew, and he reached up to yank it off and tossed it aside.

"Come in my bedroom," Sarah said urgently. "Before anyone else gets here."

Liam wanted to. Good God, he wanted to. But she deserved more than a frenzied, silent quickie. Hell, that might be fun some other time, but not for their first time crossing the finish line together.

Before he could tell her that, the door to the suite swung open and Mason joined them, followed by Jillian with a fully loaded cardboard coffee cup holder. Sarah stepped back from Liam as he turned to more directly face the newcomers.

"I got four coffees," Jillian said. "All with a splash of milk and two sugars. No special requests today."

"You know, not everyone likes sugar in their coffee," Mason sighed.

"Deal with it." Jillian rolled her eyes. "Everyone else isn't afraid of a little sugar."

"I'm not afraid of... never mind." Mason shifted his attention to Liam. "You ready to go over final details?"

"Yeah."

"What did I miss?" Callie chimed in, joining them from the bedroom where she'd been resting or sleeping or whatever. "Oh, thanks for the coffee."

"The highlights are that we still don't know if Cross or Collins are attending the fundraiser tonight. The plan is for you both to attend either way. If one or both of them show, you'll see if you get the opportunity to find out anything."

"Maybe we'll find out something either way," Sarah said.

Liam admired her determination, but he didn't want to encourage it. Her lack of training and experience didn't support her boldness.

"If I see an opportunity, I'll take it," he assured her. "I promise you that."

Sarah opened her mouth to say something, and snapped it shut. Liam really wanted to know what she self -edited – then decided he was better off letting it go.

Chapter 51

Sarah

Sarah gazed out the massive window and into the darkened gardens she could see below. Flickering flameless candles positioned artfully around the huge ballroom reflected into the glass in front of her, beautifully mimicking authentic candlelight. The string quartet in the northwest corner of the room played a piece that even Sarah recognized, although she wasn't quite sure about the name. Was it Vivaldi? Something about Spring? Summer?

She felt the heat of him when Liam moved behind her, and the scent of him embraced her as it had the first time they'd met, and every time since. It was enticing and comforting, a dichotomy of sin and safety that was irresistible.

Sarah didn't turn to look at Liam immediately. Even though Collins knew she was linked to Infinite Security, they didn't want to make that connection appear to be a personal one. An intimate one.

"It isn't fair to look like that when I'm not supposed to touch you," Liam murmured. "I'm already on edge from those couple of minutes in your hotel suite."

"I could say the same." Sarah gazed higher, meeting his eyes where they were reflected in the window.

"Don't. The thought of you wanting to touch me is more temptation than I can handle."

She turned to face him directly, her fingers tightening on the wine glass in her hand.

"Did you just get here?" she asked. "To the ballroom, I mean."

After he'd left her earlier, in the mindful company of Mason, Callie, and Jillian, they hadn't spoken again.

"Yes." Liam nodded. "Within the last half-hour, Rick told me they heard from New Jersey that she isn't coming tonight."

Sarah didn't need an explanation to know he meant Mrs. Cross. "You mean they heard from what you left behind there?"

"Yes. Since Collins isn't on the guest list, and neither is Milligan –."

She couldn't hide her disappointment. "We're not going to find out anything here."

His eyes made a slow, thorough examination of her before he gave her a heated look that warned her he was about to say something he shouldn't. One corner of his mouth lifted in a hint of a smile. "Except maybe how strong my zipper is."

Before she could stop herself, Sarah glanced down at the zipper in question.

"You can't say things like that, not here," she hissed, trying to keep her voice low. Sarah looked around, making sure again that nobody was close enough to overhear.

"No one can hear me. Don't worry."

Sarah looked around the immediate vicinity, noting how the big ballroom was filling up more and more quickly. "People are constantly walking around. You don't know who's coming up behind you."

Liam stepped a little bit closer. "I have good situational awareness. I always know when someone is nearby."

Despite the stressful situation, Sarah couldn't help but tease. "Another of your many talents?"

"I do have a lot of them," he winked. "I haven't shared most of them with you yet."

The tone of his voice made it clear that he wasn't talking about investigative talents, or dealing with money laundering, book auctions, or anything else except what was going on between them.

The heat of his gaze was palpable, and she could've sworn she felt his touch on her bare shoulders even though he never lifted a hand. Her silk jersey gown was closely fitted, in a rich shade of dark red that she knew complemented the auburn tones in her hair. Sarah could feel the pebbled proof of her attraction to him and hoped the lining in her bodice was thick enough to hide the evidence.

She sipped her cold Chardonnay. It was nowhere near cold enough to cool down the fire he'd ignited. Sarah watched him watch her lick a drop of wine from her lower lip. Liam raised his right hand, lifting his tumbler to clink with her glass. There was a rough note in his voice that she recognized from their all too brief afternoon interlude.

She cleared her throat, "To what are we toasting?"

"To picking up where we left off when we were interrupted by the arrival of my team."

Before she could offer a flirtatious response – or any response at all – she glimpsed an unexpected face near the entrance to the ballroom.

"She's here!" Sarah exclaimed in an excited whisper. "Mrs. Cross. I think that's her, by the entryway."

Liam turned around with feigned casualness, looking where she'd indicated. He clicked on his comms. "She sees someone she believes is Cross. Approximately 5'9", very thin. Hard to age, maybe early 60s. Black cocktail dress. Short silver-gray hair. Bracelets right arm. Low heeled shoes."

"Copy. Ethan is heading that way."

Sarah heard the ice in Liam's glass clink as he shifted to set it on a high-top table beside them. His eyes held steady on hers, no sign at all of their personal exchange still showing at all.

"Keep your glass to help occupy your hands," he told her. "We're going to approach. Follow my lead."

Sarah fell in beside him as he walked across the room, periodically stopping to make an innocuous comment about items in the silent auction catalog. She tried to pay attention, to actively participate in, but her mind was racing.

Victoria Cross isn't supposed to be here. Why is she here? What changed? Does it mean anything? Is Collins here? What does it mean?

When Liam stopped a couple of feet behind Mrs. Cross, Sarah took a sip of wine to wet her lips. Ethan was facing the older woman, proffering a tray laden with champagne flutes, and glasses of both white and red wine. A dark- haired, younger man accompanying Mrs. Cross took two glasses of champagne from the tray and handed one to her. Ethan moved a short distance away, presenting his tray to another group of partygoers.

Liam circled around the front of Mrs. Cross. "Veronica Cross?"

Sarah hadn't expected him to walk right up to the woman, but she probably should have. He'd defied her expectations from the moment they'd met.

"Yes?" Mrs. Cross's dark eyes traveled slowly down Liam's fine form and back again. "And you are?" As she spoke, her gaze shifted to the side and took in Sarah, as well.

"Liam Connolly, ma'am. It's a pleasure to meet you," he said, the words accompanied by a smile that combined friendly and sexy in an irresistible curve of sensuous lips and flash of white teeth.

Mrs. Cross focused on him again, a smirk touching her own lips, calling attention to her heavy lip liner. "What are you doing here today, Mr. Connelly? Do you have anything up for auction, or are you a hopeful buyer?" Her eyes moved to Sarah again. "Maybe a philanthropist?"

"I buy when I can, but my pockets are often not deep enough." Liam indicated Sarah. "Have you met Sarah Prescott? She's a buyer's agent."

The stocky man accompanying their target leaned close to her and spoke in her ear, his black eyes remaining on Liam. He looked out of place in a tuxedo, even though it fit him well. She brushed him off and remained focused on the conversation.

"No, I haven't had the pleasure." Mrs. Cross offered a tight smile to Sarah.

"It's good to meet you." Sarah tried to smile back, but knew it looked as false as it was.

"It's unexpected to meet you both here." Mrs. Cross's expression grew serious. "I can't say that I am entirely displeased. Being straightforward is usually the most effective way to conduct business."

"What business do you want to conduct?" Liam's charming manner vanished along with Mrs. Cross's.

"We can adjourn to my room to continue this discussion," Mrs. Cross said.

"Not happening."

Something in Mrs. Cross' bearing had changed, although Sarah couldn't identify exactly what it was. "It cannot be discussed here."

"I have access to a small meeting room we can use."

Mrs. Cross shoved her glass at another passing partygoer, and Sarah realized that man must also be with her. "Do you really think me a fool? You think I'll follow you to a private space you happen to have at your disposal?"

Liam's voice was mild. "No, I didn't think you would."

"I'll presume you also realize I'm not only accompanied by Carlos."

"Of course." Liam looked as relaxed as if they were discussing the weather. He tilted his head to the side. "If you're so amenable to civil discussion, why the aggressive tactics with Edward Collins acting on your behalf?"

A group of people passed behind them, laughing and talking. The ballroom was getting even more crowded than it had been a couple of minutes ago.

"I'm not going to entertain your fishing expedition, Mr. Connelly." Mrs. Cross sipped her champagne again, "I wasn't hiding my appearance here tonight, although yours is a surprise. But I'm always prepared for any eventuality."

Several people passed behind them, laughing and talking. Somebody jostled Sarah, mumbled an apology, and moved away.

"Sounds like we are at an impasse," Liam said.

"I don't think so." Mrs. Cross directed her fake smile at Sarah again. "What do you think?"

The sharp point Sarah felt to the left of her spine took her by surprise.

"Liam!" she hissed.

"Is it always your way to target innocent women?" Liam stepped closer to Mrs. Cross. "You know I could snap your neck before anyone could save you."

"What would be the point?" Mrs. Cross shrugged like the threat was no big deal. "Neither of you would make it out of here alive, and what would be the point?"

"Again, the impasse then?"

"I have a room prepared with a special guest waiting there. Rest assured, Ms. Prescott, he is rendered unable to hurt you. By my calculations, we have approximately 40 minutes to conclude this matter, and then I have to get back to the auction here. What you do with the rest of your night will be entirely up to you."

Sarah could still feel someone close to her back, although the sharp knife was no longer pressing against her. She desperately wanted to know what Liam was thinking. What was Mrs. Cross talking about? Who was her special guest?

Chapter 52

Liam

Liam kept his voice low. "Where is this room with your guest?"

Mrs. Cross reached out a hand to pat him on the sleeve. "I'll give you the room number to share with your team as we walk."

"We've already figured it out," Dax said in Liam's ear. "We'll have you covered."

Liam wanted to ask questions but couldn't; all he could do was stall for as many seconds as possible to give his team more time.

He maintained his focus on Mrs. Cross. "If we go with you to this room, how do I know we'll walk out of it?"

"Because as of right now I don't have an issue with you or Ms. Prescott." She cocked her head to the side. "Or do I?"

"I don't randomly hunt for trouble," Liam said. He wasn't a vigilante, and neither were his colleagues at Infinite. His interest in this matter began – and ended – with Sarah and her father.

Not that he condoned or in any way accepted the violent, criminal horror that was the hallmark of the drug cartels. In his opinion, those people were the business of government, official special ops, and mercenaries who had no hesitation about plunging headfirst into those dark worlds. None of that was his job or his mission any longer.

He and Sarah were escorted out of the ballroom by Mrs. Cross and several men who looked ill at ease in their evening clothes. They were stopped multiple times for people to greet the "philanthropist" and seek to engage her in conversation about auction -related topics. Liam had to admit that she was a pro at greeting people and yet barely stopping.

The woman had the skills of a seasoned politician.

Liam caught Sarah's gaze around the bodyguard who walked between them. He mouthed the words, "You okay?"

She gave him an almost imperceptible nod. He knew Sarah was scared. She had to be, after one of Mrs. Cross's goons shoved some kind of weapon in her back. She was tough, and resilient, but the chaos she was caught up in was far outside anything she knew.

Jack and Jillian were in formal attire and actively engaged in intense conversation near the doorway. Their heads were bent together over an auction brochure, and Jillian was smiling. Neither looked up as Liam, Sarah, and their companions walked by.

It was comforting to know that his team was on-site and ready.

The ballroom was on the second floor of the lavish hotel. Following the lead of Mrs. Cross and her escort, they quietly waited for an elevator down to the first floor. From there, they walked to the end of the corridor and around several large potted plants to get to the service corridor. Two passing leaders looked at them strangely, but both kept walking with their heavily laden trays in hand.

The first service elevator was empty, and Mrs. Cross stepped right into it. There wasn't much choice but to follow. They bypassed the kitchen level and went to the floor below that.

In the lower level of this luxurious hotel, there were corridors leading in multiple directions. They passed a couple of huge supply rooms stacked with tables and chairs, and a warehouse style space that appeared to be stuffed with furniture of all types. Everything looked ominous, most of it covered in protective materials.

Their footsteps echoed as their small group traipsed down a narrow hallway. There were a couple of offices and a bigger door at the end. The bodyguard in the lead knocked sharply and commanded whoever was on the other side to open the door.

Immediately, it swung open.

The room inside was another storage space, this one almost empty. Two men were slumped forward on metal chairs that faced one another, both of them bound with knotted rope to their own seat. Bloodstains discolored the remnants of clothing they wore. Liam quickly noted that multiple small body parts were missing, and there were layers of cuts causing much blood loss.

He scanned the breadth of the plastic sheeting. Damned if Mrs. Cross hadn't had a kill room set up in the basement of this luxury hotel.

Another quick look at Sarah and he was amazed she was still standing; she was visibly trembling so violently. Still, he wasn't sure she realized what she was ultimately looking at. The men in those chairs were going to die.

Who were the unlucky bastards? Why were he and Sarah here if they weren't next?

The comms unit in his ear had been silent, but as Mrs. Cross spoke, so did Dax.

She jerked her chin in the direction of her prisoners. "Wake them again."

"We're in the supply room closest to you," Dax said.

"Sarah doesn't need to see this!" Liam spoke over the sounds of water sloshing and muffled screaming as the prisoners regained consciousness.

"Oh, but she does," Mrs. Cross said, her voice eerily calm. "Don't you recognize them, my dear?"

Sarah stood there, visibly horrified at the sight and sound of the scene in front of her. She covered her face, bent forward, and tried to twist away from the guard at her side.

The older woman sounded gleeful. "Come on now. This is for

you. Vengeance on your behalf." Then her tone changed. "Collins didn't have my permission for *anything* he did involving you."

Mrs. Cross started pacing in angry strides that belied her age. "He was skimming money from everything he thought he could get away with. The worm was going to use you as another of his tools. He thought you were talented at acquiring books and that he could train you to tamper with them. He decided he'd control you every which way. All of it completely unauthorized by me. Ronnie went along with everything, forgetting his loyalty to *me*."

When Cross identified them in her rant, Liam could recognize both men. The swelling in their faces, torn clothing, and extensive damage inflicted by Cross's men had left them grossly disfigured.

He tried to reach for Sarah, but Cross snapped an arm out toward him. "Not yet."

Liam and the cartel boss were both focused on Sarah, but he knew that the soldiers in the room were focused on him.

Cross announced, "I will not be dealing in rare books anymore. It's not efficient. The accounts hidden in the volume that was left in your hands, they are gone. These two worthless pieces of scum will be forgotten." She smiled as only evil could. "It'll be like they never lived at all. You're safe from me, Ms. Prescott, and so is your father."

"Now," Mrs. Cross signaled to one of her men.

Liam shoved the guard between him and Sarah out of his way and grabbed Sarah into his arms, spinning her away from the grue-some sight of Ronnie having his throat cut from ear to ear. He couldn't block out the accompanying sounds –muffled screams of both doomed men, feet scrabbling on the plastic-covered floor, mocking laughter from the cartel soldiers. Or the metallic smell of death delivered without mercy.

"You made your point. Enough!"

"It better be. You told me your reasons for involvement and you can see it is complete and ended." She snapped down her manicured fingers at one of her men. "Let them go."

Even though he wanted to carry Sarah, Liam also wanted to have at least one hand free if anyone decided to get in a parting shot.

"One more thing. . ." Cross said, stopping them midstep. "Forget about David Milligan, or I will make sure somebody regrets it."

Liam was startled at her words, but he nodded his understanding and said nothing more. One of Cross's men opened the door, let them walk through, and slammed it shut behind them.

Dax, Mason, and Jace were in the hallway. All were armed and wearing Kevlar. Liam knew they were poised to act if needed. Thank God it wasn't necessary, because Sarah could've been caught in cross-fire or taken hostage.

She was still shaking and still hadn't spoken.

"Let's get the hell out of here," Liam said to everyone in general and no one in particular as he swept her up into his arms. She burrowed her head against his tuxedo clad shoulder.

"I've got you," he whispered for her ears only. "I've got you."

Chapter 53

Sarah

Sarah still had her head on Liam's shoulder, although she was in her own seat next to his in a company vehicle. For the drive out of the city and to Infinite's Long Island headquarters, Sarah hadn't paid much attention except to ask if her father was truly safe again. Liam gave her his word, and even put her on the phone with one of the guards at Highland Hills so she could hear for herself that everything remained quiet there.

"We're almost there," he murmured in her ear, capturing her hand in his.

"Good." Sarah felt relief wash over her. She wanted to get out of her dress, her heels, and everything else. If only she could get the memory of those men in that room out of her head.

The memory of what happened to those men in that room.

Sarah cleared her throat, trying to make sure her voice sounded strong. "Will there be a meeting when we get there? To go over everything that happened? Talk about it all?"

"A debriefing. Yes, but not until everyone has a chance to rest and get it together." He squeezed her fingers. "Don't worry. You won't have to be there."

"What if I want to be? What if –."

Liam interrupted her half-panic response. "You can decide later, Sarah. No pressure."

"You're not going to tell me what to do?"

"Of course not." He sounded almost insulted. "I'll only ever do that in situations where you're in danger, and I have skills and experience to handle it. I'll never tell you what to do or not do, just for the hell of it. That's not me."

She'd known him such a short time on the calendar, such a long time in her heart. Sarah certainly couldn't tell him that, especially not here and now. She settled for saying, "Liam, I don't doubt you at all."

"Tonight," Liam said, "we're going to get some rest, and that's it. You need to talk about what you just went through. I know it wasn't easy."

After Mason pulled into the garage at headquarters, Liam helped Sarah step down from the vehicle. When he moved to sweep her up into his arms, she quickly shook her head.

"I can walk."

It was obvious to her that he wanted to disagree, but he said nothing. Instead, Liam settled for retaining his hold on her hand and leading her into the house. Other members of the team that had been involved that evening were parting ways in the foyer.

Sarah hated to sound needy, but she couldn't stop herself from asking, "Could you stay with me? I don't think I can handle being alone right now."

"I was going to insist on that." Arm around her waist, he led the way to her suite.

Sarah let him guide her, even though she remembered where to go. If Liam and his team were convinced she and her father were safe from Collins and Ronnie and Mrs. Cross, then she had to put her faith in that. Right?

My God, she thought as the gruesome scene careened through her memory, *I know for a fact that we're safe from Ronnie and Collins.*

Liam opened the door for her. Sarah knew it was safe, but still she hesitated before crossing the threshold. He didn't comment on it, simply went with it like her behavior was normal. She knew it wasn't.

He said, "Stay here; I'll check the room."

Less than a minute later he was in front of her again. "All clear. Come on in, Sarah."

She wanted to justify her behavior, but what was the point? They both knew it wasn't rational, and she wouldn't put him in the awkward position of trying to justify it for her. Sarah nodded and walked into the room.

Everything was just as she'd left it. She hadn't expected otherwise. Not really. But still...

"Why don't you get ready for bed?" Liam closed the door and locked it.

Sarah nodded. She didn't want to speak, not yet. If she said anything, she might say more than she intended, and that would be a mistake. She took shorts and a T-shirt from the top left drawer of the dresser and took them into the bathroom with her.

In the bathroom, Sarah stood like she was lost. Should she take a shower? Wash up in the sink? Just change clothes and be done with it? It was a simple decision, and it felt monumental at the same time.

She didn't know what to do. The foolish tears came on like a sudden storm, maybe trying to wash away the blood-soaked horror of the night.

"Sarah." Liam's voice was calm and quiet. Gently, he took the clothing she clutched to her chest like defensive armor against the nightmare she'd been living.

His arms were strong and solid around her, coaxing her to rest her head on him. He swayed with her, back and forth, murmuring words of comfort and reassurance that were just right, although she'd never be able to recall what he said.

Gradually, the emotional storm passed.

Liam guided her into the bathroom.

"Do you think you can handle the shower on your own right

now?" There was no innuendo or seductive intent in his tone. "I can help you, or just stay right here as backup."

"I can manage. I think." Sarah studiously avoided looking at herself in the mirror, not wanting to see the look on her own face. "But please stay." The last three words emerged as a whisper, but he nodded his agreement, so she knew he'd heard.

Silently, Liam knelt to remove her high heels. She braced a hand on his shoulder as she shifted her weight from her right foot to her left. He set them against the wall and stood, then gently turned her away from him. Sarah could feel the hidden zipper slide down to the base of her spine. Instead of tugging the dress off her, Liam kissed the top of her shoulder and stepped around her.

He opened the glass shower door and started the water. It cascaded down from the wide showerhead, and he adjusted the dials until she could see curls of hot steam rising in the enclosure.

Liam returned to her. "Are you sure you're steady enough?"

"Yes." She hoped she sounded convincing. "I won't be long."

The care and concern in his expression almost made her cry again. With the soothing sound of the shower running in the background, he turned to the shelves outside the shower and took down several bath towels and a washcloth. Liam carefully set them on the decorative chair next to the shower itself.

"I will be right outside the bathroom door, and I'm leaving that open a little so I can hear you easily over the water."

Sarah wondered briefly what he saw when he looked at her with those intense eyes.

Did she really want to know? Did it matter? He was here, sincere and caring for her, and it was time she trusted in that, at least.

"Thank you," she said. She wanted to say much more, but it was all she could manage.

Sarah expected him to leave the room, but Liam stepped directly in front of her. He framed her face with both his hands and pressed a lingering kiss to her forehead. "I'm here for you, sweet Sarah. You're not alone."

She turned slightly to watch him leave the room and pull the door partially closed behind him. For a full minute Sarah stood there unmoving, and then she pushed herself into gear. Liam *was* there for her; she didn't have to deal with everything alone.

Her shower was quick and efficient. Even though she didn't waste any time, when she emerged she was surprised to find her discarded clothing had been taken away, and comfortable sleep clothes for her neatly folded on the bathroom counter. Sarah used the hairdryer and brushed her teeth.

When Sarah pushed open the bathroom door, she wasn't really surprised to find Liam still standing right on the other side. He'd obviously stepped away at some point; the bed was turned down, and he was wearing generic athletic shorts and a T-shirt from the stash that had been in the room when she'd arrived. But he hadn't left her.

"Come on, honey. Let's rest." Even though the room wasn't particularly large, he held her hand and led her to the bed. "I put a water bottle on your nightstand in case you get thirsty. Are you hungry at all?"

"Thanks, but no." Sarah sat on the edge of the bed. "And thanks for leaving a light on."

The base of the lamp on her nightstand was illuminated, just enough to chase away potentially scary shadows. Darkness never bothered her before, but tonight she felt better with less of it. She didn't object when he coaxed her back against the pillows and pulled the top sheet up over her. Sarah watched him go around to the other side and claim the space next to her. Liam brought her into the circle of his arms.

"Do you want to talk right now? Or try to sleep?"

"I don't know if I can sleep," she admitted.

"Fair enough. How about you close your eyes and let me hold you?"

Chapter 54

Sarah

Wakefulness returned gradually. Sarah's first thought was how warm and secure she was. Liam's arm was draped across her waist, his hand splayed wide, thumb resting directly below her breasts. And then she realized she hadn't suffered any nightmares or other sleep disturbances after what had happened last night.

"Morning." Liam's voice was a deep rumble in her ear. "How are you feeling today?"

"Better than I expected," Sarah said.

"Good."

She shifted on the bed and turned towards him when he released her. Sarah pressed a kiss to the underside of his jaw, then to the faded scar on his left cheek. His eyelids drifted shut as she continued her path to his temple, his forehead, his nose, and back to his mouth. Her fingers joined her exploration, slipping up under his T-shirt to the warm skin beneath.

"Sarah." His voice was rough, probably a combination of the early morning and arousal.

Sarah pushed the shirt up more, revealing his lean, sculpted torso and all the places that beckoned her attention.

"We should wait until later," Liam said, sounding more like he was convincing himself than convincing her. "After we get through the day. After dinner."

Sarah raised her head to look at him. "Why do we have to wait until after dinner?"

"You've been through so much stress. Yesterday was shocking." He was clearly trying to do what he thought was the right thing. "I don't want to take advantage."

"Do you really think I don't know my own mind?" Sarah whispered. "I know what I want, and I want you."

He raised his hand to stroke her forearm, to touch her hand where she touched him. His fingers lingered against her skin, offering comfort. Liam touched the backs of his fingers against her jaw, then down her throat to her collarbone, where he swept her hair back over her shoulder.

Eyes locked on hers, he tucked it behind her ear, then slid his fingers forward to cradle her head. She felt the warmth of his palm there when he drew her forward and down to meet his lips. Lost in the wonder of his kiss, Sarah was startled when he flipped their positions and she found herself looking up at his morning-stubbled jaw and the expanse of his shoulders.

She didn't have time to admire the view before his mouth was working its magic again and all she could do was *feel*. Touches enhanced the kisses, and the heated desperation grew, expanding, until it seemed to have a life of its own. The fabric between them was discarded with quick, efficient movements until nothing remained but skin on skin shrouded in a haze of desire.

Liam ran a fingertip down her slit with a featherlight touch that made her breath catch in her throat. When he leaned in and followed the same path with his tongue, she couldn't stop the low moan that escaped her. And then when he added two fingers to his erotic play, her own fingers began grabbing at the thick bedding, trying to find a way to anchor herself in the maelstrom of sensation and emotion.

Her thighs trembled. Her muscles tightened. She pressed against his mouth, and he pressed his mouth more tightly against her until she shattered into what felt like a million shards of light. Liam eased the pressure, gentled his touch, softly kissed his way back up her body. Sarah looked at him with slightly dazed eyes, even so still appreciating his handsome face and the way her own hands had tousled his hair while he'd given her such pleasure.

Liam braced himself on one hand and reached toward one of the nightstands with the other. Before she asked what he was doing, he kneeled back and held up a foil packet.

"Sarah?" He simply said her name, but in the one word she heard much more. Was she still into this? Was she too tired now? Not in the mood? Had she changed her mind?

"Liam." Sarah hoped she'd managed to say his name with enough passion that he understood it amounted to her eagerness to have him inside her. With sudden clarity she knew that this wasn't a moment to leave room for interpretation, like when one read a poem, or analyzed a book. She wasn't taking any chances.

With one hand she caressed her own nipple, with the other she trailed a path down, down, down to her core. "I need you," she told him clearly.

"I need you, too," he said.

Liam sheathed himself while she watched. He slid his hands up her legs, the slight roughness of his skin stimulating her nerve endings and heightening her anticipation. Gentle kisses scattered across her abdomen gave way to the lavish attention he then paid to the swells of her breasts. Sarah squirmed, unable to keep still under the passionate onslaught.

Hands braced on either side of her shoulders, poised at her entrance, he met her mouth with his own. His kiss was everything.

When he joined with her, the rightness of it was overwhelming, and Sarah's breath caught in her throat. Her fingers tightened on the curve of his biceps, and she held on desperately, like a woman adrift in a storm-tossed sea.

The air carried their breathless words, the sounds of passion, pleas for more and pleas for mercy because the pleasure was too much. Too intense.

When it was over, they both fell silent, their ragged breathing the only sound that remained. And it said so much without needing words to define it.

Epilogue – Liam

Almost 3 months later

Sunglasses on to combat the surprisingly bright November sunshine, Liam strode under the familiar royal blue awnings with their crisp white lettering. When he pushed inside the doors, the well-dressed man who greeted him grasped his trusty tablet device.

"Good morning, sir, and welcome. How may we help you today?"

"Good morning, Brett," Liam said. "I'm here for the rare book auction."

"Excellent. There's quite a lot of excitement for that auction today."

"Glad to hear it. I have to say, I'm very excited for it, too. Is it in the Cascadian Salon on the lower level?"

"Indeed it is, sir."

"I know where to go." Liam reached out to shake Brett's hand. The auction house employee was visibly startled, but hurried to reciprocate and said, "Enjoy your day!"

"Thanks. I know I will."

Liam headed for the back of the first floor. He chose the stairs instead of the elevator and made his way to the correct room.

At the check-in table there was another familiar face.

"Tom, right?" Liam said.

The older man looked up from the papers he was organizing and stared for a moment, perhaps startled by the familiarity. A slow smile creased his face.

"Good to see you, young man. You're preregistered again, I suppose?"

"Yes. Liam Connolly."

Tom quickly checked him in. When he handed him the credentials, he leaned forward conspiratorially. "You're not the only familiar face here today."

Liam's smile got bigger. "Is that so? Then maybe I won even before the auction began."

When he got into the bidding room, his gaze was immediately drawn to her. Sarah was sitting in approximately the same place as she had been the first time they'd met. Her high-heeled shoes were on the floor, ankles primly crossed, heels slightly lifted. He much preferred when they were wrapped around his waist or draped over his shoulders.

The edge of her black pencil skirt caressed the backs of her legs above the knees, around where he knew she was ticklish. He couldn't see the front of her rose-colored blouse from the angle where he stood, but he knew how good it looked.

Sarah looked over her shoulder at him, enough that he could see the edge of the smirk that curved her luscious lips upward. Liam cut across the room, needing to take his place by her side.

"Mr. Connelly, so good to see you," Sarah said.

"The feeling is mutual, Ms. Prescott." Now it was his turn to smirk. Liam indicated the chair beside her. "May I?"

"Of course." She had both her iPad and her phone on her lap. "I'm glad we can communicate in person today."

"It's my favorite way to communicate with you, too," he said.

She completely ignored his suggestive tone. "I emailed you the item number and relevant facts about the lot you are interested in."

"I did receive that email," Liam confirmed, going along with her professional routine.

Before she could reply, the chief auctioneer and an assistant took their places at the podium. The assistant *wasn't* one he recognized, and Sarah indicated that she didn't either.

The familiar rhythm of the auction began. Liam lost interest almost immediately. He enjoyed his 19th century poetry books, but he loved the woman sitting next to him. Watching her work was a pleasure unto itself.

When the session was concluded, Sarah was smiling as she gathered her things together. She turned to him. "Are you happy with the price you paid?"

"Absolutely. I have the best buyer's agent around."

"I definitely think you do," Sarah agreed. "I have to finish the paperwork for my other client and you. Then, would you like to celebrate?"

Liam leaned closer to her; close enough to almost taste her smile. "I'd love to celebrate with you."

Sarah stood and gently stretched her back. He stood next to her, trying to maintain a bit of professional distance in what was her workplace. "Do you have anything in mind?"

"Yes, I do, Mr. Connelly. What do you think about having lunch at the hotel suite I booked?"

It was a fun twist on the day they originally met, and he was wholeheartedly on board with it. "I think that's an invitation I wouldn't even consider turning down."

Epilogue – Sarah

3 ½ months later

"This one is beautiful, too," Sarah told him. She looked out the window and despite the rain she could see the Long Island Sound in the distance, beyond the bare trees. "You even have a view of the water."

"I noticed that. The unit comes with rooftop access, and you can see better from there. "

She watched the rain sheeting down harder than before. "Probably not the best weather for it today. We're lucky it's not below freezing, or this would all be snow."

Liam ran a hand through his damp hair. "Yeah, the weather is definitely not cooperating."

"Do you want to look at the apartments again when the weather is better?" Sarah asked. "I mean, do you have to be out of your place by a specific date?" He hadn't mentioned a deadline, though.

"Not really. But I know the time is right. At least I think I do. Know that."

Sarah wandered away from the window. It really was a great unit. The large kitchen was modern, with new appliances and sleek finishes, but the great room area was somehow spacious and cozy at the same time. A half-bathroom at the juncture of the foyer, kitchen, and great room was undoubtedly useful.

"Does *this* have two bedrooms or three?" she asked, trying to remember what he'd said. Liam had taken her to see three other apartments that day, and two the day before. As important as the decision was for him, some of the details were starting to run together.

"Three." Liam shrugged out of his insulated winter jacket. "Give me yours. We can dry off for a minute while we're here."

"The lockbox things make apartment hunting a lot simpler, don't they?" Sarah relinquished her own parka to him. "We probably shouldn't stay too long, though. It wouldn't be good to get stuck here."

Liam hung both coats on the coat rack near the front door. "It's not supposed to get that bad."

No, it isn't, Sarah thought. *More's the pity.* She wouldn't mind being trapped with him. Nearly 8 months after they'd met, Liam still made her life better all the time.

She wandered down the long hallway that led off the main living space. The first door opened to reveal a bedroom, and the next revealed a full bathroom. Across the hall from both was a room with a desk and some built-in bookshelves. Past that, another bedroom. At the far end of the hall, double doors indicated the primary suite lay beyond.

Sarah pushed the doors open and walked into the vast space. Large windows, like those in the great room, revealed the rainy day and struggling to brighten the sky. There was no furniture, but on one wall part of a well-known poem was neatly stenciled in curling script.

She read aloud. "Come live with me and be my love, and we will all the pleasures prove, that valleys, groves, hills, and fields, woods, or sleepy mountain yields."

"That's so amazing, isn't –" Sarah turned toward him, and the words froze on her lips because Liam was kneeling there, a book in his hand.

"You're what's amazing, Sarah. No poetry ever written compares with how you light up my life. I wasn't really *me*, until I met *you*. You make the world a better place, and make me a better man, just by being yourself."

He showed her the book in his hand, of Christopher Marlowe poetry. She saw how his famously steady hands trembled ever so slightly when he opened it to reveal a pocket cut into some of the pages. Liam withdrew the ring box nestled there.

"Marry me, Sarah. You're already my love. Stay with me. Live with me. Marry me. Let me show you over and over how much I cherish you."

Sarah tried for a moment to pull him up to a standing position, then dropped down next to him instead. "I will. I will, and I do, and I cherish you, too."

Her mouth found his and they again professed their love for one another loudly but without words, in a timeless language that was all their own.

About the Author

DENISE DEMARCO, a lifetime New York resident, often uses her knowledge of the tri-state area in her stories. Genealogist, researcher, history buff, and collector of information about anything and everything, she creates stories from the heart from all that—plus, lots of imagination and iced coffee!

Available November 2024
Pre-Order Now

Infinite Weekend

* * *

From the moment they glimpse each other behaving suspiciously at the Renaissance Festival, their paths were destined to intertwine. Now Lance and Callie are

**swept up in the twisted dealings of a counterfeit antiq-
uities ring that will stop at nothing to achieve its goals.**

Lance is known on the fairgrounds by his joust persona, the Dark
Knight. He's a skillful horseman, and wields the tools of the joust like
he was born to it. No one knows he's working
undercover in pursuit of a counterfeit antiquities ring using the
Renaissance Festival marketplace to conduct their dirty business –
raising money to fund terrorist activities.

Callie routinely buries herself in work at Infinite Security. She reluctantly agrees to take a holiday, intending it to be nothing more than a
long weekend. Callie never thought she'd stumble
upon a suspicious character in the woods, or that he'd turn out to
actually be a modern knight.

Working together in an uneasy alliance, Lance and Callie must prove
who's behind the black market trade and put a stop to it. But their
mutual attraction is a dangerous distraction that threatens their focus
on the mission. If they aren't careful, their first weekend could be
their last.

www.ingramcontent.com/pod-product-compliance
Lightning Source LLC
Chambersburg PA
CBHW061118310726
48974CB00002B/594